Emotional Charades

A Novel

Taylor Bianca B.

Copy Right

Acknowledgments

In terms of best friends, Anisha Maze really lives up to the title. I cannot tell you how many conversations she's had with me about this book. She'll probably never read it again, and I completely understand.

To my brother, Jy'mel, and my niece, Asya. Thank you for your patience. Thank you, Stacy and Josh, for being my writing buddies back when I could barely call this a book. Every beta reader has been crucial to the fruition of this dream. I cannot express my gratitude.

I wish my mother were here to see me publish this story.

Authors Notes

While reading this book, be conscious that the characters are individuals. In our society, we often do not extend individuality to marginalized groups. If you find yourself curious about any of the communities represented in this book, learn from the source. Read works written by members of that community. Watch movies, shows, vlogs, and other medias created by them. Diversify your social media so that multiple communities are presented.

If you do start to follow any creator to learn, do not flood their spaces with questions just to satisfy your curiosity. Do not center yourself. Instead, listen and learn from them.

I set out to write a diverse book. I worked with sensitivity readers to identify my cultural blind spots.

That does not mean this book is unflawed. I look forward to hearing all feedback, especially from the communities present in this book.

Chapter 1: The Golden Promise

*O*h lord, I'm going to fail this class. I just know it. I shouldn't have taken it. I should've gone with something in my wheelhouse. An extra biology class. Maybe even an advanced chem class. Anything but creative writing.

Is something wrong, Rebecca?" Eric asked. His voice snapped me out of my mental spiral. I looked up to find his mixed amber and green eyes inspecting me.

I stilled myself, slowly smoothing away any signs of agitation from my body.

"How could you tell?" I smiled at my fiancé.

His hypnotic eyes locked on mine. "You snoozed your alarm five times this morning. I had to get you out of bed. You are biting your nails, tapping your foot, and you have not even touched your breakfast and coffee. They're already cold."

The surface of my oatmeal had long since congealed.

"You got me," I sighed, dropping my head to the table in mock despair.

He maneuvered his fingers expertly through my twist out, somehow leaving every curl in its exact position, undisturbed. The soft massage made my eyes roll to the back of my head. I was drifting on a calm current.

"Will you tell me what is wrong?" Eric asked.

"This one class will delay my graduation plans or bring down my GPA. I don't know what to do." I needed to maintain my 4.0 GPA, prepare for and take the MCAT, and be the best maid of honor for my best friend, Khadijah. My parents were even covering my living expenses for that year.

Now, I was going to let everyone down. All because of this stupid elective class.

He stood, grabbed my hand, and gently pulled me to my feet. His arms locked me into a warm embrace as he rubbed my back. Tentacles of stress receded from my head, neck, and shoulders. My slight headache lightened to just a memory. With my body eased, I could enjoy the feel of him, like a hoodie on a chilly day. It was like being wrapped in a blanket while sitting directly in front of a fan.

"Rebecca, you are smart and resourceful. You are going to figure this out," he assured me, his voice deep and confident. He tilted my head up, bringing my eyes to his level, "You will figure it out."

His faith in me replenished my confidence. I stared at him. I couldn't find the words to express my gratitude. "Eric, I love you."

He hugged me tighter and rested his head on my shoulder, "I love you so much," Eric replied, then kissed my neck. He dragged his lips up my neck, across my cheek, and to my lips. His lips were soft and firm.

Beads of arousal traveled throughout my body. Instantly, my mind cleared. I wrapped my arms around his shoulders. "I could miss my first class." I bit my lip and tilted my head.

His smile turned devilish as he considered. Then, his expression changed. A raised brow followed by a quick furrowed brow. It meant *are you sure?*

It was our Morse code. It started as a game we played when we were kids. Now, it was our second language. Our love language.

He was right.

I shouldn't skip the class I was struggling with. Even if the feel of his hands on my hips was sending tingles down my spine. I wrinkled my nose—our expression that meant *I shouldn't.*

He exhaled, "Skipping class would not help you pass." His voice was a little sour, almost as if he were trying to convince himself.

"No, I just need a miracle," I joked, "or a tutor." The idea solidified. "I do need a tutor."

I'd registered for this class thinking it'd be an easy A. Silly me.

Eric nodded unenthusiastically. He'd likely seen it as an obvious solution, and not the epiphany I did.

Ten minutes later, Eric dropped me off to the Michigan State Normal University campus, which was filled with stone-faced historical buildings and contemporary additions that didn't meet the charm of their predecessors. Fresh grass clippings scented the air. The trill of a lawnmower reverberated in the distance.

The beautiful stone structure of Scarlet Hall loomed over me as I entered the building to attend the class I hated. The rectangular room had floor-to-ceiling glass windows on one side. Clutters of dew clung to them. Bright September sunlight clashed with the fluorescent light that collided with the cream-on-cream décor, making me feel groggy.

I rushed to my seat, trying to avoid—

"Grand rising, Miss Dangerfield. I'm so happy you're with us today," Professor Lamb greeted.

—exactly that. "Good morning, Professor Lamb."

She shuffled a stack of paper on her desk. She insisted on hard copies because, for some reason, she thought handwritten feedback was easier to absorb. I didn't tell her what I thought of that.

"Miss Dangerfield, would you like to get us started?"

I flinched at the request but managed to mutter a hesitant, "Uh…Sure."

She handed me back my assignment: A modern-day fairytale. There was a purple *C* handwritten at the top with a stream of feedback that ran to the very last page. I'd spent hours researching classic fairytales and composed a piece that combined several themes with modern situations. Clearly, it was for nothing, though. She wasn't impressed.

I speed-read my work. She opened the floor for feedback. I opened my laptop.

~~*Notes*~~ *Reasons I hate this class:*

1) The seating arrangement. This class has small side-entering desks, each less than a centimeter apart, forming a circle. A tall, plus-sized girl who sits next to me has to extend her long legs under my desk for comfort.

I thought about asking her to be my tutor. She had a voice and passion in her writing. Everyone paid attention when she read. But maybe she was too good to waste her time on me.

2) Reading stories out loud is pure torture. I hate making eye contact with other students as they listen in judgment.

"Rebecca, description is what your writing lacks. Right now, you have an outline but no color. Paint with your words," Professor Lamb urged.

Her words reminded me of feedback she'd given to another student, Christian. Only his was the opposite. She'd told him that unnecessary words act as a film, obscuring a genuine idea. That he was drowning his writing in details.

Maybe I could ask him. Maybe my lack of color could even help him.

"Thank you, Professor Lamb. I understand." I didn't. I returned to my list.

Scuffs against the floor and chatter pulled my attention. The class was over, and Christian was leaving the room. I rushed to catch up with him.

"Christian?" I shouted down the crowded hallway. His head jerked in my direction, and he stopped to wait for me.

"Rebecca? Right?" He asked when I was close enough to hear him.

"Yes, nice to officially meet you." Until now, we'd only exchanged comments in class. "Professor Lamb's something, isn't she?

"Yes, she's a character." He paused then smirked, "I sense she's trying to dissolve the particles of our soul into increments then reassemble them to create a superior writer's spirit with her overly colorful criticism."

Emotional Charades

My mouth twitched in an almost smirk, but I didn't know him well enough to be sure that it was a joke. "Criticism can be uncomfortable," I responded, simplifying his sentiment.

The hall was still loud. He took a step towards me, leaning in so I could hear him. His cologne smelled like mint and evergreen.

"Yeah. That. Or it's her excessive use of metaphors, similes, and alliteration. Anything to hammer in that we're in a creative writing class."

He had wide-set brown eyes and full pink lips. Large white teeth shined against his light brown skin. His smile was contagious.

I smiled back involuntarily. "Yeah, it's disorienting. She once told me, *'Rays of light can't shine through without color reflecting the true emotion.'* I'm almost sure she was on something."

We both chuckled the awkward chuckle of people becoming friends.

"If I'm honest, I hate this class. I spend most of my time writing detailed lists about how much I hate it." I pulled on a few ringlets and disturbed the shape of my afro.

"Oh, really, what are your top reasons?" He crossed his arms and leaned against the wall.

I took a beat to recall my list from class today.

I told him reasons 3 and 4: *Mrs. Lamb's excessive perkiness* and *her too cute attire.*

"So, you're not a morning person," he deduced.

I smiled. He had me there. "I wouldn't normally take such an early class. But my schedule is packed this semester, so I had no choice."

"What else is on that list?" His eyes were bright and engaged, like reading between the lines was his social sport.

I told him reason 2: *Reading stories out loud.* I rambled a bit, telling him all about the girl who used yawns as shorthand, but he listened attentively. He even chuckled a bit.

"I take it that you're not comfortable with your writing ability." His polite smile softened his frankness.

"Not when it's creative writing," I admitted. *Wow, he was good at reading subtext.* "See, I'm pre-med. I only took this class, assuming it would be an easy A to fulfill a Gen-Ed. That's why I stopped you. For this observation assignment, maybe we could work together? If your writing is too colorful and mine is too bland, we could balance each other out, maybe?" I asked.

He looked pensive for a moment as he arched his left eyebrow.

What if he thought this was a stupid idea? What if he thought I was insulting him? I wrapped my arm around my belly, trying to quell the slightly nauseated feeling that was growing ever so quickly.

"Why not?"

My nerves dissipated. I pulled out my phone to find time on my packed schedule. Maid of honor duties overlapped study sessions, which overlapped scheduled naps.

He peered at my phone. His brows pinched as he took in my schedule. He pointed at the sliver of time I had right before my next study session.

"You're free now and I know a place," he suggested with a smile and slight tilt of his head.

"Why not?" I said, repeating his words back to him.

The place was a hipster café a few blocks from campus. It was shabby, missing a sense of chicness by miles. It was all mismatched furniture, local art, and random books. The room smelled of coffee and staleness. It was the kind of made un-trendy-on-purpose place that I normally avoided.

"Have you ever been here?"

"No, I don't…" I paused because I was about to be too honest to a stranger, "don't normally come to hipster cafés," I improvised.

"And here I am wearing flannel?" he joked with a wink.

"Are you going to order, or just flirt?" a pink-haired barista barked at us. We both stared at her. She stood, unfazed by her rudeness, waiting for our order.

This was why I didn't like these places. Snarky customer service. The last time I came to a place like this, I'd ordered a caramel macchiato when I meant a caramel latte. The barista refused to serve me, lectured me on the differences, stated that Starbucks was the coffee devil, and that I should do my research before coming back. So, I never did.

"Let's just get seats," he suggested. We found two tattered recliner chairs and a small table awkwardly placed where the L-shaped room curved. We settled into them.

"I wrote an observation in class today. Do you want to hear it?" he asked.

"Sure." I leaned forward and sat my chin on my palm.

Taylor Bianca B

He flipped through his notebook that was covered in doodles on the header of every page and began, "Mornings assault her. A mere bother that she endures with no effort. Her curls carelessly secured near the top of her head in the approximation of a bun. Dark brown hair scattered with highlights that mimic the rust color of her almond-tilted eyes. Crescents lay beneath her eyes, not specific enough to indicate whether she is well-rested. No paint is present to enhance or hide her bare skin. Cedar smudges alter her dark brown skin as a relic of the times when acne disturbed her pores. She continues her statement against morning by spending the same lack of effort on her attire. Her loose clothing allude to the figure they believe they are shielding. It's the effortlessness in her beauty that makes her astonishing. Being captivating without trying is her natural talent."

Oh no.

I sat back in my chair, scrambling to find a way to respond when a handsome man calls you astonishing, and you're engaged. "Um," I started, then stopped because my voice was in the falsetto range.

"You should do your observation on the touchy couple in the corner," he suggested, pointing behind me, sparing me the awkwardness of having to address the moment.

I had to peer around my recliner to see them. Their lips were locked. They were completely unbothered by the room full of strangers. Handwritten notes were never my thing, so I started typing, creating a symphony from the sounds that echoed from my worn-out keyboard.

From the angle I was seated, I could see his back and quick glimpses of her profile. The motion of their kiss moved her in and out of my line of sight. I finished, reread what I'd written, and felt dirty—wrong. I shook my head at the words.

"What's wrong?" Christian asked.

"Um…" What was wrong? I couldn't put my finger on it. "I just feel like a pervert. I spied on that couple," I whispered. Still, I turned for another glance. Drawn to them. They pulled apart and my head jerked forward.

"Writers are perverts…Oh, shit." He pinned me with his eyes. "They saw us," Christian said. "Let's get out of here."

I peered over my shoulder to get one full glimpse of the couple. For the first time, I saw his face. The touchy guy stared at me, and I froze. Christian was laughing. He grabbed my hand, trying to pull me to my feet to flee. I was rooted.

The touchy guy's eyes began to water. The tears made his mixed irises glow. The same ones that woke me up for class this morning. They belonged to the giver of the diamond promise on my left hand. His tall, thin frame stiffened and mimicked mine. We faced each other, stunned.

Then, all I could see was color as tears obstructed my view.

Taylor Bianca B

Chapter 2: Exhaustion

"Eric," I called, hoping that he was just a doppelgänger.

"It's not what it looks like," Eric insisted.

"What the fuck is going on?" I shouted.

Heads started to swivel; waves of chatter buzzed in the café. Christian let go of my hand and backed up a few paces. The girl Eric had kissed backed into the shadowy end of the café. Should I charge him or her?

Before I could decide, the stares and the chatter of the crowd started to feel like pinpricks against my skin. Mortified, I rushed out of the coffee shop, our story damp on my cheeks. Eric chased after me.

"Rebecca!" he shouted.

I turned. The sunlight half obstructed my vision. I could only see his gray cardigan blow in the slight breeze. "What?" My voice was hoarse. My head was spinning. The sunlight felt too heavy and hot on my skin.

"Can we go home?" Eric stopped in front of me. His frame blocked the bright glare of the sun. He gestured to the people watching us.

Cameras spotted the crowd. I imagined someone shouting "WorldStar!" I didn't want to go viral for being an oblivious idiot. I nodded and followed him to our car. I spent the 10-minute drive to our apartment in silence, constructing my arguments and concealing my tears.

Taylor Bianca B

Our apartment was light-washed from the sunlight streaming through the patio door. The stark white walls bounced the light. I felt like we were center stage.

"So, you're fucking cheating on me." My voice rang out like a bell at the beginning of a boxing match.

He stiffened. "I know what it looked like but no I am not...or...I can explain. Let me retrieve my notes," he said while he sprinted toward his backpack near the door.

Shouldn't he be begging for forgiveness? He was behaving like we'd just experienced a different day.

"Eric," I cracked. His casual tone had ruined me. My breath came in large swallows. My throat felt dry, like I'd gone without water for days. The taste of dirt and sand filled my mouth. I'd never been heartbroken before.

Noticing that he changed course and ambled towards me, I shouted, "Eric, don't come near me!" I shuffled around our couch to keep the distance between us. "How long have you been cheating on me?"

"Rebecca" he paused, his eyes darting around the room, "It's complicated," he managed after a moment.

"Make it simple."

He sighed. "What you witnessed was research for—"

My ears perked up at the word *research*, then the conversation took a needed pause as the wooden fruit bowl I flung across the room collided with the wall. It wasn't intentional, but I felt a deep satisfaction when it crashed.

"What are you doing?" he asked, looking at the splintered bowl. I'd surprised us both.

I stood tall, feeling both stupid and vindicated for throwing it. "Eric, I watched you. Don't lie to me. Don't make this worse. Answer my questions." Pools of anger and grief clashed, leaving me disorientated. I was in two places at once: Here trying to get answers, and there at the café, re-watching all the answers I needed.

"I was testing a theory." He held my gaze as his body inclined toward me.

I searched him. His brows were smooth. He wasn't fidgeting, and he was making comfortable eye contact. I was searching for telltale signs that he was lying. None. He believed what he was saying. That didn't make his words make sense. Had I missed something that reduced the significance of the scene? A camera, a script for a play, perhaps? I couldn't wrap my head around it.

"Eric, explain to me what I saw today, and why it happened," I insisted.

"A Prosen study conducted at the University of Groundwood concluded that romantic relationships that originate in youth and continue to adulthood, like ours, have higher rates of divorce. Evidence suggests it is provoked by a lack of varied experiences."

I rolled my eyes, but I didn't interrupt, giving him the time to explain this misunderstanding. Because it had to be a misunderstanding.

"It occurred to me that we could increase our chance of a successful marriage by identifying and synthesizing the areas we lack varied experiences. After evaluating the physical and emotional changes in our relationship, I selected…public displays of affection… You witnessed a trial run. The premise was encouraged—almost assigned—by my professor." He

14

tacked on that sentence like it validated his actions. "Also, I want you to do an iteration of the experiment."

I stared at him in disbelief. His voice was irritating me—calmly presenting evidence that supported his case. As if he were going to break even and convince me that today's actions were forgivable. More than forgivable—the solution to issues that we might have in the future.

"You no longer condone PDA, not since high school. In the experiment, I determined that I am comfortable with public exchanges of affection and was only restricting myself to fit your needs. An acceptable modification in a relationship, but had you asked me before the experiment, I would have said I didn't condone it, instead of saying the truth, which is that my fiancée doesn't like kissing me in public. At least not anymore," he finished shyly.

I stared at him, still trying to process the words that were spilling from his mouth.

"I presume you might want to iterate with a candidate who does not get overstimulated or need to leave social events early," he continued with his gaze to the floor, blinking rapidly. His eyes flicked to mine. "Someone who doesn't embarrass you when they inadvertently say the wrong thing," he added.

Something inside me shifted. I felt like I was in an alternate universe. I glanced around our apartment. It all looked right. Our trinkets, our pictures, our ugly couch, the life we'd created together. I cherished him and us and our future. I thought he felt exactly the same. So, where was this coming from?

My jaw clenched, "I have never complained about any of that."

"No. You never have. Not once." He shook his head and his eyes darted back to the floor. "Factually speaking, those are basic experiences you have not had because of me. Because I am autistic. Five or six years from now, you might start to wonder if you are missing out. This process could remedy that."

I cocked my head to the side, too confused to be properly angry anymore. "So, you cheated on me thinking it could *remedy* a problem that hasn't even come up yet?" I said, sifting through his bullshit.

"Yes, but there is more to it. I am not explaining this well."

"Sure, you are. That wasn't the extravagant answer I was looking for. It wasn't the one that was going to make me instantly forgive you. Is there a bomb on a bus that would have exploded if you hadn't kissed that girl?"

"No, there was not a bus involved," he responded, insecure in his answer.

"I guess you weren't rehearsing for a play either, huh?"

"Rebecca, are you teasing me?" His finger started to tap against his thigh.

"Yes! It's stopping me from saying god-awful things to you. You betrayed me. Now you're explaining it to me with babbling bullshit. Eric, that entire scenario dissolves into you cheating on me. It still hurts, and I feel betrayed, despite your explanation, or your bullshit projection on how I might feel in five years." Tears irritated the skin on my cheeks. A burning sensation followed their trail.

There was finally a moment of awe, clear in his eyes. He rubbed his chest and backed up a few steps. He

16

seemed to have been laboring under the assumption that his motive for cheating would lessen the blow. He shook his head in absolute shock. "I should have told you first. That's what I was going to do originally—"

"But you didn't because you didn't care about my opinion. You knew I would say no."

He tucked his chin. His lips pressed together. "I did not believe you would admit that there are oddities in our relationship that you might wish to live without. I knew you would find scruples with my plan. I thought if I complete an initial cycle, prove that we can grow from this process, then I could convince you. I knew I was violating our trust, but I thought," he raised his hands palms up, "that the ends would justify the means."

"So, you didn't care about my opinion," I repeated. My eyes weren't focused on anything. I was lost as I took in his words. He hurt me on purpose.

For the first time in 10 years, I regretted the person I found love with, resented his inability to detect subtlety, and resented his matter-of-fact communication style. I flinched at my thought. It wasn't true. I didn't regret him. It was frustration. He cheated on me and was telling me like it was the morning news.

Angry, vile thoughts swam through my mind, trying to break through—trying to hurt him back.

He continued to tap his finger against his thigh. "A year from now, you are going to start med school. You are going to spend 80 hours a week with men who share your passion. I cannot construct a timeline where you do not outgrow us." His voice sounded thin. He looked sunken.

I felt like I was falling to pieces. My heart dropped, heavy as a stone. It must have crushed my stomach on the way down. That would explain the nausea sneaking up my throat.

"Are you blaming me for this?"

"Absolutely not. I made an error in judgment. I deluded myself into thinking this was necessary. I am completely sorry. Rebecca. please." His voice broke, "You can contact Juliette for confirmation. I messed up, but the experiment is all true. You can confirm that it wasn't romantic." His words rushed together.

Juliette.

Her name made everything feel more real. At that moment, I was back in the café. There was something familiar about her name.

He was all apologetic now, sobering to the effect of his action. His apologies weren't taking the sting out of my chest. My lungs sizzled with every inhale.

He grabbed my arms below the elbow and tightened his grip. The pressure pulled my attention back from the café, from their kiss.

"Rebecca, I love you. I swear it. I am an idiot."

His eyes locked onto mine. He slid his hands down to mine. My skin still reacted to his touch. My anger parted for the world of tenderness that still existed between us. Somehow. Now, his murmured apologies felt more impactful. Like I believed them. Or like I desperately wanted to.

I stared into his eyes, wanting to see a path through this, wanting to forget it ever happened. Then, he blinked. In that instant, the memory of the kiss flooded me. The way his hands had danced on her neckline.

I yanked away, "I can't listen to this anymore." I ran towards our bedroom.

"Who was that man you were with? He was holding your hand," he asked.

I stopped in my tracks. He thought we had both been caught in acts of betrayal today. I turned to face him. He couldn't look at me.

"That *man* is Christian. He is my tutor." I enunciated every syllable. I slammed the bedroom door and locked it.

My mind wandered while I sobbed in bed. I tried to sleep, but the film of today's events played on the back of my eyelids. Her name echoed in my mind, fanning small fires of anger. I realized that it wasn't just any girl. I knew this girl. I knew of this girl.

She had the type of reputation that made women nervous. I'd watched women's nervousness transform into fear, which turned into slut-shaming. I heard those nervous women spread the word of supposed misdeeds, isolating her from the other women, which ironically forced her into the company of their men.

I'd dismissed those claims or shut down the gossip. I was above that type of behavior until the day I wasn't. Now, I could only think of that cursed day as I drifted off to sleep.

Chapter 3: Share with the Class

I woke up that evening with more questions. Eric wasn't home to answer them. He'd likely gone to class. It infuriated me. He left like we weren't in the biggest fight we'd ever had, like he was sure I wouldn't leave him.

My ears rang. Sirens, fire alarms, a cacophony of alerts sounded in my mind. They all told me to leave, just like he had. I yanked open drawers, stuffed my overnight bag, and left.

Freshly fallen gold and orange leaves tumbled by me as I walked lead-footed against the breeze. Hot with anger, the chilly wind against my skin made me sweat. Droplets of condensation irritated my skin underneath my hoodie. I ignored it.

That kiss. The way his hand lingered on her collar. I was lost in thought.

I reached my best friend's dorm. I knocked, hoping she was home.

Khadijah opened the door.

She looked immaculate as ever with her beautiful hair in one thick braid. It hung over her shoulder and reached her waist. She was Indian with her mom's copper brown complexion and her thick, long, wavy hair with her father's dark brown color.

Taylor Bianca B

Act casual, act casual, I told myself as I kicked off my shoes and placed them on the mat she designated for them. Her room was small, maybe the size of a single car garage. She'd filled it with bright colors and textured fabrics. A light lemon smell of cleaner lingered in the air. Every visible surface in her room was spotless.

I didn't plan what I would say. My hands felt clammy. I wasn't ready to tell anyone.

"What are you up to?" I asked casually.

She tilted her head and narrowed her eyes in suspicion. "Nothing much. I was going to go to Jamie's later."

"Do you mind if I spend the night here?"

"You don't even have to ask." Khadijah gave me another searching look. "Give me a second." She grabbed her phone and slid into the hall. Her room was cozy and comfortable. Pillows, plushies, and a fuzzy pink rug loaned softness to the space.

I paced the length of the room. Every seven steps I had to turn or collide with a wall. Although, banging my head against a wall wasn't the worst option. At least my head would stop spinning. I couldn't stop rehashing the day's events.

To distract myself, I pulled out my phone and perused my Instagram feed. I came across a picture of Eric and me. There was a new comment: *#relationshipgoals, you guys are too cute!*

Impulsively, I deleted the picture. The dense tension in my chest lightened as I confirmed. I went to my page. My stomach turned. I couldn't stand my curated gallery of us. The smiles and sweet captions felt like lies now. I scrubbed us from all my recent posts. Deleting memories and moments until tears swelled in the corner of my eyes. It was childish and meaningless, but it gave me a slight satisfaction.

The door hinge squeaked. Khadijah bobbed in, carrying vending machine snacks.

"Change of plans. We're hanging out tonight." She tossed the snacks in my lap.

"You don't have to do—"

"Shut it," she ordered. "Eat. We'll lay down and watch a movie. If you feel like talking, we'll talk. If you don't…" She shrugged, lifting a single finger to her lips.

I obeyed my bossy best friend.

She put on a horror film and got in bed with me. When my shoulders heaved in time with quiet tears, she rubbed my back in gentle circles.

***

My post-kiss-memory bank shifted from moment to moment, losing chunks of time. I'd spent the last two days at Khadijah's place, ignoring Eric's single text. '*I know you are with Khadijah. I am ready to talk when you are comfortable. I love you and I am sorry I caused this,*" I reread it in my mind for the hundredth time. I simply didn't know how to respond.

Suddenly, it was Wednesday, and I was back in class. Sitting in this classroom made me itch. It felt like I was allergic to its connection to Eric's betrayal.

Christian had assumed the seat next to me, kicking my plus-size acquaintance out of her familiar place. I placed my bag on the desk on the other side of me. No reason for her to have to search for a new person willing to share legroom.

I watched the door and waved her over.

22

"Thank you. These desks are small as shit," she whispered. "I'm Ambrosia."

I almost laughed at her frankness, but my sense of humor was on an emotional hiatus. "I'm Rebecca, and it's no problem."

My attention to her arrival removed Christian's chance to start a conversation. He had questions and I wanted to ignore them.

"Class, are you all ready to share your observations?" Mrs. Lamb asked. Like clockwork, she looked at me. "Rebecca, could you share what you have?"

For the first time, I didn't resent her for her request. I was waiting for it.

"Love has a look to it, and so does lust. He isn't aware of how he looks to the rest of the world. She is his only audience, and he is her only critic. The room of people is completely capable of ignoring their constant affection. They continue their conversations as if the couple is invisible. They have to because the couple isn't aware of them. His hands are a testimony to his addiction. He repeatedly traces her collarbone with his fingertips, lingering in the space between her neck and her shoulders. Slipping his lips to her neck…he whispers kisses there. Their desire radiates out, infesting secret viewers who ardently pretend not to watch, pretend not to be affected, not to be jealous."

I lost a few moments again. I was at the end of my story before I remembered starting.

"How was that? Terrible, unimaginative, intrusive?" I prompted Mrs. Lamb, knowing that nothing could distract me like her idealist input on assigned journaling.

Emotional Charades

"No, you captured a moment. I believe, had you let the story go on, we would have a nice romance." It was her first polite critique of the year.

Not a single fucking metaphor, nothing inflated. I'd wanted her to say something ridiculous so that I could bury myself in sarcastic lists for the rest of the day. No one was living up to my expectations lately.

"Rebecca?" Christian whispered. I glanced at him and focused on his eyes. They were worried about me. It was only then that I realized the pressure on my hand was his. He was holding my hand, and everything I was holding in wanted to escape. His hand felt as solid as steel. Like he was cultivating reassurance. Warm waves washed over me, easing the anxiety.

I blinked back tears. His concern seemed to be the catalyst to my personal Pompeii, but I refused to explode. Closing my eyes tightly, I turned my head to remove Christian from my sight, making myself dormant.

He squeezed my hand. The pool of grief welled up in me again.

"I can't do this." I pulled my hand free and bolted out of class.

Christian followed me. The hall was empty and bright, our steps echoed.

"What's going on?" he whispered, as if the hallway would overhear us.

I felt it building—the emotional eruption from class, the desire to let it all out. But I hadn't told anyone. I was too embarrassed. Then, I realized he already knew. He'd been there. So, I erupted.

"On Monday, you and I watched my fiancé publicly fondle another woman. We went home. We

24

fought. He explained that he was conducting an experiment, not cheating."

Christian looked aghast.

I raised one brow, "Right. Oh, and at some point in the fight, I realized I knew her. Juliette. I didn't recognize her at the café. She used to have red hair. The blonde pixie look is new. I was a complete bitch to her the last time I talked to her." I buried my face in my hands, letting out a sigh that sounded more akin to a grunt.

That day kept replaying in my mind.

Last year, Khadijah and I were meeting Eric and Jamie at a bar. When we walked in, Jamie, Khadijah's fiancé, was talking to Juliette. Her red hair was hanging in her face. He reached up and gently tucked it behind her ear. It was nothing, but with his reputation, it was everything.

Khadijah stormed off in tears. I followed her. Jamie followed us. He was begging Khadijah to listen.

He stopped us. "Nothing was going on. We were talking about class. I've changed. I love you!" Khadijah calmed, then Juliette walked up to us. She echoed Jamie's words.

Khadijah lost the bead of composure she'd regained. "You'll never be the type of woman he'd take home to his mother," she said. Khadijah pulled off her engagement ring, stepped forward, and handed it to Juliette, "Since you'll never earn one," she admonished.

I could have defused the situation, but my best friend was hurt.

I said, "The campus whore with the university slut. They might make a powerful chlamydia-infested couple."

Emotional Charades

"Now, this all feels like cosmic retribution," I whispered on the brink of tears.

"Okay." He paused, shaking his head as if to clear it. "How are you?"

"I'm spiraling." I leaned my head back, looking up to the ceiling. There was a well in my chest, a pool of tears that were trying to get out.

He placed a hand on my shoulder, "You know it's not your fault. You didn't do anything to make him cheat."

My lip quivered; I took a deep breath. I needed that confirmation. I snapped my head down, "You know, he thought that I was cheating with you."

"I thought he might. We were holding hands. I tried to DM you on Instagram to…I don't know…defend you, or back up your story?"

"My account is suspended. I deleted a few pictures. It was reported as suspicious behavior by my friends and followers." I smiled, shaking my head with disbelief. "They blocked my access, pending an investigation." It wasn't a joke, but out loud, it kind of sounded like one. I tongued my cheek to stop an involuntary smile. He bit his bottom lip to contain his. With that moment of levity, my avalanche of emotions settled.

We found a courtyard. Purple petaled trees adorned the manicured lawn. The edges of their petals were browning a little in the cool, fall air. We sat on a bench and just talked. For a moment, I wasn't the girl whose relationship troubles were broadcasted in a café, and he wasn't a stranger, oddly entangled in the mess of someone else's romance.

We were just friends catching up.

Taylor Bianca B

Chapter 4: Awkward Introductions

Ｍy phone's alarm chimed, pulling me back to reality. It was time for my study session with Khadijah. Christian walked with me. His company was comforting. The 5-minute walk seemed to take seconds.

I knocked on Khadijah's door.

Christian touched my arm, and it went from a stagnant touch to a gentle stroke. "If you ever need to talk, just let me know," he offered. His hand was there to politely console me, but his soft touch left trails of pleasant sensation. My skin was starved for it.

My breath caught.

"We set our date! January 4th," Khadijah shouted, she pulled open the door. I jumped; my head whipped toward her. She clapped her hands over her mouth and shrieked. "Oh, I'm sorry." She extended her hand to Christian. "Hi, are you joining us for our study session?" She looked from him to me.

"Hi, I'm Christian." He extended his hand to meet hers. "No, I have to get going," he said, peering at his watch.

He grabbed my hand and squeezed it. "I'll see you later." He glanced back at Khadijah and said, "Nice to meet you," before jogging away, clearly late for something.

Khadijah's face was screwed up in suspicion. She eyed me as I entered and then glanced down the hall in the direction Christian had gone. I could tell she was concocting her own narrative about my relationship status.

"Congratulations on setting a date," I said.

"Who was that?" she asked, her eyes narrowed.

"A friend from class. We were just…"

"No, he isn't your friend because I've never heard of him." Khadijah used her ipso facto best friend logic.

"What's on the study agenda today?" I inquired, changing the subject.

She rolled her eyes at me but pulled out her phone to look at the agenda she'd created. "Well, you'll study for your test in A&F, and I'll study for the GRE."

If superpowers existed, hers were planning and organizing. Since our freshman year, she'd insisted that we maintain a study schedule and share calendars. Every semester, she copied my syllabuses to plan out an effective schedule.

I set my backpack on her desk. Something was different. "Khadijah, is there more stuff here since I left this morning?"

"Yes! I woke up this morning and cleared out nearly five Dollar Trees." She skipped to an inundated bookshelf. Khadijah grabbed an ornately designed plastic plate from a large stack. Her parents didn't support her getting married before graduating. So, they placed the onus on her to plan the wedding. They agreed to pay for the dress, venue, and the cake. Everything else was up to her.

Her room was neatly crammed with lights, chair covers, candles, centerpieces in different stages of construction, and the newly added plates. All things she'd found at a discount. Everything she needed to plan her wedding on a budget.

"What are you going to do with those?"

"Spray paint them gold and use them as plate settings."

I pulled out my phone to look at her schedule, "Khadijah, when are you going to have time to spray paint 50 plates?" I estimated from the stack on the bookshelf.

Khadijah's schedule was jam-packed. She was a full-time student, studying for her GRE, applying to grad school, working 12 hours a week, and planning her wedding.

"150 plates. My mom and aunties are picking up all the plates in their area."

I gawked at her. She was insane. How was she going to get this all done? "I can help."

She sucked her teeth, "Oh, how nice of you to offer. It's already on your schedule. I'll see you Saturday."

I side-eyed, then switched back to my calendar. Sure enough, she'd scheduled over my "couple's time" block. As her maid of honor, I'd given her free range over my schedule. Any time not blocked off could be absorbed by wedding planning. A week ago, I would have raised hell about her invading my couple time, but today, I was thankful for a distraction.

I switched to her calendar, "It says you're tutoring on Saturday."

"It's online. I can do both."

I looked at her, and she turned her head to avoid me. "Khadijah…"

Taylor Bianca B

"Don't start."

I threw my hands up, "Not starting."

I sat down at her desk and opened my study guide. Khadijah pulled out a box of GRE prep cards and sat next to me. I read through my notes, distracted.

Four months. That was…it was crazy.

I started, "Honey, are you sure—"

"Rebeca, you don't understand," she sighed, dropping her head into her hands.

"Planning a wedding in four months seems crazy, and you're already so busy."

"I have to be married by the time I graduate so Jamie and I can move in together."

"You can postpone it a bit. A summer wedding?"

"I'd have to move back in with my parents. I'd have a bedtime and daily reminder of *'is that top a bit small, beta?'*" She mimicked her mom's rich voice.

"For like a month. Or you can live with your fiancé. They won't like it, but they will get over it."

She frowned, "You don't have Asian parents. You don't have Muslim parents. You're already living in sin, and your parents pay your rent," she joked and gave me a *no offense* smile. "And as much as I sometimes reinterpret the rules, I want to be married before we live together. That's important to me." She sat her hand on mine.

I nodded, "Move in with me for a month then."

"Oh, move in with the newlyweds so that I can study how a perfect couple does it firsthand," she joked, referring to us by that dumb nickname. It certainly didn't feel like we were in the newlywed stage anymore.

My head shot down to hide my glassy eyes. Discreetly, I wiped my lash line and cleared my throat.

Emotional Charades

"No one is perfect," I said softly so that my voice didn't crack. Focusing on her had distracted me from the café. Now, the pain was creeping back in.

"Rebecca, I know you're worried, but you don't understand. I haven't been a great Muslim daughter. My sister has taken over that role," she huffed. She and her sister, Amara, were in a lifelong battle to be their parents' favorite according to Khadijah. Amara doted on her little sister every time I'd met her. To me, the rivalry was one-sided.

"I'm engaged to a non-Muslim, and he's a white boy. I act *'too American,'* as my mom would say, but I can do this one thing right. Give my mom something to gossip to her friends and frenemies about. And I'm going to do it before my sister can." She raised her hand for a high five.

I begrudgingly slapped her hand. "Dork."

As I sat and thought about it, this was her domain. Organization was her superpower. She'd managed to organize decorations, a dress, a venue, and a date. Instead of being another hindrance, I needed to help her.

"I do understand. I will do anything I can to help you, I promise."

"Thank you." She put her hand on my cheek and dragged her thumb underneath my eye. "Are you ready to talk? I normally wouldn't push, but watching you cry isn't easy. Plus, you and Eric never fight. Now, some new handsome guy is hanging off you in hallways."

I took a breath; telling her would make it more real. It'd be followed by pity and advice. Tears forced their way through my guard.

Taylor Bianca B

She wrapped me in a hug, "Oh, sweetie." She pulled back and grabbed my hands. "You can tell me anything."

"Eric cheated on me."

She laughed—more of a cackle—in pure disbelief. "No, he didn't," she said confidently.

I nodded. "I caught him kissing a girl at a coffee shop a few blocks from campus." I looked up at her with tears in my eyes.

Her jaw dropped. "Rebecca, I'm so sorry." Khadijah pulled my head to her shoulder and held me there.

I sobbed in her arms.

Why had I been so afraid to tell her? She'd understand better than most. I could confide in my best friend.

"I just didn't think this could happen to us. I thought we were better than this. This happened to other people. Couples who can't communicate or people who ignore the signs. Or people who don't really love each other. I thought if someone cheated on me, I'd just leave, not dance around my living room arguing semantics. Now, I just feel so fucking weak and stupid. I just didn't think it would hurt so bad." I wept on her shoulder, venting mindlessly.

Khadijah pulled back. Her eyes were bursting with tears. I was so grateful to have her sympathy.

Her eyes narrowed. "Is that what you think about me?" she asked. Her tears were for the insult I'd laid on her shoulder.

"No, Khadijah. I didn't mean you!" I grabbed her hands, trying to force reassurance.

Emotional Charades

"What must you think of me? I forgave. I worked it out with Jamie. It damn sure was more than a kiss. You think I'm pathetic, don't you?" Khadijah ranted, her tone on the cusp of anger.

My eyes flittered down for a second. There'd been a time when I didn't understand how she forgave him. He'd made a fool of her, and she let him. That didn't mean I thought she was pathetic.

My eyes flashed back to hers. "No, I don't." She pulled her hands free, slid her chair back, and stood. She'd seen that moment of indecision.

"Khadijah, I'm sorry I hurt your feelings. I wasn't talking about you."

"Yeah, yeah, just girls like me though." She waved her hand, dismissing my apology. "You guys didn't break up over this? That stupid Instagram breakup was a hack, right?" Her eyes inspected me.

"We fought and we…" I paused, struggling for the words.

She looked incredulous. "No! No! Absolutely not. You two can't break up. You're the perfect couple," Khadijah said matter-of-factly. She shook her head. "Rebecca, please don't be childish. Over a kiss? Nonsense." She paced the small room, muttering under her breath.

"Clearly we aren't perfect."

"I shouldn't be getting married. If you two can't make it work, Jamie and I…we're fucked." She turned and looked at me with tear strained eyes. "You two are the role models. You set the example."

"What?" How had we gotten here?

"I need to call off this wedding. What was I thinking?" she said frantically, roughly running her fingers through her hair. She was panicking as she held my relationship on a pedestal, suddenly finding hers wanting.

She lifted a trash can and brushed several completed centerpieces into it. She grabbed her phone and started to dial. I shot up and pulled her phone from her hands.

She reached for it. "I need to tell him," she cried.

I tossed her phone on the bed behind her, then grabbed her hands. The contrast of her inflamed green eyes against her dark skin looked cartoonish. She looked like she had been photoshopped into a Disney villain. I did this. Pushed her over the edge of her insecurity.

She struggled against my hold, "Khadijah, stop. Listen."

"You said it. I'm weak."

"You're not weak."

Her eyes were piercing me. I didn't know what to say. Apologizing hadn't worked. Explaining hadn't worked.

"Were you pretending before?" I asked.

Her breathing slowed and she blinked a few times. Strings of tears raced down her face. But she didn't pull away. I released her.

"What do you mean?"

"You were excited about your wedding date. Excited about plastic plates from the dollar store. Was that all pretend?"

She backed up and sat on her bed. Her eyes were cast down. I waited for her to collect her thoughts.

"I wasn't pretending," she answered tentatively, then sniffed.

"Do you want to marry Jaime?"

"Yes." She grabbed a tissue and blew her nose.

"You're not weak. I'm hiding out here instead of talking to Eric. I'm the weak one."

I sat next to her on the bed and took her hand.

"I'm sorry, Khadijah."

She looked at me, "I'm sorry, too." It's all the stress from the wedding. I just freaked out." She leaned her head on my shoulder, talking more to herself than to me. "That was all in the past. He's not like that anymore. We've moved on and we're better."

Chapter 5: The Times Before Now

There was a weakness in avoiding Eric, in hiding in my best friend's bed. Avoiding the reality that his answers wouldn't align with my expectations. I'd prefer something like, *'I had to kiss her, or a train would have derailed at the airport, destroying a fleet of passenger-packed planes.'* With an excuse like that, all the pain would go away. We would move past it and go on to the happily ever after in our love story. The reality was, there might not be a happily ever after. Avoiding him wasn't going to change that.

So, I called him.

I sat hunched over on the side of Khadijah's bed, hoping he'd miss my call.

He answered on the first ring. "Rebecca, I am so sorry."

"Eric, I…" I clenched my fist and held my breath. *Don't cry. Don't cry.* "Um, we need to talk."

"Do you want me to come get you?"

I sighed, "No." I couldn't hash this out, and then try to function in class the next day. "This weekend. Maybe?" I offered.

"We are supposed to drive home on Thursday. Since you do not have Friday classes, would that work for you?"

No, because I never want to fucking talk to you again, a voice in my head rang out. It was followed by another voice that said, *You're a damn liar. You miss him.* The truth in both statements made me sick.

"Sure," I agreed. I tossed the phone on the pillow and hugged my stomach, ending the call before my conflicting emotions could escape.

Now, I had a day to mull over what I wanted. A part of me wanted to get over this. The other part of me wanted to leave, to move on, or to get even, but every breakup scenario I constructed ended with us getting back together. I hated that I couldn't imagine breaking up with him.

In what felt like a blink, my 24-hour grace period was over.

I heard the engine before I saw him. Eric pulled up in our Ford Focus. It was so loud it raddled the car a little. The familiar rumble offered me a little comfort as I climbed in, shifting my position as close to the door as possible, and as far away from him as I could get.

Then, we were headed home to see his little brother, Landen, off to his first high school homecoming.

"Thank you for coming. I know everyone would have missed you," Eric said. He put the car in drive and eased into traffic.

I nodded, "I've missed Landen. I would've regretted it." I considered canceling, but why should I exclude myself for Eric's mistakes? Plus, the two-hour drive from Ypsilanti to Grand Rapids was an open opportunity to talk.

"How was your day?"

"Fine," I huffed.

"How is your writing class going?"

"Better. I have a tutor now, and I got a decent grade on my last assignment."

"That is great. I knew you could do it. You can do anything." He glanced at me and smiled.

His smile covered me with warmth, like a blanket at a movie theater. His mixed eyes have been the start and end to my day for so long. They still soothed me like Epsom salt. I smiled back.

He reached for my hand. I recoiled.

Instantly, I pictured his hand cupping *her* face. A slow simmer of anger, hurt, and embarrassment rose in my chest. My jaw clenched.

"I am sorry. Habit," he corrected, then he started to tap the steering wheel.

His gaze shifted from the windshield, then at me a few times. He frowned, his features contorted. "Do you want to break up? I do not."

I don't know," I said.

My hands started to shake. I stared out the window, trying to hold back tears. Green, gold, and orange leaves blurred as we drove past trees on the highway. This landscape, this route home, was tied to us. Memories of happier drives blurred by like the trees. Times when we sang off-key, and passed love taps back and forth. Everything was bubbling up again. I couldn't go home like this, tear lined and festering in anger. Our parents would interrogate us. "Maybe we should save the heavy topic for the drive back."

"Yes. We can talk later."

This could be the last time we all get together as a family, I thought. I didn't want it dampened by this drama. I tried to let my mind drift off to better times to assuage my mood.

***

Emotional Charades

The day I met him, I saw his family move into a house across the street from me. He looked about my age, so I was excited to make a new friend. I waited for what felt like months for the opportunity to meet him.

Later, my mom told me I had only waited a week.

During that time, I watched his older siblings coming and going, playing outside, and meeting other teens on the block, but never him. I only ever saw him in transit.

I sat at our bay windows with my jacket and my gloves on. As soon as I saw them, I bolted for the door, screaming, "Mom, I'm going to meet him."

She'd follow me at an adult's pace.

I remember waiting for her at the curb. My mom grabbed my hand and walked me across the street. The moment my feet touched the curb, I ran to where his family was loading up their minivan. The whole family froze at my approach.

"I'm Rebecca Dangerfield," I announced to everyone. But I held my hand out to him where he stood near his father.

He looked at me, but his eyes darted to the ground too quickly. He repeated this sudden head movement a few times. Awkwardly, he stepped towards me, paused, then turned around and walked behind his father, hiding behind his dad's puffy winter coat. A moment later, he was climbing into the minivan and closing the sliding door. He repeated the awkward head gesture a few more times, then made no more attempts to look at me.

"Well, he's rude—" I started to say aloud.

My mom expertly slid into the conversation to prevent me from vocalizing any more of the conclusions

I'd reached. "Hi, I'm Teresa Dangerfield. You just met my energetic daughter, Rebecca. We don't want to hold you up. She just wanted to let you know that a kid around your son's age lives close."

His parents introduced themselves as Bette and Paul Bridgeport, then introduced their kids: William-14, Joan-11, Eric-8, and Landen-6 months. They pointed out the kids and then apologized for Eric's behavior. At the time, I didn't understand why. The three parents seemed to be speaking in an adult code.

When we got back to the house, my mom tried to have a big talk with a little girl.

"Rebecca, you know that some people are different, right?"

"Yes, of course," I responded smugly, "Some people are tall, some are short, some are black or white, some are girls, and some are boys."

"Okay, so among all those types, there are people who have—who are different in another way."

I sat there while my mom tried to explain Eric's behavior. To convey what she'd been told during the adult conversation. What I took from the conversation was that I should be kind and patient to him.

A few days later, I went to his house with my mother's permission. He was playing, kicking a ball against the side of the garage. At 8, he was already tall— 5 feet and rail thin. His arms hung like branches on a snowman and reached well past his waist. He was a winter's pale during a warm fall.

When the ball rebounded, he would stop it, reset it in front of him, then kick it again, softly. I recognized the game as the lone kid's soccer. Your adversary: an unmoving wall that could never miss a shot. He removed the excitement from the game by slowing it down to a toddler's pace.

Eric ignored my presence; his sole interest was in the game. I introduced myself, again, and practiced the patience my mother instructed me to employ.

After playing 7 rounds of his scoreless game, he said his first words to me. "Hi, Rebecca Dangerfield. I am Eric Bridgeport. It is very nice to make your acquaintance."

It was the most formal introduction I had ever heard from a child. He paused between every sentence, speaking in an odd pattern.

Excited, I rushed to his face, "I have a dog, and she loves me. My dog's name is Lucy, short for Lucy Lawless. I'm an only child, but I have lots of cousins. My mom brings them over a lot so that I don't get stingy. Their names are Kyle, Mike, Lauren..."

His brief sentence allowed my 8-year-old mind to believe that my patience had worked. That I had overcome whatever was different about him. Somewhere in the middle of my ramble, I noticed that he wasn't looking at me or kicking the ball. He began to rock back and forth while tapping his thumb to his fingers. I could hear him muttering, but I only made out a few words: occipital lobe.

Panicked with the belief that I had broken him, I took a few steps back, toeing the ball so that it would follow me. I kicked the ball to him slowly, he stopped it, and in his own time, returned it.

"We have a dog named Biff and a cat named Lady. I like her more. The cat, I mean. I have three siblings, William, Joan, and Landen. You met them *briefly. I have more cousins than I would like to list, but if you were to insist, I would list them."*

Eric released a huge breath after he finished, like the effort of responding had tired him out. He stopped the game while he spoke and restarted after gathering his breath.

The rest of the day went like that. I'd list details about my life, and in his own time, he would respond with his version of the same list.

Our interaction mimicked a conversation, but it wasn't one. It was more of an exchange. Our next interaction happened pretty much the same way. We played a mostly silent game of kickball. We exchanged information and from a distance, we may have looked like two kids playing.

After a while, I became bored with the pace of the game. I began to kick the ball without stopping it first, adding a little force with every kick. His posture became strained and unbalanced. He struggled to reach the ball before it could pass him, and he lost his breath. I could predict what was going to happen, but I couldn't stop myself. I kept kicking the ball harder and harder until he ran for it, misjudged it, and tumbled down.

He sat there expressionless. I couldn't tell if he was mad or wanted to cry as he wiped debris from his clothing. Frightened, I stood in silence, guilt radiating from me.

Luckily, Mr. Bridgeport offered salvation from the side door. "Does anyone want hot chocolate?"

"Yes, sir," I responded quickly, desperate to leave the scene of the crime.

Eric stood and walked into the house. I worried that he was furious and that once he told them what had happened, everyone else would be, as well. Nervous, I followed him into his house, glancing at my own with the hope that someone would come to my rescue.

I walked into a dated kitchen and accepted a seat at a red table with silver legs. Mr. Bridgeport boiled milk and made three cups of hot chocolate, complete with marshmallows. He sat all three mugs on the table and took a seat across from me. Eric picked his cup up and walked away. I watched him leave the room, confused about my placement.

"So, how is school going, little lady?"

"It's good. I mean, it's going well."

"Do you go to Hope Academy?" Mr. Bridgeport asked.

"Yes, I'm a third grader, and I'm on the honor roll," I told him proudly, careful to use proper grammar like the teacher taught me.

"Eric goes there, too."

"No, he doesn't," I stated firmly because I hadn't seen him in school.

"Well, actually, he does. He is in a special class for—"

"Different kids," I responded, excited to have the answer.

"Yes. He has a condition called Asperger's. It makes it hard for him to get along with other kids," he explained. Though he didn't tell me at the time, I later learned that Mr. Bridgeport was a doctor and felt that it was important to casually talk about Asperger's, to remove the stigma associated with social disorders.

My curiosity was sparked because I wasn't sure what he meant. Several questions prepared to burst out of me because I needed to become an instant expert on "ash-burgers."

But just then, Eric walked back into the room, mug still in his hand and hot chocolate still filled to the brim. "Do you like video games? Do you like Sonic the Hedgehog? I have the game. If you want to play, you can follow me to my room," he said without waiting for me to respond. Even back then, I could tell when he had practiced what he wanted to say before he said it.

We played for hours, and it was the first time we interacted like kids. While playing the game, he was jovial, relaxed, and competitive. He talked more; it was mostly directed at the game, but it was in my presence, so I accepted it.

We were friends.

Mr. Bridgeport knocked on Eric's door after it was dark. My dad was at the front door to call me for dinner. I exited his room without an actual goodbye. I waved, and he darted his eyes away. He probably hadn't had time to practice his goodbye speech.

I followed Mr. Bridgeport to the door. The whole time, a tiny seed of guilt still weighed on my conscience.

"I'm so sorry about making Eric fall. I didn't do it on purpose. I didn't push him or anything, I just kicked the ball too hard."

He laughed at me, kneeling to my level. "Well, it's alright, sweetheart. Eric isn't hurt and it wasn't a malicious act. Eric has trouble with hand-eye coordination, and you couldn't have known. Plus, falling is good for you."

He led me to the door, and I jumped into my dad's arms. I was a little too old to be carried around, but my dad didn't mind.

Emotional Charades

The moment the door closed behind us, I asked him, "What does malicious mean? And how could falling be good for you?"

Over the next few years, our families became very close. We'd take family vacations together, spend holidays together, and support each other in times of crisis.

Eric and I were the closest. We were like any other best friends, but there were small oddities unique to our relationship. I learned to have an analytical conversation about anything: toys, sitcoms, ice cream cones. He learned that hurt feelings outweighed logical correctness and that apologizing was the solution. Also, all comments or complaints about a movie needed to be held until the end. That sentiment was seconded for books.

I had after-school activities like soccer and gymnastics. He had sessions with a speech pathologist and an occupational therapist to help him with social skills and his speech cadence. As with any skill, practice makes perfect, and I was the perfect practice partner. We made his therapy homework into games like emotional charades. We built a private language of expressions based on those games.

For four years, our friendship was isolated. He was still uncomfortable with most people. When I was with other people, he preferred to stay home reading or playing games. It made me sad because I loved his company and I was sure my friends would, too. I could tell him anything. He was funny. He was cute and tall, and when his eyes caught the sunlight, they were mesmerizing.

He mentioned to his therapist that I got sad when he refused to meet my other friends, so Dr. Wallis challenged him. He wanted Eric to accompany me to a social outing, to push his comfort zone by interacting with people outside his circle.

He refused. But our parents insisted, his professional family encouraged it, and in the end, a bowling outing was chosen. My co-ed soccer team had won an important game in our conference. As a reward, the coaches scheduled an event at the bowling alley.

I knew he was nervous because he was tapping his fingers together while repeating the list under his breath. I knew it by heart now, the anatomy and function of the brain. He'd memorized it from a poster on his wall—one that his father had used while in medical school and given to Eric as a keepsake.

It took about 15 minutes for the whole experiment to dissolve. I introduced him to everyone and he managed to offer a general "Hey" to the 15 kids in the alley. He sat down while we picked the teams and the bowling order. The group was super cheerful and gossiping about school. It was Eric's turn to bowl. I was worried that he would fall or throw the ball in the wrong direction. He got a strike.

It caught everyone's attention because he rolled the ball slowly. Everyone erupted in chatter and cheer.

"Wow, that's crazy!"

"That's impossible."

More praise ran through the crowd. They were laughing and pointing, and Eric misinterpreted their polite intention. I was caught up in the chatter for a minute. Then, I noticed Eric, his eyes darting to the floor then to the crowd.

"What? What is so funny?" he asked.

I couldn't hear him. I could only read his lips. He was backing up toward the lane, speaking too softly for anyone in the group to hear him over the noise.

I jumped up, trying to get to him before he stepped into the waxed lane. But up he went, his feet slipping from under him. With the splendor of the uncoordinated, he somehow landed on his stomach, looking down at the pins.

This time, the crowd laughed at his expense. With his head held down, he got up and walked directly to my side. He didn't say anything. He grabbed a free chair and sat down as close to me as he could get. My skin prickled from his nearness. His face flushed, and his breathing was irregular. Still, he sat calmly, determined to get through the outing.

"Do you want to walk home?" I asked, releasing him from this social experiment.

He answered with a head nod, so defeated that his eyes never made it to my face. I wanted to comfort him, hold his hand, or give him a hug, but I didn't want to bring any more attention his way.

Once we were outside and a few feet from the alley, I could see him coming back to himself. His skin returned to a shade of pink instead of periwinkle.

"You know that they weren't being mean the first time they laughed, right?" I said.

"What was so humorous? I was confused. A strike is the objective of the game, yes?"

I laughed a little, but not harshly. "Yes, a strike is the goal. Most people bowl harder, throwing the bowling ball down the lane with all their might." I demonstrated a bowling technique for him. "It looked like you just sat the ball down and somehow it knocked the pins over one at a time. Everyone was surprised."

"So, the contrast was amusing."

"Yes."

"Thank you for your clarification and reenactment."

"I'm glad you came," I told him, all warm and giddy inside. I was proud of him. He had faced his fear.

"Are you? This was a celebratory event for you, and my presence ruined it," he responded guiltily.

"It's no big deal." I waved it off. I wanted to lift that guilt. I had agreed to this evening. It wasn't his fault. I wasn't even expecting a perfect night, but I didn't want to tell him that.

"I had hoped to impress you tonight. All week, I practiced appropriate conversation topics and listening skills with William and Joan."

"Why?" I asked. I knew what I wanted him to say, but I wanted him to say it all on his own.

"Because I often discuss topics that do not interest others and I do not recognize the signals that indicate their lack of interest, like their body language and facial expressions. You know…Asperger's syndrome." The biggest smile broke across his face at his own joke.

I closed the space between us to bump him. It was flirting, although back then, I didn't know what to call it. He followed me back to my side of the pavement, walking close enough that our hands touched after every step.

"Why did you want to impress me?" I asked hastily, eager to hear his reason.

"I had hoped that this outing would give me the opportunity to kiss you," he blurted.

Emotional Charades

The grin on my face forced my dimples to new depths. Eric didn't look at me. I think he was too nervous to see my reaction.

"Why did you think that kissing me and coming tonight were connected? Did you think that coming tonight would earn you a kiss?"

"No," he hurried to explain himself. "No is the answer to the second portion of your question. I did not think my attendance earned me anything. At our homes, we are surrounded by our parents. I hoped that without them around, we could discuss a possible kiss or the prospect of you becoming my girlfriend." He rushed the words as if he were afraid he would lose his nerve.

We were in front of my house. The walk from the bowling alley had revealed our mutual crushes.

"You should have asked. It could have saved you a fall and you would have gotten the kiss," I advised before fleeing into my house. I could see him running to his own house as I closed my front door. Twenty seconds later, my house phone rang.

"Rebecca, I think you are beautiful and kind. You are the best best friend I could hope for. Would you like to become my girlfriend?"

"Yes, I would like that!"

Two seconds later, I heard the dial-tone, and twenty seconds after that, there was a knock on my door. I answered it, and by the time I closed it, I had had my first kiss. It was immediately followed by my first grounding.

We had walked home without calling our parents.

Taylor Bianca B

Chapter 6: Moms and Dads

Memory lane was supposed to be a distraction from my anger, but it was actually the remedy. By the time we reached the Bridgeport's house, I was on the pleasant side of neutral. Stepping out of the memory of the café reminded me that we were more than that day.

Looking out my window, there were new memories to hold on to. Landen was posing with his date. He looked like Eric, tall and thin with sandy brown hair. His date was short and curvy, with pale skin and red hair. They wore matching suits.

My parents and Eric's were taking more pictures than they could ever print. Colorful fall trees created a cozy backdrop. Mrs. Bridgeport was using a tablet to take pictures. It made me smile. She was simple and sweet, with dark brown hair that was always kept at chin length. Her eyes were mixed like Eric's.

My mom was using a digital camera. I knew she wouldn't upload the pictures for months. She was pretty, even now in her fifties. Her dark brown skin had escaped wrinkles. Her coily hair reached the middle of her back.

Our fathers were both snapping with their phones. They were like carbon copies of each other, other than different careers—my dad a professor, and his dad a doctor—and different complexions. My dad was a deep brown and his dad a fair-skinned redhead, but both were

6'2" and outdoorsy. Both were selective with their words and wise in their delivery.

The pair rushed to my car door to hug me. They play tussled over who would get the first hug. My father won, opening my door and bear-hugging me the moment I got out. The moment he released me, Mr. Bridgeport hugged me and kissed my temple, "We've missed you, baby girl."

"I've missed you all, too."

"This is my other sister, Rebecca, and this is my brother, Eric" Landen introduced us. "This is Makenzie, my girlfriend." His smile was ear to ear. We all greeted each other politely.

"Get together. Say cheese!" Mrs. Bridgeport said.

We bunched together, arms wrapped around each other. After several rounds of *'look here, smile'*, I asked, "Have you all taken pictures with them?"

"Not with both my boys," Mrs. Bridgeport welled up. She handed me her tablet as we exchanged positions. I took a few shots, but I kept hearing low voices from the tablet. I looked at the taskbar. FaceTime was open. I tapped that icon. William and Joan were there chatting together.

"Hi, guys."

"Oh, thank goodness. We'd been staring at mom for five minutes," said William.

"We've gotta get Mrs. Dangerfield an iPhone. She's the only one I trust to operate facetime properly," said Joan.

I laughed, then turned the camera around and the volume up. We all had a little laugh about the mishap. Landen took the iPad and introduced Mackenzie to William and Joan. Soon, Landen's school friends showed up. There were more photos and then they were off in their limo.

My dad turned to us, "Kids, I know you're not staying the night, but how about dinner?"

Eric and I looked at each other. After exchanging a few expressions, we decided to stay.

"Dad, if you cooked, I wouldn't dare miss it." My dad wrapped his arm around my shoulder and led the way to our house across the street.

"I'm not going to take that personally, baby," My mom interjected, grabbing my other hand.

Everyone followed us. I walked into a time capsule of my adolescence. A stranger wouldn't be able to tell whose house this was. There were as many pictures of the Bridgeport's as there were of the Dangerfield's.

Dinner with my family was pleasant. Time flowed by with light conversation, but it was getting late.

"Oh, we should leave soon. I need to get back to Khadijah's before she falls asleep," I said, scooting back my chair.

"Back to Khadijah's?" My mom asked, one brow raised.

My heart skipped a beat. How the hell had I let that slip?

"It'll be nearly 2:00 am when you get back," my dad added.

"Is this some late-night rave?" Mr. Bridgeport joked.

"Um, we have to drop something off," I improvised.

All the parents looked at me suspiciously. I could see Eric out of my peripheral vision. He was staring dead at me, waiting for me to direct him. Maybe Eric could withhold the truth, but a direct lie was beyond him.

"It can't wait until morning?" Mrs. Bridgeport asked. She squinted at her husband.

"She has an early morning." I looked at Eric to give him the expression to go along with it.

"Yes, she has an early morning," Eric repeated.

They exchanged suspicious looks. Eric's jaw was tight, and he looked like he was going to be sick.

"Dear, Landen told us you scrubbed your Instagram," my mom said gently, her hand clenching my dad's. They all nodded reassuringly. "He said that means you broke up." She put her hand on her chest and rubbed in gentle circles.

I could feel my heartbeat racing. That moment was the bane of my existence. I'd invited other people's opinions into this situation while I was still processing mine.

I peered at Eric. He was stimming, tapping a melody on the table. We were busted from his body language alone. He looked at me with a question on his face, *What should we do*? I answered with an expression that meant *just tell them.*

He nodded.

"Unfortunately, I have to inform you that our relationship is on hiatus. Recent indiscretions on my part have violated the terms of our relationship," Eric explained. His shoulders eased and he stopped tapping as hard.

He summarized our demise in two sentences, where I would have needed a prologue just to set the scene at the café. My version would have lingered on minor details, devoting several paragraphs to describing the kiss as accurately as possible.

The silence grew heavy in the room. Confused glances darted among our parents. Soothing looks were directed at me and suspicious glares towards Eric. They were quiet for a while as they figured out the best way to continue.

"What happened?" my mom asked.

He took a deep breath, then cast his eyes down, "Rebecca caught me with another woman," Eric responded concisely.

Mrs. Bridgeport stiffened and reached for her husband's hand. My parents both sat back in their chairs, creating space between them and Eric. Mr. Bridgeport looked bewildered, as if we had shown him proof that aliens existed. They must have willfully misunderstood his use of the word *indiscretion*. Indiscretion always meant cheating.

"You cheated on Rebecca?" Mrs. Bridgeport blurted in surprise.

"Yes," Eric responded curtly because that was the answer to her question. They all wanted more.

'Details, the color,' Mrs. Lamb's voice echoed in my head. Out of place, a smile parted my lips.

"Last Thursday, I walked into a café and watched Eric make-out with—" I paused, my anxious smile dissipating. It was her name that stopped me, "a girl from his class."

"You were seeing someone behind Becca's back?" My dad practically growled the words.

"No, I was not seeing her."

"It was just physical?" my mom asked, furious.

"No," he answered.

"So, do you have feelings for this girl?" Mrs. Bridgeport wondered out loud.

"No."

"Were you and Becca on bad terms… fighting… about to break up? What happened?" My dad was searching for the smoking gun, the information that led to the crime. His tone seesawed between upset and hurt. A new level of embarrassment engulfed me, watching my dad negotiate with his desire to protect me against his understanding of and love for Eric. We had all become one family over the years, and this situation stirred up dueling feelings.

"No. Rebecca and I were doing well."

"How long has this affair been going on?" my mom demanded.

"I would not classify this as an affair. An affair implies a prolonged sexual relationship and emotional attachment."

"What would you classify it as, Eric?" my mom asked, not bothering to hide her frustration.

"Mom, there isn't a good answer. No normal reason why he cheated on me. His professor suggested that long-term relationships like ours are flawed. He said that we couldn't know what we wanted in a relationship because we'd never experienced anything else. Eric went out and tested the theory by kissing another girl. He determined he liked PDA and I don't."

"I sabotaged our relationship," he explained, shaking his head, unable to meet anyone's gaze.

The conversation halted. Everyone needed a moment to process.

Emotional Charades

"Eric, you kissed a girl in public, just to see if you would like kissing in public?" my mom asked, bewildered.

"Yes."

"Would you cheat on her again?" Mrs. Bridgeport asked.

"No! Had I anticipated this reaction, I never would have done it."

"What reaction did you anticipate, Eric?" I demanded, amazed at his line of thinking, aggravated by it.

"That you would disapprove initially, but that you would understand the overall motivation. I never could have imagined you would just leave."

"Leave?" asked my dad, his curiosity following the wrong trail.

"Yes, Rebecca began the process of moving out."

"Wait, so it was only a kiss?" my mom asked delicately. The question was directed at Eric, but I felt the implication.

I grew furious at the use of the word *only,* paired with the *it's not that bad* tone she had used. My mother had formed an opinion, and as I looked at my dad and the Bridgeport's, I could tell that they had picked sides also.

"She witnessed this portion of the experiment, but there—"

"Wait, what do you mean *only?*" I interrupted, unable to shake it from my head. "Like a kiss isn't enough. And if I hadn't caught him, he probably would have slept with her, too." I started tapping my foot to siphon off the frustration in my voice.

I will not cry. I will not cry.

58

Then, Mrs. Bridgeport broke me with a single question. "Do you believe that, sweetheart? That he would have slept with her if you hadn't caught them?"

"No." And it was the truth. I didn't like it, but I did believe Eric's explanation. I wasn't worried that he would leave me or that he would continue to cheat on me. And maybe that was the smoking gun, the important piece to this romantic puzzle. Maybe there was no real crime, just a poorly conceived experiment. At least that's what it felt like they were saying.

The silence in the room was now for me. My hands started to shake. I hid them under the table. Everyone emptied their cups and Mrs. Bridgeport began refilling them without being asked. I sat, trying to consider their opinions. They loved me, too. They wouldn't knowingly misguide me. They were trying to offer me perspective. But it felt like their investment in our relationship was overshadowing my feelings.

I cleared my throat. "You all know that's not the point. He planned this—he calculated the risk and decided that I would forgive him in the aftermath. He omitted the truth, deciding that my opinion wasn't important enough to be considered. Plus, I saw them. It was a lovely kiss. It was deep and passionate, and before I realized that it was him, I was a little jealous of their lust for one another. Damage was done, and I'm allowed to react however I want." I trembled as I tried not to cry.

This was embarrassing. Laying out the sorted details just so they could understand.

Worse, deep down, a part of me agreed with them. Deep down, past the anger, past the hurt, I just wanted to skip this part. To delete it from our story.

Despite my fury and fear, I still loved him. And I'd missed him over the last few days.

The contradiction made me feel stupid. Made me mad at myself. Made me want to react more extremely. I sighed, trying to wrestle my mixed emotions.

Eric covered his face for a moment, then turned towards me and whispered, "I am so sorry."

"I know," I said, just as softly.

At the same time, my mom, dad, and the Bridgeport's started to offer their retractions and apologies, but it turned out to be a brief intermission before they quickly trailed back to defending the state of our relationship.

"Sweetie, all we're trying to say is that you and Eric are engaged." Mrs. Bridgeport grabbed her husband for support. "That ring you're wearing is a prelude to thick and thin. If you're ready to leave after a kiss, what's going to happen when you encounter more complex issues?"

"This happened a week ago! Is there a time frame for how long a person is supposed to be hurt? Am I just supposed to pretend I'm fine because we love each other?"

"We're not saying that," Mrs. Bridgeport added quickly, "but because you love each other, you should be handling this situation more maturely."

They all nodded their heads in agreement. I shifted back in my seat, annoyed. No one was listening to me.

"I agree with Rebecca. Please, the focus of this conversation should be on me. You all should examine the decisions I made, not their consequences," Eric said in my defense. "If we are capable of repairing our relationship, it will not happen tonight and not solely because you disapprove of our separation."

I looked at him, surprised and appreciative. When our eyes met, I felt we had reached an understanding.

This wasn't helping.

"You want us to discuss your behavior. I'm the most disappointed in you than I have ever been in my life." Mr. Bridgeport looked at Eric and added, "I'm ashamed of you."

Eric's father had picked a side. *Mine.*

Eric stared at his father. His eyes became glassy, and he started tapping his pattern on his thigh. I watched his hand fidget with anxiety. He and his father were close. I couldn't recall Mr. Bridgeport ever saying a single hurtful thing to his son. I felt bad for Eric despite my anger.

Mr. Bridgeport grabbed my hand, "I'm sorry, Rebecca. I'm sorry that this *man* that I raised could betray you." He was talking to me but staring at Eric.

He stormed out of the room; the chair legs scratched against the floor. His steps echoed until he slammed the door to my father's office.

It didn't take long for me to negotiate our exit. We walked to the door in silence. Words seemed costly. The wrong ones could instigate a family feud.

At the threshold, Mrs. Bridgeport took a chance to speak her peace. "Rebecca, please tell me you two will try. You belong together." I wanted to tell her that she was overstepping, but I couldn't disrespect her.

"We will try," I answered with my teeth gritted.

Chapter 7: The Ride Back

This time, it was Eric who needed to be alone with his thoughts. He sat rigid in the passenger seat. I could tell that Mr. Bridgeport's opinion had devastated him. I focused on the road. It would've been just our luck for a deer to saunter into our path. We'd already had an eventful night.

I stopped by Khadijah's. I needed to get my things, plus I wanted to check on her. She'd called a few times during my drive, but I didn't have the energy to talk. Eric decided to accompany me to her room to ensure the visit didn't veer off into an unending conversation.

My knuckles rapped the door lightly. "Hey, guys, it's us."

"Come in. It's unlocked," Jamie called.

Fire.

Lace.

Khadijah was surrounded by the shredded remains of her red wedding dress, a cell phone to her ear. My pocket vibrated again.

The glow of a flame died. My heart palpitated.

Khadijah cut another small section from her dissected dress. A click of the lighter. A meeting of flame and lace. The room glowed in firelight for an instant. She dropped the burning section into a small, metal trash can, where it burned to nothing.

I was in shock. The sounds, smells, and actions in this room registered out of order.

The dress. I remembered she'd picked that dress to pay homage to her Indian and American cultures. The structure of the dress was close to a traditional American bridal gown. It had three-quarter length sleeves made of lace that were connected to a strapless corseted bodice. The skirt mirrored the wrap of a pleated sari. Now, it was just disjointed fabric.

The air in the room was hot. It felt thinner and thinner with every breath. My skin felt cold and clammy.

Khadijah and Jamie sat calmly amidst the flames, watching like you would a campfire. Jamie had the window open and a box fan inserted backward to clear the smoke. On the desk near him was the smoke detector, battery-less. His dark hair was slicked back. The fire danced on the sheen of his silk strands.

I grabbed Eric's hand and we backed against the wall.

"Khadijah's calling off our wedding," Jamie explained casually, pointing at Khadijah on the floor with a pair of shears.

"Stop making jokes! This is serious," Khadijah said, mascara tears streaming down her cheeks.

"Right," he said, then turned to us to continue. "To prove her seriousness, she's destroying that very expensive dress." A twinge of a smile curled his lips. "We can get married in robes and slippers for all I care. So, it's not affecting me the way she wants it to. Her dad, on the other hand, he's going to be pissed considering he paid for it." Jamie gave us the recap, like a stand-up comedian setting up a punchline.

How could he crack a joke? Why was he so calm?

"You can't take anything seriously," Khadijah scolded.

"You're practicing arson and I'm protecting you." He pointed to the fan and smoke detector. "So, there's nothing left to do but joke about it. Hell, I think this just shows what a great future husband I'll be. I'm supportive."

"It would never work," she cried, new tears tracing the mascara tracks down her face.

"Is that a fact or an opinion? Because if you haven't suddenly developed the power to see the future, it must be an opinion. A newly acquired opinion that seems to have more to do with the separation of our friends," he gestured to Eric and me, "and absolutely nothing to do with us."

Khadijah lit a small piece of lace and let it go. It floated, pulled up by the flame, and faded into nothing as the lace burned out. A muted smell of burned leaves eased around the room.

"Don't you see? If they can't do it, we can't. Their relationship is so much stronger than ours."

Jamie cocked his head to the side, examining us. "Nope, I don't see it. Can we call the wedding back on now?"

"You only proposed to atone for cheating," she shot back.

"So, we're going back there again?" Jamie's tone wasn't light anymore. "You never forgave me, and I never earned back your trust?"

"It's not that," Khadijah said quietly. She grabbed the dress and cut down the length of the skirt. "We have messed up so much. We can't put it back together like it was," she said.

The room was quiet except for the crack and pop of the fire.

"So what if we're messed up? We don't have to be what we were. I did something terrible early in our relationship. We made it through. Now, we can move on to the no-sex portion, or the nothing-to-talk-about-portion. Everyone makes mistakes, even The Newlyweds," Jamie reasoned.

Khadijah stared at us. We had shrunk into a corner, watching them warily.

Khadijah's attention shifted back to Jamie. "They're what a lasting relationship looks like. We've been together three years, but we have more deceit and grim memories than they do."

"We're not them," he said softly. "They've been together since before his testicles dropped. That doesn't mean they're going to be together forever. I can't go back and fall in love with you when I was 12. But I love you now," he continued.

"You're not a good enough man to be my husband."

Jamie sat back in his chair. The color faded from his olive skin.

She started throwing large sections of the dress into the burning bin, feeding the flame until they raged and threatened to escape, raising the temperature in the room. I lurched back, towing Eric with me. I patted behind me for the door.

Emotional Charades

Jamie grabbed a fire extinguisher from beneath his chair, the picture of calm, as he put out the fire and returned to his station next to the window. It only existed for a second or two.

"I shouldn't have covered for you." He pointed to the smoke detector. "The cops would have been called. I could see you in real handcuffs, not the cloth ones we have." Jamie paused, losing his humor. "Would you please talk some sense into her, Rebecca? I can't anymore."

He rubbed his beard and slunk back in his chair. His head lolled back. I'd attributed his red eyes to the smoke. Now, it seemed like exhaustion. How long had they been at this?

His use of humor had rubbed me the wrong way, but at least he was doing something. He was trying to address her feelings. Keeping the cooler head for the two of them.

I'd just been an audience member. While standing there, I should have been preparing a speech, a rebuttal, but I wasn't. I'd been too engrossed in the spectacle. Now, it was my cue to chat with my best friend, who'd been calling me for hours. Who'd needed me, and I didn't pick up the damn phone.

"Sweetheart," I started, but with nothing to say, I stopped. I looked at her and then at Jamie, trying to drum up a platitude that fit the room.

What could I have said to her?

Eric knelt and slowly made his way to sit beside her. "Khadijah, you are focusing on the story of our relationship and allowing that to act as a standard. You are ignoring the people in the relationship, and how they contort to each other. For instance, if Rebecca were ever to react to her emotions in this manner, I would not know how to handle it. I could not be as calm as Jamie is."

Khadijah laughed a little.

"That was not for amusement, Khadijah. I would have had you arrested and suggested an evaluation for mental stability. Second-guessing your nuptials is rational considering his history of betrayal, but it should not be a direct reaction to our relationship."

Jamie scowled at Eric. I assumed it was for implying that her reason was logical.

"Are you guys back together?" Khadijah asked.

Eric rubbed his temple. She hadn't been listening to Eric. What she wanted was solidarity.

Finally, I knew how to reassure her. I sat in front of her. "We worked it out because I hated the idea of being apart. You were right. I shouldn't have left him."

She looked at me like I was preaching her personal gospel. I eased her fears, but betrayed myself with every word. She sputtered out a few more tears and dropped the lighter. Khadijah clung to me, crying on my shoulder.

Her co-dependence on my love life felt tangible, like a rope binding us to their survival. Nothing was solved, though. Her execution was dramatic, but if she had doubts, then the relationship needed to be reevaluated. I needed to tell her that her feelings were valid.

"Would you like to go outside for some fresh air?" I asked.

She snorted, then composed herself, "Sure." She wiped her face with a tissue from a box on her desk. She pulled on a hoodie and a pair of shoes. Jamie shot me a glance and a *thank-you* nod.

Emotional Charades

I felt a little treacherous. Jamie looked at me with solidarity. From his perspective, I almost understood why. He probably felt he could depend on me to get Khadijah back on track.

I could equivocate, and say I wasn't his friend. I could claim that I only tolerated him for Khadijah. That was only half true. Before his tawdry affairs, Jamie and I were close. He used to roast me for being Khadijah's protégé, and I roasted him for being her shadow. Mostly, we both loved Khadijah. For the first year, Jamie seemed perfect for her. He brought her snacks when we were locked in long study sessions. He always volunteered to drop us off and pick us up from our girl's night out. He wasn't intimidated by her bossiness, and never asked her to be less.

After, I hated him on Khadijah's behalf. But it didn't last because she didn't hate him. As their relationship mended, and the sweet version of Jamie resurfaced, my anger and disdain for him was an issue. Over time, I learned to hide it, then to let go of some of it. I kept a thimble-sized amount of hatred shielded, just in case. Now, a tattered version of a friendship existed between him and me.

But I wanted to speak with her freely, not for his benefit. Indirectly, his actions were the root of this breakdown.

The night air was crisp, hovering just above chilly. We walked a few paces, then stopped near a bench on a well-lit path with a glowing blue light that illuminated our steps. She blew on her hands and rubbed them together.

"What a crazy night," she said. Her lips were pressed, but her cheeks rose. An inauthentic smile.

I turned and caught her eyes. "Are you okay?" I couldn't tiptoe around tonight's events.

She took a beat and looked off. "Of course," she responded, then took a deep breath, "I'm fine." Khadijah stared at her hands, then started cleaning her nails.

I placed my hand on her shoulder to comfort her. Khadijah peered up.

"It's okay if you don't want to get married."

Her eyes narrowed to slits. She shrugged her shoulder free, as if I were assaulting her. "What! This wasn't that big of a deal."

"You burned your wedding dress in a dorm room."

"Oh, that," she scoffed, waving her hand dismissively. "That was nothing. Jamie had it under control. It's not his first rodeo."

"You've…you've done this before!" She could be dramatic, but this was too much—too dangerous.

"He's lost a few gym bags over the years." She sounded cavalier.

My jaw dropped. Her eyes gleamed over. Tears rushed to aid her pain. "This is why we don't tell you anything," Khadijah shot.

Taken aback, I murmured, "What?"

"None of us can talk to you about this stuff. You don't understand because your life is almost perfect. You have a living, breathing prince charming, and you were ready to walk out over a kiss. The rest of us in the real world, we've kissed far more frogs. We struggle. But you. Eric adores you. You say never do that again, and I would bet my life he wouldn't even kiss his mother."

We don't tell you.

Emotional Charades

Our mutual friends came to mind. Had they talked about this behind my back? No, my friends could talk to me about their relationships. They did. But…when I tried to recall a time like tonight with Khadijah, when the pain was fresh and unfiltered, nothing. I always got the consolidated version after the drama was over. I'd always considered it their comfort level, but maybe I'd made them feel judged.

"I didn't mean to make you—"

She cut me off, "Oh, and I *do* want to marry Jamie," she shouted. Lights in nearby dorms flickered on. "Outside of…" she took a deep breath, "that time, he has been perfect. He's my best friend. He supports me. He encourages me. He accepts my flaws and forgives all my mistakes. It's not perfect, but we can't all be you."

She looked defiant. Her arms were crossed. Her scowl gave clear instructions not to push the topic.

What could I say? Was she wrong? Was she just hurt and lashing out? Suddenly, I was colder than the night's air. A cloud of uncertainty engulfed me.

"I didn't mean to." I paused, trying to figure out what I needed to apologize for. "I didn't mean to judge you. I just wanted to make sure you were okay."

"I'm fine." She flicked her hair over her shoulder. "And I don't need your help on Saturday. Jamie will do it." She stalked off.

Chapter 8: The Big fight

Our exit felt like an escape from a madhouse. The first step into our apartment felt like stepping on base during an intense game of tag.

I closed my eyes and took a deep breath, "That was..." I started, but what was an accurate description of tonight? I looked to Eric for help to find the words that fit.

"Criminally reprehensible," he suggested.

I snickered. "That wasn't what I was going for."

For a moment, my guard was down. I smiled at him. Muscle memory took over. I nudged him with my elbow, and he responded with a shoulder bump. This part was easy for us. I missed our friendship. Warmth swelled in my chest.

He turned to face me, resting his hands on my hips. Our eyes locked. A moment of recognition that we didn't know where we stood enveloped us. That we were still in the middle of this. We both looked at his hands. He let go of me. The warmth faded and I wanted it back.

Without thinking, I stepped forward and laid my head against his shoulder. He wrapped his long arms around me. Warmth spread through me as we flowed right into the familiarity of our 10-year-old relationship.

"Regarding my experiment. I must be completely transpa—"

Emotional Charades

No! My chest tightened. I couldn't dive back into that pool of pain. Not right now. Not after the day we'd had.

I cleared my throat, "Are you hungry?"

He froze a moment. I felt him become rigid and then relaxed as he selected his answer, "Yes."

"Okay, let me change and I'll make us a snack." I started for the bedroom.

"Rebecca, there is more that I believe is imperative to discuss."

No! The same internal scream radiated through me. "We can eat first. It's been a long day."

He shook his head, something grim to his cheeks. "We need to talk."

I didn't want any part of whatever conversation he had in mind. I felt normal for the first time since it all happened. I didn't want to jump straight back into the pain. I pulled my hoodie over my head, then dropped it on the floor.

His head twitched. "What are you doing?"

"Changing for bed," I explained, walking away from the discarded hoodie.

He gawked at the hoodie and back to me, "This is not funny," he said, retrieving the hoodie out of compulsion.

"What isn't?" I asked while pulling my socks off and throwing them in different directions.

"Rebecca!" he shouted, his smile escaping in frustrated amusement. "I will go put peanut butter on every single dish in the kitchen," he countered.

"Hmm, seems time-consuming. In that time, I could unfold every single piece of clothing in our room."

His eyes bulged. "You would not."

72

"I wouldn't. But could we put a pin in it for the night?" I asked. I needed a night without this emotional burden. A night when tears didn't guide me to my dreams. Dreams that didn't star another woman.

His eyes darted around the room. "Deal."

My next breath felt lighter. "Deal. I'll go change for bed the right way." I put air quotes when I said *the right way*.

"Thank goodness." He slapped his chest dramatically. "I will prepare us a snack."

"Thank you."

He brought two bowls of cereal, handed me mine, then placed his bowl on the nightstand. He undressed, then sat on the floor near our dirty clothes to fold them.

"Match those socks and the pin. Look at that execution!" I narrated sarcastically.

"Don't tease me after you used my compulsion to manipulate me," he joked. I smiled.

Our house was hamper-less because he hated the intermingling mess they held. Instead, he separated and sorted our dirty laundry, folding each item and then placing them into neat, color-coded piles that occupied the floor of our closet. Our socks had to be safety-pinned to their match. He had rituals that he had to follow, or he would feel agitated. After tonight, our little routines felt like an international treaty.

He finished, then grabbed his bowl from the nightstand.

"I'll sleep on the couch," he said, then he switched off the light and walked out of the room.

For a split second, I'd forgotten that there was a reason for him to sleep on the couch.

***

Emotional Charades

The next morning felt new. I stretched and yawned and breathed in the fibers of a new day. My favorite meal was prepared and plated at the table: oatmeal with fresh strawberries and scrambled eggs with cheese, bacon, and sausage. My prepared plate beckoned me. Across our small circular table, he sat waiting.

"Good morning. Thanks for breakfast."

"You are welcome. Good morning to you, too," he responded, looking at the ground, then at me, and back to the ground again. He didn't have a plate. Instead, a folder sat in front of him.

My chest tightened. Right there, I saw the flaw in this day. The conversation he wanted to finish last night was trying to ambush me. I stood over it, contemplating how to salvage the morning. I unwrapped my headscarf, releasing bounds of kinky curls that fell toward my eyes in a bang. With one hand, I dragged my plate across the table, reassigning my seat. His lap became my chair.

"It was very nice of you to make breakfast."

"It is the least I could do," he said apologetically.

I smiled at his serious tone, trying to ease the mood. It was only a matter of time before he would ruin it.

"I would like to start by showing you this." He pointed to the folder.

I kissed him. I kissed him to stop the conversation from starting. I kissed him because his last kiss belonged to another person.

He kissed me like I was delicious. Like there was a bit of sugar on the back of my tongue that he had to taste. With one hand on my back, he pulled me closer. I wrapped an arm around his neck. His other hand rubbed circles on my inner thigh. I parted my legs, giving him total access.

Then, he pulled away, a little breathless. "I don't think it is the appropriate time to reconnect physically," he cautioned.

Were hearts elastic? My heart was stretching but trying so hard to stay whole.

"Listen," I pleaded. "I've been upset for an entire week. I've just had two unexpected and emotionally exhausting conversations with people we love." I said the words with a strong voice and a big smile, but inside, I was begging in a wretched key. "I don't want to fight right now."

"What if, after this day is over, you regret moving too fast?"

I repositioned myself, straddling his lap, so we were face to face. "Then I won't be able to blame you," I reasoned. I leaned in and kissed his neck.

"Um," he released the smallest moan. "Are you sure? There is more that I have to discuss with you."

I pulled back to look at him. "Yes, I'm sure. I want you."

He grabbed my waist and pulled me flush against him, taking my breath away for a moment. He grazed his teeth gently against my skin before sinking them into my neck. I leaned into it. He sucked the same spot. The sensation rippled through my body, hardening my nipples, and teasing my clit. I grinded against his growing stiffness.

Arousal shot through me. I could feel my wetness breaching my panties. Maneuvering my hand to his fly, I gripped him firmly and stroked him gently. He was hard and thick.

His head rocked back, "Oh, fuck," he moaned. His eyes changed—animalistic, a teaser for what he was about to do me. I smiled, giddy at the sound of his moan. I bit my bottom lip. My eyes locked with his. He pulled my face close to his, peering into my eyes. "I love you."

He kissed me hard, savagely, like he wanted to consume me.

He stood, placed me on my feet, and pulled my back to his chest. His hand slid past my stomach until he found my clit. His fingers brushed circles, squares, and ecstasy. Waves of pleasure mounted. My knees started to give.

The whole world slid away.

There was just this connection. This buzz. This yearning for release. He wrapped a securing arm around my waist to keep me standing. His hand cupped my breast as his thumb massaged my nipple. I was lost in sensation. My body burned. My heart raced.

"Oh, Eric," I cried.

Desperate to cum. Close. So close. I rested my head against his chest and let the hot sensation pulse through me. He increased the pressure a little more and a little more. I quivered. I wanted him to bend me over. His lips met my cheek just below my earlobe.

"I'm going to win," Eric whispered in my ear. For us, sex always had a friendly level of competition. It was a matter of who could get the other there first.

I tried to respond, but all that came out was a moan. He kissed the sensitive spot on my neck. My eyes fluttered closed. A wave of pleasure washed over me. It ravished me. I nearly collapsed. His arms were the only thing keeping me standing. He threw me over his shoulder and carried me to the bedroom.

We stayed there all day.

On Saturday, it was just TV and conversation, enjoying each other's company. I laid with my head rested on his shoulder. He traced the lines on my palm. Then, he turned my hand over and kissed my engagement ring.

"I," his voice cracked, "I am ashamed of myself. I cannot express how much I regret my actions." A tear slid down his face, "all last week I thought about—"

No. The word roared in my head. "Eric, can we just have the rest of the night?" There was only pain there.

He kissed my forehead, "Of course."

Chapter 9: Sex Revelation

I t's an eerie feeling, knowing you're about to be hurt.

He was dressed in a t-shirt, cardigan, and dark jeans. I was in a house coat.

He'd made me breakfast again, and I could make out abandoned tear trails on his cheeks.

"On March first, Professor Rogers presented research to my Psychology of Human Relationships class. The research identified markers for the failure of modern marriages," he began as if he were defending a dissertation. "The strongest correlation existed in couples whose relationship was initiated in youth. Focusing on how the lack of varied experience with multiple romantic and sexual partners created a *what-if* effect. The more I researched it, the more I began to agree with its assertions. Increase in average life span, social media interaction, accessibility, the financial independence of women, and normality of divorce are all attributable to a difference in the social functionality of modern marriage."

I listened as he presented his hypothesis.

"Relationships like ours do not appear to last anymore. That notion terrifies me. It became imperative that I find a way to increase our odds of a successful marriage. I created and outlined an experiment that should have strengthened our relationship by incorporating external experiences. During a set timeframe, we were both to engage socially and intimately…" He paused, searching for the most accurate word. "…including intercourse with an archetype of our *what-if* desire. My research indicated strong gravitation towards…"

I listened as he listed the variables:

- Familiar lovers—often referred to as *the one who got away*
- Sexually experienced and/or mature partners
- The physical opposite of your current partner
- Athletes
- Authority figures
- Overweight partner

"We would both pick lovers who met our unfulfilled interest or desires. Those experiences should have been capable of satisfying the *what-if* questions that typically plague couples during the rough patches. The idea was to eradicate curiosity when it came to intimacy and intercourse." He paused, giving me a moment to speak, but I had no desire to participate in my undoing.

"I completed an entire phase of my experiment with Juliette. I fornicated with her. Just one time," he admitted. "I was going to ask you to do the same with the romantic archetype of your selection." His eyes dropped.

My heart sunk.

Method…trial…I didn't know which part of the scientific method it fit into. This wasn't well-thought-out; there were no controls. This wasn't his typically prepared victory speech. Merely him rambling to justify his actions.

He opened the folder, removing a copy of his experiment entitled *SIP: The What-If Effect.* To him, this was important. It was proof that he had thought of this as an experiment. For me, it was the hammer and chisel breaking me in two. He handed me the copy and I automatically took it. My curiosity and anger were eager for details.

Synthetic Intimacy Project
Subject 1: Promiscuous Partner

The heading was all I could read before I suddenly drifted back to the café, watching the intimacy in that kiss. I questioned myself. Had I known that they had sex? Did I suspect it? I didn't know in the café, or at our parents' house. But I knew when we got home.

The "more" that we needed to talk about...the dread in his tone.

He started reviewing the notes. He talked and I listened. I listened because my only impulse was to lash out. Malicious thoughts played out in my mind. I thought about calling Eric's father to further his disappointment in his son. Tickles of pleasure grazed me as I pictured Mr. Bridgeport berating him, belittling him, and losing all respect for him. Every word I wanted to say was savage, mean, and...ultimately pointless. Nothing would stop the pain I was feeling, so I just held it all in. I sat still. My eyes swelled full of potential tears.

"I thought you knew, Rebecca," Eric amended. "It was not my intention to mislead you."

When he was done, there was a heavy silence that loomed over us. This was it, the moment where I would presumably have filled the silence with vulgarities.

"At breakfast on Friday when you tried to tell me, I was scared," I explained, still numb from shock. "I didn't want to be sure of what more you wanted to tell me." My lips parted for a moment, but it wasn't a smile. A wince of pain had caused my lips to twitch. "Honestly, I wanted to skip this conversation entirely." My voice ebbed, on the cusp of cracking.

Eric lowered his head, removing the option of eye contact. "Would it have been better if I had disclosed it then?" he asked, meekly.

A gradual shake of my head answered the question before I had the words to explain. "I didn't want to know then; I needed a break from this…" I paused, trying to come up with the word, "…experiment."

Then, I was lost. I was back at the café watching their intimacy. The same embarrassment of being a pervert crept over me. The memory no longer ended with the kiss. No, now, my imagination had them walk out the café, hand and hand, and fall directly into a bed. Our bed? Her bed? Steal and stone, I sat there filling in the gaps.

"Your reaction is baffling me. You are not exhibiting the behaviors I expected." His shoulders pinched forward, elbows on his lap as he leaned towards me.

Eric was staring at me now, watching me for our Morse code. I stayed stoic. I stared at him, purposely not giving anything away.

"Are you angry? Do you hate me, Rebecca?" He was practically begging for answers.

"Why did you assume that I knew about the sex?" I retorted, needing an answer of my own. I kept it short; I didn't trust myself with words. I could use a few of them to devastate him.

"Last week, upon returning from class, I was immediately aware of your absence, and I inferred from your missing luggage and personal items that you intended for your venture to be lengthy. This folder had been placed on my desk in preparation for this conversation," he explained, tapping the green folder that chronicled his betrayal. "It appeared that you read its contents, became infuriated, and left me. That scenario was...proportional. I could accept it. On Thursday, our conversation with our parents informed me that you only possessed knowledge of the kiss."

"Terrible communication skills. Your therapist would be ashamed of us. Especially you—you made a few big assumptions." Years earlier, his therapist taught us the *rules for fighting fair*. Eric had not followed them.

"The only woman I have ever been in love with packed her belongings and left me. No calls, no text, no explanation at all for the departure. I had to believe it was over more than a kiss." He whispered, anger in his low tone. "It didn't feel like that big of an assumption."

Sparked by his tone, my emotions flooded out. "I woke up alone to an empty apartment! You cheated on me. Then, you left as if nothing had happened. As if it were something that could be resolved later. As if it were less important than a missed class." I paused, stumbling over the embarrassment in my admission. "I saw you kiss her; I watched you enjoy it. I dreamed about it. Eric, I dreamed about her. You fucked her!" I was yelling now.

Just like the baton in a relay, he picked up where I left off.

"I did go to class, to turn in my assignment. Then I came right back. I was gone for 30 minutes! You decided to leave within 30 minutes without even a call."

"Are you mad at *me*?" I asked, amazed by his tone.

"Absolutely not. However, I am frustrated," he answered, restrained, reeling in his volume before it became a shouting match.

"This isn't a pendulum—you can't swing the fault my way. You don't get to be frustrated with me for being hurt. I didn't cheat on you."

Eric took a deep breath, shifting away from me. He tapped his fingers on the table in the pattern of the list.

"My actions were detrimental to our relationship and I deeply regret the choices I have made. I understand now how invalid my thought process was. I know that I hurt you. I am most apologetic, and I will apply my every effort to…" His voice cracked. "Are you going to leave me, again?"

"Where would I go? Back to Khadijah and Jamie's?" I asked sarcastically. "I don't want to deal with that! Should I go home to my parents? Listen to them tell me that I am in the wrong, that your cheating wasn't that big of a deal or—"

"Please refrain from basing your decision on the prospect of other people's reactions," he interrupted. "I need to know if you want to leave me." I could see the anguish in his eyes.

Emotional Charades
"That's not how it works. You don't get to be assured of anything!" I turned, leaving him with his concerns and determined to sleep away my own.

Chapter 10: Perfect

*W*here *would I go?* That had been the theme of my dreams. Not to the lion's den of opinions, not the chorus of *it was only once.*

I pulled my blanket back, trying to escape my thoughts. The brightness irritated my unadjusted eyes. Retreating from the sunlight, I pulled the blanket over my head, but it resisted. I looked towards the corner of the bed. Eric was sitting there, elbows on his knees, his hands covering his face. His head lifted and turned toward me.

"I am sorry."

"Sorry for something you planned?" I asked rhetorically.

I ripped the blankets back, grabbed my phone from the nightstand, and bolted for the bathroom. The walls, tub, and tiles were sterile white. I felt like I'd walked into a padded room. Knuckles rapped against the door. He kept speaking, explaining, and looping his apologies. I needed to drown it all out.

I reached for my phone, turning it on for the first time since Friday. Hoping that a song or a podcast could alleviate my thoughts, the screen illuminated. I desperately tapped my streaming app. Nothing. It wouldn't respond. Instead, my phone vibrated with an onslaught of notifications. A whole weekend's worth.

Emotional Charades

Mom: I'm so proud of you. For being understanding and forgiving. (Friday 6:30 am)

Khadijah: I wish we were like you. (Friday 8:00 am)

Jamie: *Hey, update your insta.* (Friday 12:00 pm)

Joan: Call me! (Friday 4:27 pm)

As I checked my text messages, tons of Instagram notifications started to pop up. My access had been restored. I read through the comments.

What happened? This can't be real. Fake news.
Is this a joke? Guys, it's not April.
No! The Newlyweds didn't break up.

It went on and on. Something became crystal clear to me. I wasn't a person in their eyes. I was half of a whole. The onslaught of messages made me feel even more isolated. They reinforced my fear. They'd eventually side with the relationship.

Even my family and friends.

Sure, at first, they'd be pissed. They'd berate him, but eventually, they'd employ the *it was only one time* logic.

Khadijah had already posted a correction: *They aren't broken up. Fake news. #hacked.* Her post was flooded with comments. Strangers claiming they knew it.

I read until my alarm startled me. A reminder that my entire life wasn't shaken by his actions, that this quake was localized. I had classes and goals to focus on. Being still and broken wasn't an option.

Move. Pull yourself together.

Taylor Bianca B

When I opened the door, Eric was waiting with bloodshot eyes. He looked exhausted and depleted. The sight of him infuriated me. *I should be the inconsolable one.*

"Rebecca." He said my name mournfully.

Just the tone of his voice irritated me. I glared at him.

"I am sorry."

"You said that already," I spat back. Then, unanswered questions surfaced in my mind. *I don't want to know. I don't want to know.* "When…when did this happen?" I closed my hands into fists, digging my nails in my palms.

"September 22, 7:32am," he rattled off as if it were a doctor's appointment instead of an illicit tryst.

"Where?"

"Her apartment."

I closed my eyes and took in a deep breath. At least I hadn't slept on the memory of their time together. I thought about asking for her address, then a more gut-wrenching question came to mind.

"Did you enjoy it?" My dignity shredded with the question.

"Rebecca..." He paused, his face flushing and his eyes turning glassy. He pinned his eyes on the floor. "I ejaculated, if that was the nature of your question."

Keys, phone, backpack, and then I was out the door. I slammed it. The thud echoed in the hallway. I pushed the heavy metal door of the apartment complex so hard it slapped the side of the building.

I slid into the car and started it. The rumble of the engine grounded me. After a few seconds, my hands stopped shaking.

Emotional Charades

This is happening. This happened. He cheated on me. This isn't my life. This isn't supposed to happen to me.

Denial wanted to take root in me. I wanted there to be an emergency emotional exit.

The inaccuracy of my words caused me to hyperventilate. I gripped the steering wheel so hard my knuckles cracked. "This is happening," I finally admitted to myself. Reality struck me so hard my chest hurt.

Motion in the rearview mirror caught my attention. Eric was coming out of the door, backpack in hand, prepared for us to drive to campus together. I peeled off.

He could walk.

My week looped. Morning apologies, classes, and restless sleep. Repeat.

Then, it was Saturday, and I didn't have a class to escape to. I showered for the first time in a week. I'd gotten by with birdbaths. My hair was matted and tangled from neglect. I washed, detangled, and conditioned my hair only to put it back into a puff. I didn't have the energy to style it. I slipped on a hoodie and fought my way into a pair of leggings.

I walked into the kitchen and Eric was at the table. He was always at the fucking table. Waiting on me with an apology on his lips. A plate of breakfast and a mug of coffee were placed on the opposite side of the table. I walked past his peace offering. It enraged me. Everything he did enraged me now.

I took a deep breath.

Compartmentalize. Focus on my goals. Focus on myself. I made myself breakfast and took it and my backpack to my desk. I put on my noise-cancelling headphones and played trap mix. I completed my assignments and started to study for the MCAT. I focused on what I could control. I could be a perfect student.

A hand brushed my shoulder. "What do you want?" I grunted. I yanked my headphones down and spun around. *What is it this time? Another apology, another excuse, another folder that might rip my heart to shreds?*

She startled and stepped back. "Whoa! Are you okay?" Khadijah asked.

"I didn't hear you come in."

"Eric, let me in," she said, nodding her head to his door. I looked just in time to catch him closing it. "I'm glad you're studying because you've missed three of our study sessions," she noted, peering over my shoulder towards my laptop.

"You taught me well," I complimented her, tiptoeing around the tension. We hadn't really talked since the dress burning.

She'd taken off her shoes and jacket. They were situated by the front door. In the nook of her arm was a glass container. I spied it suspiciously, tilting my head back while squinting at it.

"This? Are you looking at this?" She passed it to me.

I pulled the lid open. The spices from the fresh golden-brown samosas filled the air. They smelled like heaven. I'd just made breakfast, but it no longer mattered the second their scent filled my nose. *Sorry, sausage and eggs. I'm carb-loading this morning.*

"Thanks, Khadijah."

Emotional Charades

I walked into the kitchen and grabbed two plates. She joined me. I put two samosas on both plates. She unlidded a jar of chutney and sat it in the middle of the table. We dug in and let the shared meal break the ice.

A few minutes later, Khadijah was wiping her hand with a paper towel, and I was rubbing my happy, full belly.

"I didn't like the way we left things," she started.

"Me neither." My stomach twisted into knots every time I thought about it.

She sat back into her chair. Her chest rose like she was preparing to dive into the sea. "You know that I've been a tiny weensy bit stressed, right?"

I held my thumb and index finger a 10th of an inch apart. "Just a little." My eyes widened as I expanded the space between my thumb and index finger.

She chuckled and batted my hand away, then brought hers together. She fidgeted with the thin gold rings on her right hand. She took a deep breath, "You guys suddenly in the throes of a breakup, some new guy on your arm, and it all happened on the day I set a wedding date. It felt like a bad omen. I tried to ignore it because I could see you were hurting. I wanted to be there for you. Then, and I know you didn't mean to…your words threw me back to the worst time of my life." Her shoulders pinched in. Her back rounded, like she was sinking into herself.

It was uncomfortable watching her revisit her past. "Khadijah, I—"

She put her right hand up, palm out. She offered a serene smile, determined to finish. "I couldn't stop thinking about the timing or comparing us to you guys." She shook her head. "I told Jamie, but he wasn't worried.

90

He's confident in us. It turned into a fight. Then, you guys showed up. And I can't remember a time I felt more embarrassed. Jamie and I have had so many passionate fights that they started to seem normal. But the look on your faces, well, I knew I was being an idiot. I was just too far gone to reel it back in and control it." She held her right elbow with her left hand. She glanced up at me expectedly.

I sat there, torn. *Ask her. No, let it go.* A little voice in my head debated itself. She already looked so vulnerable, but we were having a heart-to-heart. This was the right time. "Did you mean it when you said I judged you?" I asked.

"I don't think you meant to judge me. Everyone wanted me to leave him. And it wasn't what you said." She leaned forward, resting her forearms on the table. "Sometimes, you looked at me like I was shrinking."

Her words connected so closely with a memory that my eyes started to water.

Two years ago, Jamie's escapades were campus gossip. He was deemed the community Casa Nova.

One morning, he missed a class we all had together. He wasn't answering anyone's calls. Khadijah decided to stop by his room. She dragged me along. I pretty much hated him at that point. Eric wouldn't even talk to him.

She knocked on the door. Then kicked. Then banged. It garnered stares and whispers. I tried to shield her from them. My heart sunk for her, while my temper flared.

He opened the door shirtless. He rubbed his eyes, then stretched in the doorway. "I overslept," he yawned.

Emotional Charades

Khadijah hugged him. Her petite frame clung to him like she hadn't seen him in ages.

"Morning, Rebecca."

"Jamie," I said dryly. My fingers inched. This felt too staged.

Jamie backed into his room, towing Khadijah. Jamie held the door open for me. A flawless smile displayed his white teeth and sharp canines.

As I stepped into his room, his suitemate's door opened, and a girl creeped out. We made eye contact. Her amused grin was a story in and of itself. I turned to get a second look. Jamie closed the door quickly.

We locked eyes. His pupils narrowed in panic.

I glared at him. "Khadijah, we should go."

Before she could respond, there was a knock. Jamie's eyes widened. I snatched the door open. He tried to stop me. That girl was standing there in an oversized t-shirt, the same grin across her lips. Jamie covered his mouth with his hand.

"Oops, I forgot to leave this," she said, then she pulled off the shirt she was wearing. She stood there in a sports bra and yoga pants. Her arm extended in Khadijah's direction. The shirt dangled on her index finger.

Jamie rubbed his neck. "Leave, Brie."

"We should go," I interjected. I extended my hand toward Khadijah. She walked toward me. Ignoring my hand, she stood in front of Brie. She eyed her up and down.

"Thanks, dear. This one is my favorite." Brie's brows pinched and her smirk disappeared. She looked dumbfounded.

Taylor Bianca B

Khadijah snatched the shirt and slammed the door. She turned and glared at Jamie, "Rebecca, could you give us some privacy?"

I gawked at her. Why was she staying? He'd just talk his way out of it. She was lost and acting like a doormat for a man who did not deserve her. I'd thought worse...And she read it all in my eyes.

"It's in the past. That's over now. I shouldn't have thrown that accusation at you. You were worried about me. Especially since I'd just burned a dress. By the way, it was a freak accident involving a candle, if my parents ask," Khadijah finished.

"I'm sorry that I made you feel that way." I reached across the table and touched her hand.

"I forgive you. I'm just stressed now. Old feelings bubbled up."

"If you're this stressed, have you considered therapy?"

She scoffed, "My sister graduated early from MIT. I'm not going to be the first person in my Desi family who needs therapy."

"Okay." I laughed at her insistence on sibling rivalry. I bit my bottom lip; a new question had sprung to mind.

She tilted her head, "What?"

"How did you learn to strategically burn a wedding dress?" I joked to lighten the mood.

She snorted in laughter. "Our parents sent us to suburban schools with spoiled rich kids. You learn more than good study habits. I've seen some things." She turned her phone over. "Oh, I have to go. I was supposed to be at work an hour ago. I offered to redo my co-worker's résumé if she stayed an hour over for me."

Khadijah walked to the door and put on her Hunter boots and coat. "I was going to do it regardless. She's a genius, but résumés are not her forte. I'm going to create her one that will get her in any room she wants to be in." Khadijah pulled her long hair from the collar of her coat. "I'm glad I stopped by."

She put her arms up. I walked into them.

"Me too," I said into her ear.

I felt a new distraction present itself. I would be the perfect maid of honor.

Chapter 11: Study Hall

Perfect. I could be perfect in the other areas of my life. For the next week, I put all my focus on my GPA, MCAT practice, and the stupid creative writing class. As an added benefit, it helped me avoid Eric. My favorite pastime now.

I was sick of his apologies. Of his guilt. Now, I only offered him silence.

"Rebecca," Christian called from behind me. The concern in his voice was palpable.

I closed my eyes. I'd been avoiding him, too.

"Christian, hi," I responded simply, unsure whether my voice would hold if I said more. The *more* was now building in my chest. The parts I couldn't tell Khadijah or my other friends.

He walked in front of me, "How are you?"

Don't tell him. Put on your mask. Be perfect.

"I'm…I'm…" I paused, trying to force myself to say fine. "I don't want to go in there," I admitted. We craned towards the class door, watching our classmates take their seats.

He nodded, then gestured for me to follow him. He led me to a small concession stand. I caught my reflection on a glass container. Did I really need to explain? Red eyes and disheveled hair had probably given him basic details of my current state.

Emotional Charades

He ordered two coffees. Black. After, I followed him to a small study room, windowless with white cinder block walls. The study nook held a slight chill. We sat at a small, round table. Smudges of ink and carvings stained it in layers.

He handed me one of the coffees and took a sip of his.

"How are you? How was your weekend?" I led, hoping for a normal conversation. I wasn't quite ready to open up, even if my emotions wanted to spill out.

"Great!" he responded, although he seemed surprised by the question. "I went home to visit my family. My younger brother was home for the weekend."

"Home from where?"

"He's a freshman at The University of Michigan, studying engineering. Dude wants to be an astronaut. I'm so proud of him," he smiled. "Rebecca? Are you—"

"Is he your only sibling?" I asked, interrupting him, begging for the distraction. Because no, I was not okay.

"Actually, I have five siblings. Two sisters and three brothers. Carter is 19, Kasey's 11, Meghan is seven, and Samuel and Emanuel are five. Twins. What about you? Any siblings?"

"I'm an only child, but I'm close to Eric's—" I froze. "Would you mind if we just talked about you for a while?" Nervously, I rotated the untasted coffee in my hands.

He reached forward and wrapped his hands around mine. "We can talk about anything you want to talk about, Rebecca." Again, his manner almost pulled the emotions out of me.

Immediately, I threw him another question. I practically interrogated him, desperate for him to keep talking. His calm tone prevented my overactive synapses from firing, from analyzing the same phrase: *Synthetic Intimacy Experiment.*

"It's nice. My parents are still in love. Watching them is fantastic inspiration."

"That's wonderful," I said, another question on the tip of my tongue.

There was a rush of noise as the hall filled with hundreds of people exchanging classrooms.

"What do you have after this?" I asked.

"I have a few hours between classes. I normally stay here and do my assignments. If I leave campus, I won't come back."

"I have a study session in an hour then class at three." While I spoke, it hit me that a study session with Khadijah would be intense. I dreaded the idea. My chest tightened. So, I texted her to reschedule.

"Stay here. We can be study buddies." He smiled, something bright and charming. "I could review your story for class today."

"That would be nice." I smiled back at him.

He provided feedback on my horror story. I made the changes, then emailed it to Professor Lamb with an *I'm not feeling well* excuse. We stayed there, quiet companions. He left for his noon class, but came back quickly. He also brought me back lunch, which I appreciated. His presence calmed me, and I didn't want to go back to the overgrowth of emotions that ambushed me in his absence.

Yet, my class was about to start.

Emotional Charades

"Thank you, Christian, for..." I paused, trying to figure out what to call this. "...spending time with me," I explained, packing my laptop and textbooks.

"Any time," he smiled, while he packed his belongings. Unexpected movement pulled my attention. I watched his hand crawl across the table towards mine. I froze. The space between us decreased to millimeters, then expanded. His hand reeled in my phone. A little flustered by his momentary closeness, I sat back down, weak-kneed.

He handed back my phone, open to a new contact: *Christian Taylor – Creative writing (333)-588-2114.*

"Rebecca, you can call me anytime. We're friends," he said, shifting around the table. He grabbed my hands, pulling me into his embrace. He was warm and firm. A sense of safety flooded me. I stayed in his arms for too long, arriving to class five minutes late. Nevertheless, my assignment was done, and I was prepared to participate in the class discussion. I flung my hand up every time the professor threw us a question, hoping to quiet my thoughts. Christian had managed to keep all the emotions at bay so far, and I wasn't about to let them all come pouring back.

After class, I went to a Black student union event. 50 or so people filed in the auditorium. Glass windows let in a beautiful glow of natural light. Through them, you could see the tree lined edge of campus. The green mosaic carpet dated the room.

"Hey, Becca, do you need a seat?" It was Ambrosia from my writing class. She signaled at the seat next to her.

Taylor Bianca B

"Thank you so much." I reached out to shake her hand.

She flashed a smile and shook my hand. "It's nothing." She pointed to the stage. "This is going to get very good." She pantomimed pulling a pair of glasses down and peering over the top of them, then pushed them up the bridge of her nose.

Her theatrics brought a smile to my face.

"What will *get good?*" I asked.

"Oh, you haven't been here the last few weeks?" She tried to whisper, but the surprise in her voice carried. "You've missed out big time. Stacy is the most entertaining president in history." She pointed to the stage, where there was a rectangular table. Seven board members were seated on the far side, facing the audience. There was a slideshow projected onto a screen behind them.

"She's a porcupine," Ambrosia exclaimed.

"A porcupine?"

"Professionally prickly."

"That's a substitute for *bitch,* I've never heard before."

She responded with a grimace. "Bitch is just the lazy way people describe women who don't care about being liked. If she were a guy, you'd call her a perfectionist. Porcupine just means that if you come at them wrong, you're going to get pricked"

For a moment, I was taken aback by her frankness, but as I thought about it, she was right. My admiration for Ambrosia's intellect increased every time I heard her speak. I followed her example and focused my attention on the stage.

Emotional Charades

A well-dressed man was mid-brag about his effort at a recent fundraiser. Stacy clicked a button and the slideshow changed. The screen behind him now displayed images contrary to his every word. Time-stamped pictures of the empty BSU Kiosk lit up the room. Then, photos of him chugging a beer at a frat party—also time stamped—flashed onto the screen.

She'd baited him.

The room was silent, staring at Stacy, at the man that stood there, then at each other.

When he finally realized, he panicked. He stumbled over his words and his mouth became dryer and dryer. After he realized he couldn't possibly salvage his reputation, he offered to donate the anticipated funds from the fundraiser. Stacy accepted. The screen powered off, and she moved the meeting onto the next item on the agenda like the whole escapade had not happened.

I smiled at Ambrosia, "Porcupine."

The meeting ended, but as dozens of people exited, I stayed seated. I desperately tried to keep Ambrosia talking—anything to keep me from going home.

10 minutes later, I was still drumming up questions. "So, did you see how she…"

Ambrosia gave me a side eye. "Girl! I saw the whole meeting. I was sitting right here." She waved her hands in front of her lap. "Next to you. I saw and heard what you saw and heard," she explained, staring at me like I was malfunctioning. "It seems like you need to talk to somebody. Well, I'm somebody. Talk!" she commanded in the most caringly assertive tone I had ever heard.

Her genuine willingness to be a listening ear warmed my heart. I caved.

"I found out that my fiancé had done something terrible." I told her everything. "So, now I'm stuck with this big decision: whether I want to stay or leave."

My stomach eased, releasing anxiety. It felt good. Letting it out. So much easier than talking to my family or friends. I wasn't scared that she'd side with him on the strength of the relationship. Her opinion didn't hold weight like my parents' and Khadijah's.

"Go on."

"I have been giving him the cold shoulder because I just don't know how to fix this." The room was empty now. Ambrosia nodded encouragingly. "I'm afraid I will lose my life as I know it. Afraid that my family and friends are going to tell me to get over it…afraid that I can't. Afraid that I will end up resenting them for their opinions. This decision is going to change the rest of my life. I might lose parts of my family." I stared at her, waiting on her to pick a side.

"I wanted you to vent, but I don't want you to expect me to hold a conversation about it."

"Oh…" I peered down, confused.

"See, I don't know him, and I don't know you. At best, I would give advice based on my experiences and that wouldn't be helpful. Also, from what you said, it seems like you're dealing with too many people's opinions anyway. I just want to be a sounding board." Finally, I understood.

She raised her hand like she needed to ask a question.

"What? What is it?" I asked.

"Although I said I didn't have an opinion, I did want to put an observation out there."

"Okay."

"At some point, you said you have to decide." I paused and waited on bated breath for her to finish. "Why do you have to make the decision now? Is there a deadline? Is there a test? I don't want to talk about it. Just putting it out there."

Her words resonated. I was carrying this decision like it was lit dynamite. Like it was going to explode any second, and I would be stuck under an avalanche of expectation. I had the timer.

I smiled at her. It felt so nice to not have to force it.

Chapter 12: Perspective

I walked home with calm resolve. There wasn't a time limit on figuring it all out. Instantly forgiving and forgetting was not a requirement. Nor was just leaving.

When I walked into the apartment, dinner was on the candlelit table. My favorite: fried pork chops, baked mac and cheese, and greens. He'd probably spent all day trying to prepare this meal. He'd probably called my mom for instructions.

The candles were melted past midpoint. It was nearing 9:00 pm. He likely expected me to be home around 7:00. I saw his effort—his attempts to right the situation.

"Good evening, Rebecca," Eric said from the couch.

I joined him on the couch, ready to burst. "I don't know anything about the future of our relationship. I'm feeling so many things. This fucking hurts, and I'm so mad at you! And all I want to do is hurt you back. Make you feel this bad…but I love you, so I feel bad for wanting that. Sometimes."

He reached his hand out to touch mine. I snatched back reflexively. "

I don't want you to touch me because my skin crawls when I think of you touching her. You slept with someone else." Then, I was lost in a sea of salt and sobs.

Emotional Charades

"Rebecca, I am..." He tried to speak, but I was too far gone, my whole body shaking.

Snot, tears, snorts, and coughs. It was all coming up at once. I felt like I was drowning. and I had no idea when—or even if—I would break the surface. This was my Pompeii.

He walked out of my sight, and I sank a little deeper in despair. I felt alone. He was never good at this part. At tears and raw emotions. He would probably wait until I pulled myself together.

In the near dark, I just resolved to cry until I couldn't anymore.

I yelped, startled by a heavy blanket falling around my shoulders. He put his hand on my back, coaxing me to my feet, then lifted me off them. He carried me to the bed wrapped in a fleece-lined, weighted blanket. I cried as he lowered us both in the bed, holding me to his chest. I let it all out.

***

A gentle rocking caused my eyes to flutter open. My eyes were swollen, and I struggled to keep them open.

Eric was still holding me close. Maneuvering myself to the opposite side of the bed, I retreated. There was something caustic about being in his arms, even when he was comforting me.

"Is something the matter?" he asked, surprisingly alert.

"I told you last night, I'm still uncomfortable with being affectionate with you."

"Yes, that is why I got the blanket. I thought a barrier may reduce the 'crawling sensation.'"

I stared at my cocoon, understanding his brief absence in a different light.

"Rebecca, regarding your first statement about not knowing how you feel. I do not expect you to just get over this."

I nodded. He understood this might take time.

"Would you like a cup of coffee?" he asked.

"No, I want to sleep some more." The clock said it was 6:00 am.

I tucked my head beneath a pillow. After a few minutes, I heard footsteps and the door closing to our bathroom. I was caught in the beginning stages of falling asleep, where your active mind controls the theme of your dreams. I was at the coffee shop again, an idle witness.

"Should I draw you a bath?" Eric asked, pulling a towel over his wet hair. One eye open, I checked the time to see if I'd slept in longer than I thought. 10 minutes had passed.

"No, I don't." I pulled the blanket over my head, taking comfort in the pitch-black.

"Are you cold? Should I turn the heat up?"

"Eric."

"Okay, I will return at any time you designate."

"Noon."

"Very well then."

Relief crept through me as he closed the bedroom door. I rocked my legs to make the bed sway, easing myself back into my dreams.

"Rebecca, do you—"

I ripped the blanket away to see him standing in front of the closed door.

Emotional Charades

"No, you know what, I'm just gonna go to class, okay. I'll see you later." I hurried out of bed and into the bathroom.

Eric stayed posted.

I rushed to take a shower and get dressed. I'd opened the door to communication, and he was determined to keep it ajar.

"Would you like a ride? Or you could take the car," he offered.

"No, I'll walk."

"Would you like me to pick you up for Khadijah's cake tasting?"

"Sure." I made a beeline for the door.

"Rebecca," he called.

I stopped, preparing for another question.

"I know that I am annoying you. It is just that you have not spoken to me in days, and I am just so eager to hear your voice. I will be more patient. I have just missed you."

"I've missed you, too." It hurt to say, but it was true. My chest felt tight, and I looked away from him. "See you later."

Is this what the healing process felt like? It felt like I had exposed an unhealed wound. I walked into class, still processing the anxiety of that small step.

Christian walked into class and hugged me.

It all went away. I took a deep breath and felt present. He took the seat to my right. Ambrosia took the seat to my left. Leaning over me, she looked Christian up and down. After taking her appraisal, she leaned back in her chair.

Very obviously, she mouthed, *"Is this your boyfriend?"* Ambrosia apparently witnessed the hug as she entered.

I mouthed back *"No,"* amused by her antics.

She shrugged, then leaned across my desk towards Christian. She winked and gave him a cute wave. Charmingly, she rested her chin on her fist then smiled at him. Christian smiled back and blew a kiss. I guess if he wasn't mine, he could be hers. My stomach tightened; a slight wave of possession wrung through me.

Christian is my… my…friend. Just my friend, I reminded myself.

All throughout class, no matter how hard I tried to focus my thoughts, they drifted instead to Christian's touch outside of Khadija's door. How his fingertips had effortlessly stoked a craving for his touch. The memory was intensified by the heat emanating from Christian's body next to me—the desks so tightly aligned.

Then, just as fast as it had started, class ended, and so did the errant thoughts of him.

Christian and I took off towards our lounge. We stayed there most of the day, attending our separate classes, then returning to study.

"Rebecca, there it goes again. That buzzing sound."

"Do you have tinnitus?" I asked. Christian had asked me about the mystery sound three times, but I hadn't heard anything.

"Well, it stopped now. Wait a few seconds." He looked around the room. "What is tinnitus anyway?"

"A condition where you hear a buzzing sound in your ear, but it's not from an outside source."

"No, I haven't suddenly developed a case of tinnitus." He nudged my elbow. "Wait and listen."

I closed my eyes and turned an ear in his direction. I leaned towards him until my head rested on his shoulder.

"You're being silly, but there is a—like a vibration sound."

My eyes popped open. "Oh, crap! It's my phone. It's on vibrate." I hastily rummaged through my purse.

"See, I told you. Tinnitus," he snickered.

"Oh shit! I've missed like 20 calls and even more texts!" My heart leaped into my throat. I couldn't handle another Khadijah meltdown.

"From Eric?" he asked gently.

I peered up, and his calmness eased my worries. "Mostly Khadijah. We have the cake tasting today. In like 15 minutes." I'd lost track of time.

"I can drive you," Christian offered.

"That would be great." I texted Eric to meet me there.

Chapter 13: Staying Afloat

I spent the short ride evaluating Khadijah's mood from her missed calls and unanswered messages. She'd called to confirm the tasting and when I didn't answer, she called again. Ultimately, she resorted to texting the same information repeatedly.

I wiped my brow. Right now, she seemed reasonable but annoyed.

"Oh my God, you made it!" Khadijah yelled, running into my arms.

"Of course. Where else would your maid of honor be?" I offered.

The bakery was small and quaint. Light pink and gold accents gave the space an elegant charm. A dark-skinned Black woman with beautiful, big eyes walked from a partitioned area in the back.

"Alsalamu alaikum, Jasmine," Khadijah greeted.

"Walaikum alsalam, Khadijah," Jasmine replied. They hugged.

"Hi, Rebecca. Nice to see you, too."

"Nice to see you, as well." I hugged her. She looked impeccable. From head to toe, she matched the aesthetic of the shop's decor. I'd met her a few times over the years, and she always looked stunning. It was no surprise; hijabis in Michigan were always serving looks.

She was Amara's best friend and had owned this halal bakery for the last three years.

Jasmine turned back to Khadijah. "Oh, are you excited about Amara's news?"

Khadijah's face went placid. "Of course." She smiled. Her cheeks pinched tightly, like the smile hurt her face.

"Yay," Jasmine cheered, shaking Khadijah's hands. "When the rest of your party arrives, join me in the back. I am gonna finish setting up."

As soon as she was out of earshot, I asked, "What's going on with Amara?"

Khadijah cleared her throat like something was stuck there. "This morning, Amara let our mom know that she is ready to start a dating profile for an arranged marriage." Her eyes never met mine.

"Khadijah..." My chest tightened.

I had never really believed in their sibling rivalry. Amara seemed too kind. But starting the process for an arranged marriage while your sister was planning hers seemed competitive. "Are you okay?"

She straightened her shoulders, then raised her eyes to me. "You didn't answer. Did you lose your phone?" she asked, while dragging her a finger under her eyes. I could tell she was trying to keep it together.

"No. It was on mute for class. Sorry about that."

She peered over my shoulder. "Where's Eric?" Khadijah asked. She didn't give me room to answer. "Why isn't he here? Did something happen?" She rambled at least five more questions in the space of a breath. She almost seemed frantic.

I took in her expression, eyes wide, a frown starting to define itself. The slightest deviation of our routine and she was a mess. This wasn't what she needed right now. She needed order.

"Let me tell you what he did," I jested, but there was a quiver in my voice. She caught it. I could see it in her eyes. They instantly shimmered with tears.

"Oh, come on," she exclaimed. "Did he look at another girl in a hallway? No, he didn't fluff your pillow. Right?" Her voice was jovial, but cascaded to a crack. "I bet he didn't cheat on you so many times that it destroyed your self-esteem. Until you had a breakdown. Until you became hell-bent on hurting him that you went against your morals, against your own values. Until you aborted the child you'd been carrying for a month just so he would know you could destroy a part of him, too." Khadijah's voice was brittle at the end. A stream of tears left tracks in her makeup.

I was frozen for a moment. What she'd said didn't make sense, but in the silence of my mind, it started to. Jamie hadn't stopped cheating of his own volition. Khadijah had motivated him. I was stupefied by the revelation.

My eyes brimmed with tears. "Khadijah, what are you saying?" I started toward her, wanting to hug her. "Are you okay?"

"No! Answer the question!" she pressed, brushing off my attempt to console her. Her eyes were bloodshot. Her hand trembled.

I scanned the room to make sure Jasmine wasn't coming out of the back. Khadijah was either having a meltdown or a panic attack. Or both. The last thing I wanted was this gossip to get back to her sister. I needed to calm her down. I needed a redo button. What could I tell her? How could I set her at ease?

"Khadijah, Eric and I are fine; he'll be here any second."

She froze, her eyes red and her makeup tear-lined.

"You two are okay?" she asked in a whisper. I needed a distraction.

Eric touched my shoulder and I turned into his arms then kissed him. This was my chance to reset the evening.

I pulled away from the kiss, "Eric forgot to pick me up. That's what he did," I lied, a forced levity in my tone. I slapped his chest playfully.

"Excuse me. What was?" he started. I shot him a look that meant *stop talking.*

He did. He stood quiet and indifferent at my side. He didn't seem concerned with Khadijah's bloodshot eyes.

"He lost track of time. I was on campus, and I forgot to remind him."

Khadijah straightened, an entirely different person than she was a moment ago. "Next time, set an alarm, Eric. I can't have you ruining my wedding because you were playing D&D," she teased.

Her light, bubbly smile was in stark contrast to the distraught woman of a moment ago. A slight red tint to her eyes was the only remaining evidence of her breakdown.

Just then, Jamie strode through the door. "Hey guys, are you ready to get a sugar high?"

"Yes, baby," Khadijah said, running into Jamie's arms. Only now, I saw them differently. Saw the deceit and grim memories she spoke of. The mistake he'd forgiven. The sour hatred I'd once held for Jamie stirred. My stomach turned. But this wasn't the time or place, so I held my anger at bay.

An hour and 10 slices of cake later, Khadijah had decided on cheesecake.

"So, everything is set here?" Jamie asked, brushing the crumbs from his hands.

"I need a few signatures, then we're set," Jasmine replied.

"Okay, I'm going to warm up the car." Jamie plucked his coat from the back of the chair and kissed Khadijah on his way out.

Eric stood. "Rebecca, are you ready to leave?"

"Yup."

"Why don't you go warm up your car? We should be out in a few minutes," Khadijah said.

Eric glanced at me, waiting for my approval. I nodded. He rushed out the door, throwing his coat over his shoulders.

Khadijah waited until the door closed, then her eyes darted to me. "So, you know what's next on our list," she asked, jumping a little with excitement.

The baker carried the dirty dishes to the back.

We were alone. "Khadijah, do we need to talk? Maybe this wedding isn't a good—"

"We are talking. What's next?" Khadijah reasserted her question.

I didn't push the issue. Another meltdown was the last thing I wanted. I pulled my phone out to look at the schedule. "Shopping. We're picking out the bridesmaid's dresses, right?"

"Well, I was thinking...you're an engaged woman, maybe you could leave with two dresses."

I stared at her with a dumbfounded look.

"Well?" she asked, a smile radiating from ear to ear.

"Oh...Um...I couldn't, it's your day and—"

"Oh pish-posh," she said, "I already have my dress picked out." Her parents had agreed to repurchase the dress, although she'd fudged the details on how it was ruined.

I stared at her. It felt like I was in the twilight zone. "Khadijah, no!" I caught myself. "I mean, my mother—his mother—they would want to be there. We don't even have a date or year. We both want to finish college, at least."

She poked out a lip. "Ugh, fine. I understand."

Jasmine appeared at our side. "Can you review this and sign if it's accurate?" she asked, sliding a pink invoice in front of Khadijah. The bill was practically nothing. It had to be Amara's doing. My stands on their rivalry wavered again.

Khadijah questioned the bill.

Jasmine only responded, "It looks right to me."

I decided to take advantage of the distraction. "I'll see you later, Khadijah. Bye," I murmured, turning for the door.

I shivered in the cold. It had to be in the 40s; the chill ached at my bones. It was dark in the distance, but the light pollution for the strip mall tented the darkness in a ghastly yellow.

I climbed into the warmed car, still shaken by the shock of Khadijah's confession. Here she was talking about wedding dresses like she hadn't just spilled a dark, terrible secret. What she'd disclosed had re-written time. The story of their relationship mending with a stern conversation and hard work was just that, a story. It was Khadijah's vindictive act of desperation that supposedly fixed it.

114

"Rebecca, why did you lie about me?" Eric asked, annoyed.

"What?"

"Rebecca, why did you lie about me? You told Khadijah I lost track of time."

"To stop Khadijah from having a fit at the bakery. She was hysterical right before you walked in." I couldn't bring myself to tell him the details.

"Maybe they should hold off on the wedding. Has Jamie done something new to betray her?"

"It was about us this time, about you cheating on me," I snapped, more than a little irritated by his moral high ground. I bit my lip and tapped my foot, irritated that Khadijah had burdened me with information that I didn't know how to process.

"You told her that I fornicated with Juliette at her cake tasting?" Eric asked, outraged.

I couldn't grasp what right he had to question me. My judgment wasn't the one causing a spiral in a 10-year-long relationship. I stared at him in awe.

"Rebecca?" He looked at me and made one of our gestures that meant *explain*.

I shook my head, flustered. "The moment I walked in without you, she knew something was off!"

He crossed his arms, his back straight and stiff. "Rebecca, why would you tell Khadijah that? It is none of her business. That is a private situation!" He took a deep breath. "What would be your intent? Khadijah is prone to overreact."

"I didn't tell her anything, Eric. She just broke down crying. But you have no right to tell me what I can and can't share."

"I did not tell you what to do, Rebecca. I only questioned your intentions."

"You expect me to lie, so you won't be embarrassed?" I shot back. I wondered if Jamie had asked Khadijah to lie—to keep the abortion a secret.

"Would it have been a lie to tell her that you came from campus and I drove from home? Or is that lie only good enough for me? It was the only reason I knew for why we arrived separately."

"No, Eric, it's not the only reason. Of course, it's not. I can barely stand being in the same room as you. I stayed on campus all day because I don't want to be locked in a house with you," I barked.

As my words hung in the air, his right hand started to tap out the familiar pattern. It only annoyed me more.

"I know I cannot comprehend the extent of your emotions, which I acknowledged. I still think it would be imprudent to discuss my indiscretion with…"

I threw my hands in the air, bumping against the ceiling. "Eric, this is such bullshit! If I cheated on you, you wouldn't tell anyone? You wouldn't need to vent?"

"No, Rebecca, I would not," he said.

"You don't know that!" I shouted, bucking back in my seat.

"I could not see myself wanting our friends and family to judge you for a mistake if I had any intention to forgive you. And I—"

I could hear my pulse race at his words, "You have no fucking idea what you would do. I have never even entertained the thought of cheating. I bet you couldn't imagine what it feels like!" I yelled. Still loving him after that betrayal was eating away my self-respect.

116

"I am sorry"

"Eric, I want to go home," I said, seeking an end to this conversation.

He complied, pulling the gear into drive, and pulling out of the parking lot.

"Rebecca, I just think—"

"Eric, I don't want to talk anymore!"

"That is fine. You can listen," he insisted. "Before you interrupted, I was only going to suggest not telling Khadijah given her history. Judging from today, it is clear that Khadijah has a profound effect on you. You said that my touch makes your skin crawl and that you didn't want to be locked in a house with me, but you kissed me to please Khadijah. Not to mention you dislike PDA."

There was a pen tip of truth there. Khadijah couldn't handle this. My relationship was a safety pin keeping her together. I'd built the perfect image. Loved it when she called us relationship goals. And there it was, my way around Khadijah's breakdown. My redo button. I couldn't let her see our imperfections.

"You're right. We shouldn't tell them."

"That is not the point I meant to convey, Rebecca. I am not insisting you lie. Express your frustration with our relationship, explain that I betrayed your trust. But disclosing the coitus seems unnecessary."

"You're right. If she has a meltdown, I might forgive you for her. Like I kissed you for her. If we keep up appearances until after the wedding, we can work our issues out on our own terms," I suggested.

Eric's eyebrows jumped up. "What do you mean until the wedding? Do you perceive her issues will just go away once they are married? They have legitimate issues; they should seek professional help."

I turned to the window, my back to him. "After the stress of the wedding is over. They'll go back to normal."

"Rebecca, nothing that has happened in their relationship is our fault. It is not our problem to fix," he stressed.

I sighed and sat back in my chair. He didn't know the whole story. I closed my eyes, "I basically told her she was weak for forgiving Jamie and that I thought that women like me don't get cheated on. I was venting about us, and I hurt her. That's why she is being so much more dramatic."

He looked straight ahead for a second, nodding a few times and acknowledging the cruelty of my words. "Still, you are not responsible for her behavior."

He wasn't getting it. He hadn't seen her that day. The way she crumbled at my words. How they broke her spirit. I had to try.

"Listen, you told me you didn't want me to make my decisions based on others. If I have to deal with Khadijah, I will. You saw it today. I've barely touched you since I found out…everything." I paused, thinking back to when I thought it was only a kiss.

He stared straight ahead, processing. Not wanting to overload him, I sat quietly.

"We would be lying to them. The logic seems impractical," he responded after a minute.

"You cheated on me to supposedly protect our relationship."

"That is equally impractical. More clearly so, in hindsight, and stated out loud in plain language."

118

Taylor Bianca B

"So, do you agree, Eric?"

He sighed. "Rebecca, is this something you really want to assign yourself to?"

I turned to him, "Yes!"

"You and I would be working on our relationship?" he asked.

"Of course."

"We would only be pretending that things are perfect in front of her?"

"And you can't tell anyone else. Not Jamie, not your dad, not even your brothers."

He cut his eyes towards me at that provision. Outside of me and Jamie, they were his best friends.

"I don't want anyone else's opinion."

He looked unsure, but said, "I promise."

Chapter 14: Interview

One step forward, two steps back. We'd just broken the communication standoff when I leveraged our relationship to hold Khadijah's together. Eric had resentfully agreed, but now our apartment reeked of restrained animosity.

Needing to flee the tension, I sent an *are you up?* text to Christian. He responded quickly, and 10 minutes later, we met at Abe's Coney Island. The seats were old and tattered and the walls held layers of grease and grime. The food was going to be delicious. Coney Islands were a dime a dozen in Michigan. The ones with the best food were always the ones you felt a little unease at.

The waiter took our order, gave us a polite smile, and ambled away.

"How are you?" I asked, while tying the straw wrapper into knots.

"I'm fine, Rebecca. How are you?"

"Fine," I lied.

"Is that so? You always ask your friends out to breakfast at 9 am?"

"To be fair," I leaned on the table, "I didn't think you would respond. Anyway, how are you?"

His eyebrow raised questioningly. I dropped my head in my hands, giving up my pretense.

He cocked his head at me. "Talk to me.'" His eyes eased the self-conscious feelings that flooded me. I caught him up to speed. Our trip to our parents, our mini make-up, the sex confession, Khadijah's reactions, the decision not to tell anyone, how Eric and I had barely spoken for weeks, and that I'd been leaving to avoid the tension with Eric. How he, in fact, had been this morning's excuse.

"Okay." He blinked a few times, I suppose taking in my explanation. "So, you and Eric are broken up, but pretending not to be? And this is to stop Khadijah from calling off her wedding."

"Well, we aren't broken up..." I paused, embarrassed, "We're trying to figure it out."

"So, you're avoiding him and refusing to talk with him? Why?"

"I'm not refusing to talk to him anymore. Now, we're back to short, snippy conversations," I replied. There was a *why* attached to his question that I chose to ignore.

He let the silence linger.

I sighed, "We agreed to try to work it out. Part of me wants to. But every time I think about discussing the situation, I want to lash out. I want to say horrible things to destroy him. But that makes me feel shitty, so I don't say anything. And now he's pissed because of the Khadijah thing. So, he's been a little quiet, too."

He leaned across the table; his eyes narrowed. "Rebecca, have you ever been through a breakup?"

"No. One relationship, 10 years, no breakups." I paused, racking my brain for a comparable experience. "I mean, I guess we got into one fight in high school. We didn't talk for two weeks."

He gasped and gave me a look that screamed, *are you serious?*

Emotional Charades

I nodded, a little grin on my face. The old pride of having the perfect relationship stirred in my belly until reality faded my smile.

"From a person who has dealt with a few, everything you just described sounds normal. You get hurt, so you want to hurt them back. It's not mature, but emotions don't always have to be."

I let out a breath. The tension that had rested on me for weeks lifted.

He leaned across the table, waiting until he caught my downcast eyes. "My first girlfriend told me that she hoped I'd have an asthma attack and couldn't find my inhaler. Harsh words for a 14-year-old."

An impolite laugh spilled out of me. "Are you even asthmatic?"

"Not anymore, but I was diligent about keeping up with my inhaler after that." He smiled, then a visible shiver pulled him back.

"Didn't that hurt? Being betrayed by someone you cared about?"

"Well, I broke up with her because another girl promised me a hand-job. When you do something wrong, you know you deserve it. You accept the backlash because it's your fault."

Curious, I probed. "What is the worst thing you've ever said to an ex?"

His eyes dropped, and he eased back in his seat, moving further away from me.

"You don't have to tell me," I added, instantly wishing I hadn't asked.

A shallow smile creased his lips. "No, it's okay. It's just a long story. When I was 18, I was dating my best friend's little sister. She was 2 years younger. We were together for about a year. I was in love. She wasn't. I didn't know that then. I went off to college, still in love. She had a secret plan to end it over Thanksgiving break. But I drove home out of the blue. I missed her. I headed straight to her house. There was a bonfire. I went around back to join. Her whole family, my best friend included, were in the backyard. Only Clare was sitting in the lap of her new boyfriend."

"Shit, that's so messed up."

"Don't feel bad for me yet," he hesitated, and I could tell he was unsure about what he wanted to share. "Out of anger, I revealed a family secret her brother had trusted me with. I told her that her father wasn't her father. That her mother had cheated, and she was a bastard."

"Oh, that's pretty bad. I'm guessing you're not his friend anymore?"

"No," he said solemnly.

"I get it, though. You felt betrayed by the whole family." I empathized, recalling how my family sided with Eric.

"It took me a long time to feel sorry. For a while, I felt vindicated," he added.

He always made me feel better, feel understood.

After all that heaviness, our conversation slipped into neutral subjects: movies, writing, and video games. Anything to shift the layer of judgment his story asked for. After polishing off our breakfast and several refills of OJ, we had overstayed our welcome at the Coney Island.

Without a plan, we ended up at Christian's place, a large house divided into several apartments. His unit was a single bedroom loft, with original hardwood floors.

Emotional Charades

From his front door, you could see his living space, bedroom kitchen, and the entrance to his bathroom. It was cozy.

He had books, records, cassettes, and CDs sorted on the same bookshelf. Everything here had this arranged unarranged feel to it. It was cluttered with intention.

We settled in. I read some of his writing. His stories were more like screenshots of moments. Short one-character vignettes.

"These are lovely," I commented, impressed by how easily his characters came into view. It was like a watercolor painting.

"You're going to make me blush." He flashed his contagious smile. "I'm always inspired to write those snapshots. I struggle to complete a whole story. I hate ending them."

"So, you want to write books?"

I was sitting at his small desk, which was positioned to the right of his couch.

"Eventually." He was leaning over my right shoulder. I peered up. Our eyes met. Locked there, I noticed the gold flacks that warmed his brown eyes.

"You will," I encouraged.

He blinked a few times, then smiled softly. "They won't be too wordy?" he joked.

"Not these." I motioned to the screen, snapping out of his gaze. "Professor Lamb might be right—you try too hard for class," I added, staring straight ahead.

Christian gasped in fake offense. He sat on his couch, then flung a pillow at me. "What do you want to write?" he asked.

"I'm no writer. I'm just taking the class for an easy A, which I'm failing at."

He rolled his eyes. "Okay, but what would you write if you were a writer?"

"Huh." I took a moment to think about an *if* that I hadn't considered since starting college. "Medical books for kids."

"Like Grey's Anatomy for kids?"

I chuckled. "No, like books that break down, let's say Autism, on a child's level. Or the reverse. Explaining neurotypical behavior to kids on the spectrum." I shook my head, "That's probably silly."

"You don't really think it's a silly idea." He peered at me as if he could read my mind. "Don't do that. Don't belittle your ideas in search of someone's approval."

I felt abashed. He hadn't hurt my feelings, just called out an insecure habit of mine.

"Is this the first time you've thought of that?" he asked.

"No, I came up with it when I was little. When I first met Eric, my dad took me to the library to educate us on Asperger's. It's mostly referred to as Autism now. The history of the word *Asperger* is vile. But yeah, there was only scientific and medical information, nothing to break it down for kids." I smiled at the memory and the idea that I had forgotten existed.

"It sounds like a solid idea to me. Is that why you decided you wanted to be a doctor?"

I smiled, then looked down at my hands. "No, it was Mr. Bridgeport—I mean, *Dr.* Bridgeport." He never insisted that we call him that. "He always talked to me about medicine and helping others like he knew I'd understand. So, I started college with a vague passion for medicine. Then, I took a public health class. It covered medical racism. I knew it existed, but seeing it in black and white startled me. I couldn't believe the infant mortality rate for Black and brown women, or even that pulse ox readers are inaccurate on dark skin. I knew then that I wanted to be the change. So, one day, I will be a OBGYN in a BIPOC neighborhood."

I glanced up. He was staring at me. His eyes seemed to glow. Suddenly, my skin felt hot. "Too nerdy?" I managed.

"You're perfect," he whispered, then cleared his throat. "Perfectly nerdy. So, you could be a writer after all? Just medical journal and all that jazz."

The thought felt so new. What I was going to be felt so decided. No one asked anymore. "You know, I like making new friends. Old friends don't ask you questions like that. You never get a chance to update your answers."

"So, it's official?"

"That I'm a writer?

"That we're friends?"

"Well, I wouldn't come over to a stranger's apartment," I joked.

I felt comfortable here. His world was separate from mine, and my world didn't have directions to his doorstep. He was safe.

***

There were four distinct versions of me that I rotated depending on the company I was keeping. The edited version of me who was afraid of her words when left alone with Eric. The eager bridesmaid when I was within Khadijah's sight. The nonchalant museum guest, when accompanied by Christian, as I took tours in his world. Then, there was the shadow I became when I was alone, trapped in repetitive thought.

"Would you like some coffee?" Eric offered.

From the table, I raised my mug to show him I already had a cup. "Thank you, though."

"I can make you breakfast."

"I'm not hungry."

"Is there anything else I could do? I could lay out your clothes for class." He started towards the bedroom.

"Eric," I snapped, then paused to simmer down, "That won't be necessary. Just grab some coffee and come have a seat."

He complied. We sipped our coffee in polite silence. Once we were finished, I washed our mugs and prepared to leave.

"Do you want me to drive you? Or you could take the car today," he offered, just as he had every other day.

I turned to face him, "Not today, I need the exercise." I cocked my head to the side and smiled.

"For your health, I understand. Appearance-wise, you always look amazing," he said absent-mindedly, then turned abruptly, walked into our bedroom, and started the shower.

I smirked in his direction. I missed his uncalculated sweetness. A twinge wrenched in my chest. Like someone pinching me. Every tender moment brought the memory of the café. Even trying to forgive him came with obstacles.

I walked to class eager for this feeling to be assuaged.

"Morning, Rebecca." Christian hugged me before I could respond. Like magic, the pressure relieved itself.

"Killjoy," I admonished. "You're always reminding me that it's morning and I should be in bed."

He cocked a suggestive grin.

I smacked his arm. "Asleep in bed."

We lingered in the hall for a bit, then sauntered into class.

As eager as I was to hang out with Christian, I was not excited for class. Today was "Image of a Hero" day. We were to write about our real-life inspirations as legends or heroes. But to my surprise, I wasn't her target today.

Ambrosia had created her own superhero, who stored calories to fuel her superpower, thus appearing obese to keep herself ready for action.

"Ms. Stevenson, this piece is fine. I love that you took such a creative approach." Mrs. Lamb paused, her brow creasing, "But you don't have to go out of your way to place an overweight person at the head of every story you write."

"Why not?" Ambrosia challenged. "Everyone goes out of their way to place the lead as a skinny, fit, white person. In most cases, fat people are only included as the comic relief or a villain."

"I'm not talking about everyone else, I'm talking about you, and not placing yourself in a literary box."

"Bullshit. You haven't critiqued another student about only including a specific body type in their writing."

"No one else in this class has had such strong prejudices."

"Prejudices? If a person of a certain social group doesn't explore and expose those experiences, who will?"

"That is the point! You are a part of more than one social group; you have more to explore."

I was irritated for Ambrosia. I understood what Professor Lamb was saying, but she was missing the nuance. Missing the repetitiveness of certain bodies and shades absent from current media.

I tried to jump into the discourse to back her up. But neither Professor Lamb nor Ambrosia paused long enough to let anyone else contribute to the debate.

I wrote her a note and slid it across to her. *Ambrosia, you're my literary hero.*

She glanced at it. Shot a dazzling smile and winked. "Professor Lamb, be honest. What's the last media you consumed for personal enjoyment, not for work, which centered a fat person, and they weren't the butt of the joke?"

Professor Lamb paused with her mouth open. Collectively, we leaned toward her. We watched and waited, but the answer never formed.

"So, it is important to be intentional about what you consume and create," Ambrosia finished.

Game, set, match. It was inspiring to see how confident she was in herself.

After class, Christian and I bunkered down in the lounge until we had completed our classes. Being in his company was like finding the exact midpoint of a tornado. The calmness.

The thought of going home only invoked tension and awkward emotions. Right now, I craved solace, but we had no reason to linger here.

I leaned towards him, "What's your favorite classic movie?" Like pinballs, we bounced off each other. We sat there for hours talking about classic movies.

When the topic ran dry, Christian asked, "What is a famous movie you haven't seen but you feel bad about not having seen it?"

"Hum." I sorted through a few options. "Mean Girls."

"That's so not fetch," he smiled, and flicked his imaginary hair.

I chuckled, then slapped his arm. He rubbed it like it hurt.

"What about you?"

He tucked his chin and looked at me through his lashes.

"What is it?" I leaned in curiously.

"I've never seen Friday," he admitted.

My jaw dropped. I stood. At some point, someone in his family should have shown him Friday. "We've gotta fix that. You need to know how Craig got fired on his day off," I said.

We escaped and stumbled upon a food truck near campus. We grabbed two meatball sandwiches and ate them as we walked to his place for a movie.

He flicked all the lights off. The TV cast the only light in the room.

"I'm flabbergasted."

"It's not that big of a deal," Christian said, defending himself. He tossed me a blanket. The smell of spearmint wafted off it. I pulled it around my neck and shoulders. This time of year, it was hot during the day and cold at night, making a fuzzy blanket a must-have.

Smiling, I added, "I can't believe you've never seen *Friday*. It's a classic."

"A cult classic named such for being deeply loved by a niche community but not widely known by the masses."

"Yes, but we *are* the niche community," I snickered.

"Are you taking away my Black card?"

"Nope, I'm just surprised you didn't have this stamp."

"Well, I guess I'm about to be indoctrinated."

He streamed the movie and I scooted into the corner of his couch, legs spiraled out, leaving him the lone cushion. I enjoyed watching him laugh as I sank deeper into the soft cushion. I felt it getting late, but the later it got, the more I lost the desire to move.

***

Fuck.

I popped up, shifting a blanket off me. *Oh my god, what have I done?* I grabbed my phone. There were a ton of missed calls. Several texts. One stood out. It said: *Tell me that you are alright, please.*

I messaged back that I was fine and on my way home.

"Good morning, sleepy head," Christian sang, walking into the living room from his bedroom.

"Killjoy," I mumbled out of habit, still processing that I'd spend the night out. Eric had to be worried. More so, he was probably pissed.

"Did you want to go get breakfast?" Christian asked. It felt like an offer to run away from my dilemma.

"Actually, would you mind driving me home?" I asked.

Emotional Charades

I sat in his car trying to come up with a narrative for Eric. *I didn't cheat. I just spent all night with another man* seemed like a hard sell.

We arrived at Eric's apartment and I had nothing.

"Hey, let me know if you need anything," Christian offered.

"Thank you." I stepped out of the car.

The door was unlocked. I must have known it would be. I reached for the knob instead of searching for my keys. As it creaked open, there he was, sitting in an armchair facing the door, waiting. I turned toward the door to close it. I eased my backpack off my shoulders and set it gently on the floor.

I was walking on eggshells.

The room smelled like freshly brewed coffee. I walked to the pot.

Three coffee mugs sat on the table, filled to the brim. The light caramel color indicated that they had been prepared for me. The milk had started to separate in the first cup, but the third one was still steaming. I grabbed the pot and poured myself a fresh cup. Taking one that he had prepared seemed like an admission of guilt.

For a moment, the silence in the room was crushing as I sat down next to him in the living room.

"Were you with Christian?"

"Yes, but—"

"Do you feel better now?" he asked, cutting me off. His eyes drilled into me.

I blinked, unsure of what answer would deviate from the orchestrated conversation he was trying to have.

"I didn't have sex with him. I fell asleep on his couch," I explained quickly.

132

Taylor Bianca B

"Do you want to?" It sounded like an offer rather than a question.

I ignored him. "Look, I was wrong for not calling. That was rude and uncalled-for. I'm sorry if you were worried." I rose from the interrogation and started to walk towards the bathroom.

"Maybe you should have sex with him," he suggested.

"Eric…" I shook my head. Whatever conclusion he had reached in my absence, I didn't want to hear it.

"You should have sex with him. You would be vindicated."

"Eric!" I shouted.

"We would have equal experiences. It could resolve some of the anger you feel."

"Is that your new theory?" My nostrils flared. Here he was again trying to fix us with adultery.

"It may be more conducive to resolving our problems than the 24-hour silent treatment."

"Is that what you think? If I sleep with someone else, we would be equal…square?" I knew the question was unfair. I would be enraged by anything but a *no*, and it was obvious what he thought.

"No!"

I exhaled, letting out the frustration and anger.

"Your actions would be worse," he said, his tone a snarl. "You like him, spend hours with him, text him all day. You have feelings for him. I never left you home wondering if I was alive, dead…cheating." His voice was hoarse, pain interwoven with anger.

It wasn't just the last straw; it was a sledgehammer. Either way, the camel's back was broken.

Emotional Charades

"Maybe I do like him. Maybe I'm just sick of trying to forgive you. Do I want to sleep with him? Maybe, but not to feel vindicated. Maybe I just want him. Maybe I'm just sick of pretending that I still love you. Pretending that I can forgive you. Because I hate you, and I wish I had never crossed that street to meet you. I regret you," I shouted, and the words I didn't trust myself with made their full appearance.

Chapter 15: Sleeping Arrangements

I walked out with the same hastily packed bag I'd taken to Khadijah's, determined to leave but without a destination. Mentally, I thumbed through the family and friends whose hospitality I could breach.

No matter who I momentarily settled on, I flinched against it. When the time came for me to explain that I stayed out with another man and then told Eric I hated him, I wouldn't really seem like the innocent party.

Before I could even knock, Christian pulled the door open and hugged me.

"I thought you might be back." I could tell that he meant it. The blanket and pillow I'd used the night before were folded on the couch.

"Yeah, that didn't go so well," I responded as he took my bag from my shoulder.

"You can stay here if you need to," he offered kindly. "He wouldn't believe that nothing happened?"

"Thank you. I would love to stay a few nights." I paused at the absurdity of what I was about to say. "He doesn't think I cheated, but he thinks I should have."

He swallowed audibly. His head jerked to the side in what I thought was absolute confusion.

"He thinks it'll make us equal. So, I left," I clarified, then shuffled around him.

Emotional Charades

I crashed onto the couch like there were weights tied to my ankles. Now stationary, my anger started to give way to unchecked feelings. What had I just done?

Panic ricocheted through me in an instant. *I shouldn't be here. What would everyone think? That I was the cheater.*

"My life is going to fall apart. Any second now, they'll start to call." I froze, on the brink of tears. I'd lose contact with the Bridgeport's. It wouldn't happen all at once, but it was a matter of time before I would no longer be a member of the family.

"Rebecca," Christian called. He was sitting in front of me, apprehension on his face. "It's going to be alright."

Such a simple sentence, but I didn't believe a word of it.

"Rebecca, it's going to be rough for a while," he continued, pouring out a stream of platitudes and encouragement. It quieted my overthinking. I focused on his words like they were the anchor to my sanity. "People break up. Everything will work itself out."

I listened until the individual words started to blur, until only the rhythm of his speech remained. At last, my eyes fluttered closed.

***

I didn't go home for a night and then not for a few. I woke abruptly, again, scrambled off the couch in desperate search for my phone. The blue notification light wasn't blinking, but it wasn't enough. I scurried to my phone to confirm what I already knew. The fragile charade was still intact. No one in my life knew.

No messages, texts, or missed calls.

Taylor Bianca B

This time, my dream was terrible. Not of Khadijah's unending meltdowns, but of Eric's family. The Bridgeport's walking past me like they'd never known me, ignoring me as I attempted to greet them until Mr. Bridgeport turned and told me, *'We regret ever knowing you.'*

It gutted me.

I'd been here for two weeks, and time was passing in a warp. Every morning had started this way because I was waiting for the cards to fall. For Khadijah to show up distraught or my parents to lecture me about *'for better or for worse,'* but the cards were holding. Glued together by the omission of truth.

Despite our fight, Eric had kept up appearances with Khadijah. Attending wedding events as if we weren't broken-up. We were shallow renditions of ourselves, but Khadijah didn't notice. She only cared that we were there together. Her role models. Her safety net. So, my delicate treaty was keeping my life in working order.

Christian was up and politely ignoring my disheveled state. He was all too familiar with the evidence of my bad dreams. The charger stretched to the limit and my screen-lit face hovered in the darkness of the morning.

"Morni—"

"Killjoy! I'm not ready to meet this morning."

"Today, you look it." He laughed, then tossed me a t-shirt.

Fake shock painted my face. "Well, I never," I scoffed as I caught the shirt and began gathering my things for a shower.

Emotional Charades

In my haste to evacuate Eric's apartment, I hadn't checked what was in my overnight bag. I had only packed a few tops and several pairs of leggings. As his makeshift roommate, I had been wearing his clothes to round out my attire.

His laid-back style was well manicured. He had four stages to dressing. Assembling: laying out an array of shirts and pants. Accessorizing: picking out the best shoes, watch, or coat to complement the outfit. Appraisal: looking at each selection, and repeatedly asking me which I prefer. Selection: putting away the 85 items he decided not to wear.

I crept around him, trying to get into the bathroom before he noticed. He was just about to get to the appraisal stage.

"Which one do you like?" he asked, catching me steps before the bathroom door.

I turned with a guilty look on my face; a smile was plastered on his. I gunned it, completing the last few steps in a bound. I heard his steps dash, as well. Firm fingers sank into my waist just as I reached the threshold.

"No!" I shrilled in good humor. I pried his fingers off my waist and turned toward him, then jabbed my fingertips to the side of his rib cage. I'd won with a tickling strategy before.

He was prepared. His arms snapped closed on my hands, trapping them. Facing me, he pinned my arms beneath his and gently lifted me off my feet. He carried me to the bed's edge.

"Which do you like?" he asked, mid-laugh.

"The middle one," I answered, having already made my decision while he was compiling the selections.

"Thank you."

He carried me back to the bathroom, set me on my feet, then released my arms.

I didn't retreat into the bathroom. Instead, I stood there, expectantly. As the lingering playfulness died down, I returned to my senses. I shouldn't expect anything from Christian. Pacing back, I closed the door, trying to turn off my imagination.

What if he leaned forward? Pressed his soft lips against mine. The idea sparked through my body. The sensitive bead between my legs throbbed for a beat. I let the cold-water wash over me.

Simmer down, I'm just a little horny. It's been a while.

I showered quickly because Thursdays were busy for us. Our Monday schedule had expanded to the other days of the week. We rode to campus together, set up base in the lounge, and didn't leave until we were both done with classes for the day. On Thursdays, I hung out with Ambrosia after our BSU meetings.

Today, I was helping her move books from her car to her apartment. She'd gone to a $.50 book fair. After two hours, she'd left with more than 100 books. When she'd asked, I'd said yes so fast that I startled her. I couldn't have helped it; I'd gotten giddy, like I'd been invited to my first sleepover.

Her black Dodge Ram truck smelled like fresh coffee. The leather seats were weathered, but comfortable. Once at her place, we parked, strolled to the back, and she lowered the latch. Shit. I'd imagined 100 small to medium books. No, there were classics, volumes, and fantasy books as thick as my hand.

She grabbed a handful of books and started for the door. I stood at her truck bed for a moment, waiting for instructions. I was waiting for the plan—the number of books we needed to grab per trip, the projected timeline, or the order the books needed to be arranged.

Then, it hit me. Not everyone runs their favors with military precision like Khadijah. I grabbed six books and followed Ambrosia.

By our third trip, she still scaled the three flights of stairs with practiced ease, while my thighs rebelled. My lungs burned like they had their own heating system, and I was out of breath. Today was brisk, but the sun was out. Now, my coat was tied around my waist, and my sweater protested as it clung to my sweating body.

"Take a break if you need to," Ambrosia suggested. "I really appreciate the help."

"Oh, you're welcome." An idea flashed in my mind, "Do you have a suitcase with wheels?"

Her eyebrows rose with contemplation.

Our several remaining trips turned into a single trip.

"Thank you, Rebecca," she said, a little breathless. Lugging one large suitcase up three flights of stairs had been laborious.

I waved a hand and sank into a chair. I needed to catch my breath.

Books sat in every corner, and on every surface. Save for three comfy armchairs, the living room was filled with overstuffed bookcases. In contrast, a nook connected to the living room only stored a desk, a chair, and a laptop. A lit incense situated in a crack along a door frame scented the air with cherry smoke.

Her apartment was intentional. This room was for leisure and her nook was for work.

Ambrosia returned with two bottles of wine, and two glasses. She filled the glasses until wine rippled at the top, threatening to spill over. I slurped on the rim immediately to avoid making a mess.

Following Christian's example, I asked, "What do you want to write?"

"Everything," she said. Her head tilted back, and she closed her eyes for a moment, as if she were manifesting her dream.

I watched her in awe. She had…something…an aura that radiated purpose. Her brown skin seemed to glow in this dim room.

She lounged across the chair with her legs hung over the armrest.

"Tell me more," I urged.

"I want to be a multimedia creator, writing for TV, film, and books. I want to interrupt the media's harmful fixation on a perfect body type. And not just for championed bigger bodies. I want to dismantle the social swing to degrade the opposite of what's popular. So, when I center on people with larger bodies, I don't feature a slim enemy who body-shames the lead. I don't depend on a mean blonde trope to justify another character's good quality. I want to infest the industry until it's no longer common to villainize a character just because they have different features."

As she laid out her vision, I knew then that I would purchase, watch, and read anything she was involved in. She had her biggest fan already.

I took out my credit card and banged it on the nearest stack of books. "Take my money."

Emotional Charades

We may or may not have downed the wine too quickly. Ambrosia couldn't drive. Christian had to pick me up before his shift at the bar.

'Do you want me to drop you off at home, or are you going to hang out with me at work?" Christian asked.

"You can drop me off at home," I murmured. My light buzz started to wear off.

Surprised, Christian had to slam on the brakes to make the turn that led to his place. We'd been spending most of our free time together.

He pulled out front, parked, and looked at me shrewdly. I hadn't decided to be alone in the two weeks that I had been here.

My alone time had become more treacherous. Now, instead of being a sad shadow, I spent all unassigned time re-enacting my last conversation with Eric. Overanalyzing my words and his, deciding and re-deciding who was wrong. I wasn't sure if Christian realized that he was my peace, but he seemed to want to be around me just as much.

I offered him a reassuring smile. "I have to study for my anatomy exam."

"Alright, do you have your key?"

"Yes." I smiled at his concern, staring at the cute crease in his brow. My reluctance increased with every step toward the house. Determined not to look back to the comfort of his company, I made it to the door.

Breathe, it's just a few hours.

I perched on the couch with my books, laptop, and music playing in the background.

Before I noticed, my note cards were rendered to a recap of our fight.

Taylor Bianca B

Orbit – the bony eye socket of the – *Pretending I still love you.*

Conjunctiva – thin, transparent layer – *Pretending I can forgive you.*

Sclera – the white part of the eye that one sees when looking – *I hate you.*

Cornea – *I wish I never met you.*

I pushed my notes away and sighed. Maybe I should've joined Christian at work. His presence always alleviated my self-reflection.

No, I needed to sit with my feelings. I kept trying to run away, trying to sidestep the issue. I felt guilty because I had done something wrong. I sat silent, playing the memory on a loop. I listened until I stopped justifying the things I'd said. Until the words ached in my chest for their cruelty. Until my tick for tac defensive logic stopped making sense.

To: Eric

Hey, I'm sorry for what I said during our breakup. I should have handled that better. (6:28 pm)

To: Rebecca

I forgave you before you walked out the door. I am sorry that I could not contain my jealousy, and for 27 other mistakes. Originally, I typed them all in this message, but that seemed like a lot. Even for me. Unabashedly, I miss you and love you. I look forward to the day you feel comfortable loving me again. (6:55 pm)

There was no correct way to respond. We were at different stages in the breakup. He was still hopeful, while I had moved on.

I went back to studying. After that, my notes stayed on topic.

***

Emotional Charades

Christian's keys jingled in the lock. My head snapped to the door.

He stepped in, stomped his feet on the mat, and shrugged off his jacket. Small snow flurries dropped from his jacket. He hung his jacket up, while peering at me.

He smiled wide. "Roomie, I'm home." A familiar comfort washed over me.

"Welcome home." I hurried to my feet, and he swallowed me into a hug. Christian rested his head on my shoulder. His hands were firm against my lower back. I curved into him.

How might it feel if he lowered them? If he grabbed my...*simmer down, girl*. I took a step back, "Dinner's in the Microwave."

He grabbed the plate. "I really appreciate this."

"No problem." I was staying here for free. I could at least make him dinner.

He sat on the couch, then tapped the couch cushion next to him.

That's not the only thing he could tap. A smirk skated across my lips. Then, I pressed them into a line to stop. *Simmer down. We're just friends.*

I took a seat at the other end of the couch because my imagination was overreacting.

He took a bite, "Oh, this is good." He ate like he was starving. Once finished, he slid down the couch. He pulled me into a cuddle and covered us with a blanket.

"I've been waiting to watch *Hell's Kitchen* with you all day." He switched the TV on, then paused, "Unless you're still studying?"

I loved that he respected my strict study schedule. He was very relaxed about his own grades. '*C's earned degrees,'* he'd told me, but he never tried to goad me to be more relaxed.

"No," I said. I stared at the TV to avoid staring at his lips.

We'd spent last week inching closer towards each other. This week, personal space hadn't been required. Friends cuddle on the couch…Were we only friends?

His fingertips slid across my lower back. I arched up toward him a little. Maybe we were not just friends. No, we were just friends. Friends cuddled. No, they didn't.

His fingers crept under the bottom of my shirt. My breath caught. There was nothing friendly about where I wanted him to put his hand next. The aching between my legs wanted his attention. I stared at his throat. Would he like it if I kissed him there?

We definitely weren't just… Just then, his fingers, feather-light, trailed across my skin until his hand rested on my waist.

"Friends," I said by accident.

He pulled his hand back, then shifted to be able to stare at me.

My throat was dry.

"Just friends?" he asked.

I didn't know what to say. I hadn't had this conversation since I was 12.

"Okay. I guess I'll get ready for bed," he said as he shifted me out of his arms. Had he taken my slip as a boundary?

Frustration was pulling at the pit of my stomach. Of course, we weren't friends. We'd slipped into unnamed territory, and it was not friendship. For weeks now, being around him was my saving grace.

He grabbed me a top to wear to bed. I stormed to the bathroom to change, frustrated that my verbal slip might have chased him away. I wanted him to fall asleep with me on the couch, to stroke my back, to play with my hair. Hell, to pull it.

God damn it, I wanted him. I yanked the door open a bit too hard, "Aren't we?" I asked, not sure how to have a *what are we.*

He sat up on the side of the bed, shirtless. I ogled his firm frame.

"Friends? No, not reeeaaally," he responded.

My chest felt light. "Why didn't you say something?"

He smiled, dropped, and shook his head a little. He stood, then walked over to me. I watched his steps until he was right in front of me. My heart raced and danced.

His fingers gently stroked my cheek. "Becca, you're fresh out of a breakup. I don't want to rush you. But I do want to make this clear now. I don't want to be just your friend."

He kissed my forehead and returned to his bed. Everything inside me turned liquid. I was stuck in place. *Not friends then.*

"Could you turn the light off?" he asked.

"Ah, sure." I was a little dazed by the confirmation.

He was right. We shouldn't rush. My life was already complicated. This could wait. But did it have to wait? It should. I went back to the couch. But I just stared through the dark, mentally willing him to come back. I grew frustrated that I couldn't get warm, not without the soft warmth of his arms around me. I wanted his hand back on my waist. Autonomously, my body moved.

I stopped at his dresser to return his shirt. "Hey, I'm getting in bed with you tonight. It's cold," I said as I climbed into bed behind him.

"You steal my clothes, and now you want my body heat?"

"I borrow your clothes and anyway, I put the shirt back."

He rolled his eyes. "So, which of my favorite items are you sleeping in now?"

"None."

He turned to face me. The movement was so quick that he nearly pulled the blanket off me.

I held it, secure under my arms. The blanket wrapped around my chest like a tube top. My shoulders and neck were bare.

He held my gaze as his hand traveled under the blanket. He touched my bare belly. Fingertips featherlight, he traveled to my waist. I closed my eyes as a slight whimper escaped. His touch was what I wanted.

"Are you sure?"

"We're not friends." I moved closer to him.

He grabbed the back of my neck gently, angling me so that our lips aligned a breath apart. He paused for a beat. One last check that I was ready for this. I licked the space between his lips. His eyes flickered, desperate and wanting. He kissed me for the first time.

My body pulsed with sensation. Every inch of me needed him. I wrapped my leg around his waist. One of his hands stayed on my neck and the other roamed me confidently. Starting from my collar bone, gently grazing down my chest. He circled my nipple with his fingertips, then pinched it hard. Aching pleasure seared through me. I moaned. He kissed into it, consuming my desire.

He trailed his hand down my belly until he reached my aching, wanting bead. His fingers explored. He rubbed, tapped, stroked, all the while watching. His eyes were astute. When I moaned, when I pushed myself against him for more, when I started to shake, he took note. He repeated that touch.

It was so intense. I tried to squeeze my thighs together.

"Oh no you don't, killjoy," he said as he pushed me onto my back, pulling my legs apart, securing one of my legs around his hips. He had full access. He stroked me until I arched up, wanting more.

"I'm going to..." He kissed away my words. Hard. Too hard. I loved it. I closed my eyes and started to shake, tilting my hips to grind against his hand.

"Rebecca, look at me," he commanded. I obeyed.

"Christian! I'm—"

"Cum for me!" he ordered, sitting up on one elbow, sliding a finger into me. He pulsed his hand. I screamed, and the orgasm ravaged me. He clutched me against him until I was done. Then, he put his soaked fingers to his mouth and sucked.

Another shiver ran through me. I reached for him, eager to return the favor.

I woke up with wild, matted hair. I hadn't bothered with a scarf last night. Christian was still holding me.

"Morning." He kissed my neck. I tilted to give him more access.

"Oh, I'm not a killjoy today?" he asked.

Taylor Bianca B

"Not when you wake me up like this." I scooted deeper into his arms. He gripped me tighter.

"I have a confession."

I tilted my head up, "What's that?"

"I'd been watching you before we officially met. I thought you were pretty. I was so curious about what you were always writing in your laptop." He paused, "I only went to the café with you because I thought you were asking me out."

"What? I had an engagement ring on."

He brushed his waves with his hand, "I thought it was a prop. I work at a bar. Women use fake rings to ward off attention. I thought you'd forgotten to take it off."

"So, you thought I was a liar?"

"I thought you were too young to be engaged." He cocked his infectious smile and pulled me onto his lap. I saw the flicker of my notification light over his shoulder.

"Oh, I need to check my phone." I tried to get up.

His arm tightened, and he held me against him, "No. Stay. Cuddle."

I patted his hand, "I'll be quick."

Freed, I rushed to my phone. Khadijah had updated my schedule with new events. I sighed in relief. My charade was still intact.

I looked toward the bed. Christian was sitting now, head down and shoulders hunched. He looked defeated.

"It was Khadijah. She just updated my schedule." I walked to the bed's edge and sat. I reached for his hand and held it. "I know this is complicated."

"We can take things slow." He looked up with an assured expression.

I looked at the bed. We'd annihilated the possibility of slow. "I like you. We can move at the pace that is right for us." I paused, "I just...I'm responsible for some of Khadijah's overreactions. So, keeping up appearances until after her wedding is important to me."

He lowered his eyes, "What does that mean?"

"I want us to be private until after Khadijah's wedding."

His face screwed up in thought, "I've never been a side dude before."

"I slapped his arm. You are my only dude."

"Just the secret dude, you mean."

"Just no social media and no super public events. Just until the wedding."

"When is the wedding again?"

I bit my lip, "Early January."

His brows farrowed. "What is keeping up appearances going to look like?"

"So far, it's just been being civil at wedding events. Occasional hand holding. Posting to social like we're still together."

His brows pinched, "Um. Do you have to do social media posts? It already bothers me, if I am being honest," he admitted.

I could make a couple of posts about being too busy for social. That should be enough for Khadijah not to get suspicious.

"Of course. Do you have other rules?"

"Like, do I have a list prepared?" He smiled then leaned forward and kissed my neck. "I have never done this before. Just tell me if your feelings for me change."

"I don't think that will be a problem. I'm smitten," I admitted.

He gripped my chin. His eyes flashed, then he pulled my lips to his.

Chapter 16: Terms and Conditions

No one reads the terms and conditions. We agree to them with a perfunctory glance and a mild annoyance at having to answer. Now, I understood the frustration that businesses experienced. All the details are there from the beginning, but somehow, problems still arise.

It had only been four weeks since we officially weren't friends, and Christian already wanted to renegotiate the contract.

"You're going to a fitting on a Friday night?" he murmured, mostly to himself, while I stood in the bathroom wishing I were a goddess with several pairs of arms as I struggled to wield the flattening iron against my curly hair.

"A surprise fitting with the entire wedding party?" he asked, shaking his head with his hands on his hips.

I rolled my eyes. "She found a boutique that specializes in bride and groom attire. So, the whole wedding will come in together. They call this type of appointment *The Wedding Party*," I explained. "You get it. The wedding's party?"

Ignoring me, he continued. "Something is off. I just don't trust Khadijah's events."

Christian was a unique guy. Here I was about to spend hours with my ex, and he wasn'texhibiting a hint of jealousy. Khadijah, on the other hand, he did not like. On the few occasions they had met, she was rude to him, but he was more bothered by the way she treated me. How she composed texts that sounded as if they were questions but didn't allow for a *no*.

"Shouldn't you be more concerned that I'm about to be with him?"

"Who are you spending time with? What's his name?" I glared at him through the mirror. Eri—" Christian started to sound out his name, until I threw a bottle of conditioner at him, which he easily caught.

"It's just so controlling. Who plans a last-minute fitting on a Friday night? Not a Saturday afternoon." He tossed and caught the conditioner bottle in one hand.

I shrugged, not having anything to offer. "That's just Khadijah. Bossy people have friends, too."

Again, he rambled on as if I had not made a point. "What did you say she did to um, um…what's her name?"

"Antoinette." She was a bridesmaid. "Khadijah called her boyfriend and explained that she couldn't come to his family's dinner," I laughed.

"And you…you're straightening your hair. You hate straightening your hair. It gets stuck in your lip-gloss."

"She wants to see what we all look like with straightened hair in our gowns."

"For the first shopping trip?"

I exhaled, exasperated. "I can't wait until I get to know your friends, so when I don't like one, I can talk about them incessantly."

Emotional Charades

He stopped tossing the conditioner and set the bottle on the counter. "Whose fault is it that you don't know any of my friends? I haven't stopped you." The levity was gone now.

When his friends were around, I made myself scarce. I was terrified of my two lives colliding. I had to hide one of them.

I had walked right into one of our sore spots. He stared at my reflection in the mirror, waiting for me to respond with the same disappointment he had every time the subject was brought up. He abandoned his post by the bathroom door. Our relationship existed inside a bubble, away from my real life. There were terms and conditions to our involvement, and as the weeks pressed on, Christian became more and more uncomfortable with what he had agreed to.

I gave him a minute to calm down, traced his steps to the living room, and joined him on the couch, almost sitting in his lap. One half of my hair was straightened and hung past my shoulder, while the other half was pulled into a bun secured by a clip.

I'd hoped my silly appearance would force a laugh or break the tension. When it didn't, I just buried my head into his shoulder until he returned the affection. It took a minute, but his arm shifted around me. Just like that, the tension was eased.

"This will be over soon," I assured him.

"It could be over now."

"Soon," I said it with a note of finality. There were things I didn't see the point in debating now. So, I made a counteroffer. "How about I join you and your friends one night, as your date?"

His feelings mattered. I had to meet him somewhere. Even if it wasn't necessarily the middle.

Excited eyes met mine for a split second, then the light vanished. "You won't. She'll figure out a way to make you cancel."

"Christian, I know you don't like her, but you're meeting her at her worst. Her parents are type A, and they weren't supportive of her getting married before graduating. She's trying to prove that she can plan a wedding, graduate Summa Cum Laude, and get into an Ivy League grad school. At her best, she is the reason I have great study habits, the schedule that I want, and she inspires me to try my hardest. One day, you will get to know her outside this charade."

He kissed my forehead and pulled me in a little tighter.

At that moment, I wanted to give him everything. "I promise I will come."

"Don't promise." He looked at me with hard eyes. He hated when I made promises.

He drove me to Eric's apartment.

I wish I could cancel the shopping trip. I lacked the energy to put on the romantic show that Khadijah required. Plus, leaving Christian in that mood felt wrong. It made every part of my body feel like pins and needles.

"Bye," Christian called, and suddenly, I could feel the distance.

I leaned in for a kiss, and he ignored it, turning his head to look out the window.

"Bye, Killjoy," I said.

He turned his head quickly to protest. "I didn't wake you up this morn—"

Emotional Charades

Then, I stole it. I pecked his lips, giving him the kiss that he tried to leave me without. I smiled at him, and the corner of his lip twitched up. My chest tightened. I wanted to stay at that moment. I wanted to kiss away his bad mood. But my sense of obligation won; I pulled the latch and trotted into the cold as dusting snow swept up by the wind lashed at me.

Shivering, I clambered into Eric's car. It was already warm. I leaned towards the heating vent. Deafening silence greeted me, given that we had given up all pleasantries or attempts at civil conversation. This was when the entire situation felt ridiculous—playing musical cars to avoid getting spotted.

Eric's face contoured with disdain as he watched Christian pull away.

"How is your little friend doing those days?" he asked in a tone sickeningly similar to my mother's back when she used to refer to Eric as my *little friend*. My mom had used it when she thought we were too young to be in a serious relationship. Eric was being snarky.

"Eric," I admonished.

He scoffed, shaking his head like he wanted to say more, then pulled off.

The boutique was pristine. So clean and organized that I didn't want to touch anything for fear of leaving a fingerprint. Sample dresses hung on the wall next to large closets. Each dress acted as a label for what style of dress filled the closet next to it.

I shoved my hand into my pockets and joined my party.

Five bridesmaids and five groomsmen. His mother, her mother, some aunts, and a few friends. About twenty people filled the entry room of the shop.

Taylor Bianca B

A pair of arms wrapped around me, and I turned to see which bridesmaid they belonged to.

"Mom!" I screamed in shock.

"Mom?" Eric echoed.

Our moms stood side by side; they shifted awkwardly to the other's child to give hugs, which I accepted in a foggy sense of awe.

"Surprise!" Khadijah announced. "I invited your mothers. Now, you can shop for your wedding dress today!" She hugged me, then a reluctant Eric, and then our mothers.

I broke character. "Did you know about this, Eric?" I asked, needing to know if I should be angry with them both. I could feel the frown creasing every inch of my forehead.

"No, I did not Rebecca," he responded in his melancholy tone.

It was a small exchange, but I could see our mothers scrutinizing us. Suddenly, I realized the character I was supposed to be and tried to recover my lines.

"Oh, my God. This is such a crazy surprise," I said with the biggest smile I could fake. My smile felt brittle as irritation waved through me.

"You're welcome. You will have the—"

"But Khadijah—" I cut her off, "this is about *your* day. I couldn't possibly—"

"I already know what dress I'm wearing; I only need to re-order. I mean, I might look around to see if there's a better option."

"But I wouldn't want Eric to see me in my gown. It's bad luck." I was going through any excuse I thought might save me from this experience.

"No worries. We have private sections where brides can pick the perfect gown without their grooms," answered a clerk.

"Thank you," I grunted.

Our mom's scrutinizing looks returned.

Khadijah's mother walked in and greeted us in a squeal of excitement. She hugged our mothers first and rounded on me. "Was this a good surprise?" Mrs. Fawaz asked.

"Yes, I was very surprised," I replied. But really, I should have known that Khadijah would try something like this. I presented her with a problem, and she had seemingly solved it.

Mrs. Fawaz looked gorgeous in a bright red sari, complimented by her dark skin. Her long, thick braid reached her waist. I smiled because I really loved Mrs. Fawaz's personality. She didn't always dress in traditional Indian attire, so today's selection was intentional. She'd wanted Khadijah to get married in a traditional Indian gown, like a *sharara*. This was her silent protest. She supported her daughter's choices, but made sure her opinions were known.

Amara stepped from behind her mother. "My sister does the most." She cast a raised brow at her sister. "Nice to see you, Rebecca," Amara said. She hugged me tightly. There was a loving warmth to her hug, almost as if she considered me a sister by association. It melted the slight grudge I was trying to hold for Khadijah's benefit.

She and Khadijah were almost carbon copies of each other. Amara was an inch or two shorter, and her hair was a few shades lighter. They were both assertive and goal-oriented. However, Khadijah's bossiness was blunt, while Amara's influence was feather-light.

Taylor Bianca B

"What kind of dress do you want, Rebecca?" Mrs. Fawaz asked.

My smile dropped. "Olive white, mermaid, princess, ball-gown, slim-fit, backless, with ruffles, and lace, crystals, beading," I started, trying to Frankenstein a dress that couldn't exist. I hoped it would slow them down or produce a dress too ugly to purchase.

My mothers, Khadijah, and Amara dashed off too quickly to object to my description. In their eagerness to search, I was left to wander the showroom alone. I carefully avoided all wedding gowns.

The shop had separate dressing areas, but it did not work out well for our party. The moms wanted to see the attire for both parties, so the guys had to dress and then walk to the bride's section several times.

Eric hated the experience. He carried his head low; his shoulders hunched every time he came to the bride's side. His fingers tapped out his pattern on his thigh. I saw his mom caress his hand, trying to force relief into him. Still, she sent him back into the trenches.

I smiled a little at his unease. Not in a malicious way, just from the freedom. It was the first time that I didn't feel the compulsion to go save him.

A glare pierced my moment of freeing realization. My mother scowled when she saw me smiling at Eric's unease. I stepped away fast, hoping to hide from any insight my mother had distilled from her observation.

While everyone else was trying on their second or third dress, I was still searching. I came back into the dressing area to drop off four more options for my bridesmaid gown.

Emotional Charades

My mother had Khadijah cornered, and they were wrapped in a private conversation. I could guess the topic.

Spotting me, Khadijah marched toward me. I stepped back, half-expecting her to attack me, to cry, or to ramble off secrets. They must have pieced the whole thing together, and she was going to have a breakdown.

"Don't bother picking a maid of honor dress today. Let the other bridesmaids pick their dresses first. I decided I want you to wear a unique dress," she ordered.

At Khadijah's words, the clerk retrieved all bridesmaid dresses from my dressing room, leaving me in a sea of ugly tulle.

Annette broke. "So, she isn't getting her dress today?"

"No, we can come back when my dress comes in," Khadijah said.

"So, I didn't have to cancel my plans to be here?" Her tone was a barely restrained yell.

I fled into the dressing room to skip the bickering between Annette and Khadijah. The second I entered, the volume skyrocketed as everyone else offered their opinion.

Mothers and aunts sided with Khadijah as Annette's tone neared tears. Then, the sound faded and died, as if Simon Said it.

I walked out, simply to see what spell had calmed the crowd. Amara was talking to Annette. She was patting her on the shoulder comfortingly. Her other hand discreetly waved the clerk over with a glass of champagne. Everyone of age, except for Khadijah's family, was sipping champagne. The helpful clerk sped from glass to glass, topping them off. Khadijah looked miffed. Her arms crossed; she watched Amara with a scowl. Their mom and aunties watched her intervention with nods and smiles of approval.

I couldn't blame Khadijah this time. Maybe it was a little petty to be mad about, but Amara was upstaging Khadijah with her own friends. Intentional or not, there was a contrasting picture being painted. I didn't like how it framed Khadijah. My teeth gnawed on the skin of my cheek. There was something to this rivalry.

"Well, that one is fucking ugly," Jamie said to me. I was in a champagne dress that had had strips of tulle that started under the bust. It looked like it had been dipped in glue, then dipped into a pool of party streamers.

He was modeling a baby blue polyester suit. "Same to you," I retorted with a grin. He gave me a conceding head nod.

A choir of supporters challenged Jamie's comment, even though he was right. The knee-length tulle skirt looked like a ballerina costume.

After that, a guard was posted at the door to keep my potential dresses from view.

After the sixth hideous dress and several glasses of champagne, my reveals became a gaggle of laughter. The other girls had settled on their dresses. Everyone was enjoying the absurdity of my costumes. I buried any dress that had promise in a heap of the ones I had tried on, letting the clerk sneak them out for me.

On my last dress, I explained to the buzzed crowd that I hadn't found *The Dress*. There was a clamor of *'ahs'* and *'maybe next time.'*

Emotional Charades

I returned to the dressing room to change back into my street clothes. The clerk was standing at the door with yet another dress.

"Who picked this out?"

"I did," she said tactfully. "You're about an eight, right? We have this dress. It's on sale, and this is the last one. I think it would be great."

"Thanks," I murmured.

I stepped back into the room. Might as well get it over with. She followed me with her tag and pulley to make the dress appear to fit, even if it was too big or too small.

The delicate ivory dress looked like a fluid crystal. I stepped into it, hoping that something was defective.

"I think it's a perfect fit," the clerk cheered as she zipped me up. She stepped back, beaming. "I knew it!"

I peered in the mirror, already in tears and overwhelmed. The dress was amazing. The attendant dashed from the room, returned with a veil, a belt, and a pair of pumps. The accessories added, I saw her vision. In a different timeline, this would have been The Dress. It was the most beautiful dress I could have imagined.

She grabbed my hand to lead me to the showroom. Sadness hit me like a physical blow. I had found the perfect dress, but my dream of getting married was over.

The room awed, then there was a solemn *oh*.

I knew instantly. My eyes shot to him. Eric was in the room posing in a blue tux with black lapels. The same emotion seemed to overtake him. He stared at me open-mouthed. He stopped tapping.

Everyone in the room started to make a fuss and yell at him to leave. Unthinkingly, I followed him out of the room, still in my gown.

"Stop, Rebecca!" the bridal party protested.

Khadijah stepped in front of me, so I pushed her gently aside. Undeterred, she and my mother followed, mumbling concerns about bad luck. *We already have enough of that,* I thought.

I grabbed his hand and pulled him to a stop, forcing him to face me. Now, face to face, I had no words for this. He was the only one in the world who could know what I was feeling. I hugged him and we both sobbed a bit.

It felt like I was losing it all again. 10 years of friendship ending in an instant. I turned my head into Eric and kissed him. I meant it to be a small kiss, a sweet kiss, a goodbye kiss.

It wasn't.

My lips buzzed with a fresh, familiar sensation. It was like I had forgotten that I enjoyed this part. His hand found my lower back and pushed me closer to him.

"Now, now, kids, save it for the wedding," my mother said, grabbing my hand and leading me back to the dressing room.

As we separated, our eyes locked. I wanted to be pulled into his arms like we were magnets. Longing coursed through me for a moment. I looked away, avoiding the contact. Where had that come from? I hadn't wanted to touch him since I learned everything.

Khadijah's eyes found my mine. Her head was craned to the side, inspecting me. My heart sunk a bit. Eric and I didn't kiss in public. That moment had been a flaw in the charade. Even now, her eyes watered and reddened. All the sound in the room seemed to die out.

No. Not here. Not now. She couldn't have a breakdown. A meltdown in front of her family—in front of her sister—would crumble her. If she freaked out now, it would alert my mom and Mrs. Bridgeport. This moment could collapse my life. What could I do?

I smiled like I'd won the lottery. "I found my dress." I hugged her, hopping with manufactured excitement. She was stiff in her arms. A chill of worry trailed my spine.

Then, her arms locked around my waist. "I knew you would," she said confidently. I pulled back. She was smiling, and her eyes no longer brimmed with tears. However, they were trained on Eric as he walked away. She'd noticed something, and I knew from now on that we'd have to put on a better show.

My mother paid for the dress—a steal at $300, originally priced at $1300. There wasn't any argument in existence that could sway my mother from purchasing the dress that had caused me to dissolve into tears. Now, she was sniffling as she passed the credit card to the clerk. I could tell her the truth, but we'd come this far. I'd have to find a way to pay her back.

The subject of the groom's wedding attire had become a battle of too many opinions. His parents, her parents, Khadijah, and Jamie all had different expectations. The classic tux, a modern suit, casual, formal, color, and fit had been discussed to no end. Jamie needed to come back and select the style. Eric and I said our goodbyes and left.

"What is his address?" he asked.

"I can Uber back home from your place."

"Allowing me to drive you is a safer alternative."

"I don't mind taking an Uber."

"You did not have an issue with him driving you to our apartment."

"*Your* apartment," I corrected and rolled my eyes.

He took a breath, louder than our conversation.

"The point remains, I could—"

"536 Wilder Street," I said, refusing to have a debate he'd clearly already planned.

I was having my fill with this day. Christian, Khadijah, our moms, and that kiss. I pulled out my phone to write about it, thinking maybe that would temper my confusion. It was a habit now. I wrote when my emotions felt like they'd spill out. This one had come out as a poem and focused on the kiss. After I composed it, I realized I had been naïve, believing that kissing him would feel different. He had spent half of his life kissing me. He knew what I liked.

I looked up to see that we were parked outside Christian's. How long had we been there? The engine was off, and the car had a slight chill to it as the heat mingled with the cold Michigan air.

"Here, this is for you," Eric said, passing me a folded sheet of paper.

"What is it?" I asked, reflexively taking the paper from him.

"I scheduled your MCAT Exam. Two weeks after the end of next semester. If you need to reschedule, the phone number and registration code are on the back."

I unfolded the paper as he rambled on. It was a receipt. He'd paid the $320 fee.

"I think I picked an excellent date. Two weeks is enough time to focus on studying, but not enough to get burned out. But also, not enough time to get complacent," he explained.

It was too much. "Eric, I can't take this," I said, passing him back the paper.

He wrapped his hand around mine, gently pushing the paper towards me. "Please, Rebecca, it is the least I can do."

His fingers rested on my wrist. An electric sensation traveled up my arm. I pulled away before it traveled through more of my body.

He leaned towards me, pinning me with his mixed eyes, "Please, take it." His expression was doing most of the talking. It read, *pretty please.*

I stared at him. A montage of memories surfaced. The times we'd used that expression, playfully begging for hugs or kisses. Lazy moments when we asked for small favors that we could have done ourselves. A warmth traveled across my chest. I could see this as a favor. A parting gift.

"Thank you." For a split second, I forgot the world. I started to lean towards him for a kiss. Then, realization struck. I jerked back in my seat. *What is happening to me today?*

I scrambled out of the car, hoping he hadn't noticed.

"Rebecca," he called. I froze, knowing I would have to dissuade him of any hope that today meant something.

I spun around. "What?"

"You have forgotten to take your dress. I assume you will want to return it soon."

Taylor Bianca B

"Oh." I cleared my throat. I looked down as I walked back to the car to retrieve it. My chest was hot from embarrassment.

I walked into Christian's apartment with the dress raised over my head to prevent it from dragging. Christian stopped and eyed me like I was a piece of art. He tilted his head to the side, a spoon stuck in his mouth, the bowl of cereal in his right hand ignored.

"Why are you holding a wedding dress?" he asked after a few moments of thoughtful examination.

"Khadijah surprised me. She invited my mom and his mom so that I could go wedding dress shopping." I paused and shrugged. I was sure that didn't explain why I was currently holding a dress. "Amid all my interweaving lies, I couldn't figure out one to convince my mother not to buy this dress. Also, it fit like a glove, needed no alterations, and was on sale for a fraction of the original price."

He moved toward me with a smirk. "I like it, so maybe it won't be a waste," he teased, pecking me on the lips. He walked into the kitchen to empty his bowl. "I told you that Khadijah was up to something."

"Yeah, you did." I made for the bed, undressing and redressing in his t-shirt in seconds. I had an emotional hangover. "Come to bed. I have so much to tell you about today." Although, I didn't know how he would take it. It hadn't gone well when my ex tried to justify a kiss.

He smirked and leaned against the door frame. "What's your reason to break your promise this time?"

"What?" I asked, still distracted by the events of my day.

"The bar. Shouldn't you be getting dressed, considering you're my date?"

Exhausted, I sighed. Christian was redeeming that promise *now*." I had a hard—"

"I know. You always do." He paced backward to the door and waved. He was gone without debate.

I never had time to confront one mood before another was edging in on its territory. Guilt settled in. Guilt for dismissing Christian's feelings, for breaking promises he didn't even trust me to keep.

With no internal debate about who was wrong, I slipped on a pair of black leggings, with his t-shirt and his light leather jacket. I walked the six-familiar blocks to the bar where Christian worked.

Friday nights were busy, and the music was too loud. The room looked artificially smoky. It made it hard to spot his rag-tag group of friends from the door. I was forced to walk the bar, peering into booths.

I finally spotted them in the back near an opening in the bar. Christian was playing dual roles, both patron and bartender, to his group of friends. He slid from behind the bar with a tray filled with drinks.

My stomach seized. I had avoided his friends to keep our worlds separate. What impression would they have of me?

Deep breath. It's not an actual lion's den.

I went directly to my source of comfort, walking up behind his chair and wrapping my arms around his shoulders, planting a peck on his neck. With ease, he pulled me over his shoulder and into his lap.

"Hi." I smiled.

"Oh, it's you. I was wondering which of my girls had kissed me."

I swiped at his face.

"Hi, I'm Rebecca," I said, turning to greet his guests.

Christian adjusted me into a comfortable position on his lap. Now facing the group, I shot my hand out for proper introductions. I was sure that they knew of me, but this was the first time I had officially introduced myself.

Marty, Ronan, and Yara all offered their names and a handshake.

"Nice to finally meet you," Ronan replied.

I smiled back and let go of any hope that this wasn't going to be an interrogation. So, it began. Each friend offered a series of questions, reviewing my answers, and determining their stance on me. Like speed dating, I could almost hear the bell telling one person their time was up because the next person was ready to jump in with a new question.

I answered and answered. Christian did nothing to help, sitting there smugly instead. It wasn't until the ear-splitting screech of a guitar being plugged into an amp interrupted us that the questions died down. Marty pulled out a pill bottle filled with earplugs and passed them around.

"What kind of music do you like?" Yara persisted. I eyed her now, curious about her interest in me. She struck me as the type of person who spoke their piece. She was slim, with dark hair and a copper complexion. Sexy in an effortless way.

"I don't know. I, um, I'm not sure how to define my taste."

"So, you just listen to the top 40 and call it a day." There was a slight chuckle from the group. It didn't seem like she was trying to be mean. More like she highly respected her taste in music and didn't find my response inspiring.

"No, actually. I don't really listen to the radio," I offered to clarify. "Everything on the radio seems to be a sample of someone from the past. I always find myself looking up that original artist and listening to their album."

"So, you only listen to old music?" she continued, ignoring the introduction of the band. Now, the whole group was holding their earbuds inches from their ears, trying to hear the chain of conversation.

"Can music get old? I mean, it doesn't spoil. If you've never heard it, it's new to you."

Smugly, she stuffed her earbuds in her ear and turned to the stage. She smiled though. I think I earned her approval.

Christian stared up at me like he was drunk, and I was performing a magic trick. He was delighted, and all it took was my presence. I wanted to give him that feeling all the time. It thrilled me, making him this happy. *In a couple of weeks, maybe it could be like this all the time.*

"So, are you guys a couple?" Yara asked, defensiveness in her voice, a best friend protecting one of her found family.

I pulled back to look at him. To see if he was having the same trouble as I was. We hadn't talked about a title.

"Um…" I began.

He had a smirk on his face. "We are just…friends," he said, coming to my aid for the first time tonight. I kissed him, un-answering the question.

170

Taylor Bianca B

Chapter 17: Fruit of the Soul

"Christian." I called from the couch. He didn't answer, but sputters of laughter resounded from the bathroom. I walked to the bathroom door and leaned on the frame. "Killjoy, what is this?" I asked.

I turned my phone toward him. It was on his latest Instagram post. A picture of me sleeping on his chest. The caption read, *when you know what this feels like.*

I frowned at him, but the post made my heart sing. My jaw strained from holding back a smile, but we'd agreed to no social.

He was brushing his teeth; the mint scented the air. Still, the grin on his face was unmistakable.

He scrutinized the screen. "A soft launch," he said with the toothbrush still in his mouth. The words came out muffled.

"Christian, we agreed." The edge was missing in my voice. I bit my lips to hold off my smile.

He rinsed his mouth, and then smiled at me. His dimpled smile could melt the polar ice cap faster than global warming. "You can't tell it's you, so it doesn't count," he argued. We had some version of this conversation all weekend.

Taylor Bianca B

The night out with his friends had given him a taste of normalcy and left him wanting more. Since then, he'd posted a picture of his hand on my thigh, one of our hands interlocked, and one of me seated on his lap. All of them toed the line of our agreement. He didn't tag me, and you couldn't see any distinguishing part of me.

"Look, I won't post anything that identifies you until after the wedding," he reassured.

He was revising our terms and conditions, behaving like a person in a relationship, not one hiding it, and I liked it. I couldn't bring myself to demand that he take them down, but I could feel my divided worlds begging to collide.

Christian put his hand on the back of my neck. His thumb stroked my chin. I closed my eyes, then leaned into his caress. I felt weak in the knees. He kissed the base of my ear.

"Deal," I folded.

He dragged his lips across my cheek until he found my lips. He planted a peck then pulled away.

I looked at him with the expression for *what are you doing*? I wanted more than a peck.

When it dawned on me that he didn't perceive my expressions as complete communication, I tugged him toward the bed.

He resisted my pull, "Ahh," he titled his head, "we can't. We have to leave for class."

Oh, that wasn't fair. He'd gotten me hot and bothered just to update the contract. "Killjoy."

He laughed at me as he towed me out the door.

***

Professor Lamb began, "Poetry is the most personal form of writing. Poems are the fruits of our growing souls, the blossom, the wilt, and the regeneration. If you write a poem without genuine emotion, we will be able to tell from the absence of intimacy."

She didn't speak in prose to express her creativeness. She did it to remove our fear of expression. She wanted us to be comfortable saying anything, so she spoke in similes, metaphors, alliteration, and color to loosen our comfort with conventional language. With that understanding and Christian's guidance, I was doing well in her class now - enjoying it, even.

"Would you like to read yours, Miss Dangerfield?"

Not so much that part.

"I would prefer not to share today." I turned in what I'd written after my kiss with Eric.

Professor Lamb, "I think you should."

I read it just so she wouldn't harp on it.

"His flesh feels the same / his knowledge of my senses entices the same feelings to my flesh / that knowledge begets lust / I lust for sensation that is both / tacitly intoxicating and emotionally corrupt / my lust is mixed with loathing / my flesh ignorant of my heart's break / wet with wanting and wondering / my skin tingling from withdrawal / an addict in remission."

Out of my peripheral vision, I could see Christian staring. I slowly turned to meet his gaze. He licked his lips and nodded his head. I couldn't quite read his expression.

"That had emotion." Professor Lamb's shortest ever critique of my work. "Any comments or questions, class?"

Taylor Bianca B

No hands or voices responded, but Professor Lamb encouraged dialogue until a few students offered to fill the silence.

The class flew by. I rushed down the hall toward our lounge. Christian caught my hand and pulled me into a hug. We stopped in a sea of moving people. They verged around us and shot annoyed glances our way.

"We have a few hours before you have to meet with Khadijah the Terrible. We have enough time to go home. I think I can, what was it? 'Make you wet with wanting.'" He smiled devilishly, then kissed my neck. My body warmed with the thought. There was no desire to protest his public show of affection.

Then, Eric's comment cratered back into my mind. 'Before this experiment, I would have stated that I did not like PDA.' Right now, the hall was crawling with people rushing by us, and I didn't care.

So why had I forbidden it with Eric? I remembered giving him the look to stop if he tried to kiss or grope me in high school, but I couldn't remember not liking the attention, just the idea that it was unbecoming.

Lips brushed against mine. My bottom lip was snagged between teeth—just a nibble. My attention was no longer divided.

His hands suddenly left my hips, and he was a foot away from me. I gawked at him, trying to figure out why he had ruined the moment.

"Rebecca!" Khadijah called from down the hall. Several students shot her judgmental looks.

My blood froze. I stared at Christian. He shook his head subtly. He didn't know if she had seen us. I tried to breathe as I turned towards her.

She pressed through the traffic of people rushing to their classes.

She hugged me the moment she got close.

"Hey, sweetie," I said in an ambiguous tone, unsure of what she had or hadn't seen.

"Today is going to be so much fun! I couldn't wait, so I pushed up the appointment. That's why I'm here. To pick you up. We're going right now!" She hugged me again in her excitement. "Oh, hi, Chris." She tacked the greeting on at the end. An afterthought, deliberate impoliteness. I rolled my eyes, but didn't attempt to correct her manners.

"I hope you guys have a—"

"So, we best be off," she interrupted, grabbed my hand, and led me away.

Maybe 10 steps away, she started her inquisition. "What is going on with you and him?" Her eyes were already brimming with future tears.

"We're just friends. It isn't a big deal," I lied, inferring that she hadn't seen us kiss. Khadijah was much too dramatic to have handled my fake infidelity well.

"I know. But he's new and cute. Plus, you guys seem to get along too well. It seems like unnecessary temptation."

"Eric is fine with our friendship. He likes him, even. I think they'll be friends soon," I reassured her.

She huffed. "If you say so."

Chapter 18: The Process of Pretending

Dread crept in my gut as Khadijah and I walked to the door. Eric and Jamie were waiting for us in the lobby. A sickening feeling turned my stomach, and I counted down the moments until I had to play pretend at love.

Lights, camera, action.

Eric in character as the loving lead swept me up in a romantic hug. Khadijah examined us, looking for cracks in our facade. The show had to be believable. I wrapped my arms around his neck, and I smiled big for her satisfaction.

Unexpectedly, Eric kissed me.

His lips were sure and sweet. My pulse quickened. For the show, I endured the kiss that I used to be gluttonous for. When he pulled back, I gave him the expression to *stop*. He smirked and dropped me. When my feet hit the ground, my smile was genuine. I was amused by my short fall. I shoved him jokingly, and gave the expression for *why*?

He laughed. "You told me to stop."

I smiled, "You know that's not what I meant." I bumped my shoulder against his side.

This isn't real, I remembered. I looked down, ending the moment. I hated this part, the moment when it felt so normal to be comfortable with him. Moments when it didn't feel like I was pretending. When I glanced at Eric, he seemed crestfallen and annoyed. Khadijah, on the other hand, was beaming. She'd enjoyed the show.

Her re-ordered dress had arrived. Today's agenda: have her dress refitted, find me a maid of honor dress, and Jamie had to make the final decision for the groom's party.

Full glasses of champagne were dropped in our hands and kept topped off by our two pleasant clerks. Khadijah was taken for dress alterations while I searched for my maid of honor dress.

The alterations only took a few minutes since the seamstress already had her measurements. She was placed on a plush love seat in the viewing room with her third glass of champagne. My selections were moved to a dressing room, and I was ushered in after them with champagne in hand.

I overheard a clerk say, "Sir, we have a limited number of dressing rooms in this section. I could walk you to another dressing area."

"No, no, he can share with Rebecca. That's his fiancée," Khadijah shouted.

"Yes, I can share," Eric confirmed.

He knocked, the door opened without my permission, and Eric slid into my fitting room. He hung three suits and a tux while I stared in disbelief at his audacity. The fitting room was a nice size; we fit in there comfortably with space to move. But that didn't make this okay.

"Excuse me, get out of here," I whispered.

"Would that not seem suspicious to Khadijah? The Newlyweds unwilling to share a changing room?" Eric shot at me.

Taylor Bianca B

I stifled a scream. He had a point. "Okay, just turn around. We can share the room."

"No."

"Eric!"

"No, I have no regard for your post-relationship modesty. Now, if you are truly bothered by my presence, you can terminate this charade. Saunter into the foyer, disclose that we are no longer a couple and are only pretending to protect the farce that is their relationship. Be my guest. I am not in favor of this arrangement as it stands."

"Things have changed. You can't just intrude on me in here."

"Yes, but you wanted us to pretend that nothing has changed. It stands to reason that if you can kiss me as if you are still in love with me, then I can enjoy the privilege of watching you change."

"That's not how this works."

"Are you the only one who gets to determine how this works?"

"You agreed to this," I shrilled in a whisper.

"I agreed to keep up appearances while we were working it out. That meant attending events and being polite. Not you kissing me, while wearing your wedding dress, and pretending we are wholeheartedly in love. Only for you to completely refuse to talk to me the moment they are out of our sight. To have you and then not have you is torturous. Did you think about how much this might hurt me?"

"Maybe I put as much thought into this as you put into fucking Juliette!" I shot back, only responding to his question. His statement was too heavy to address right now.

"Those situations are not comparable. My interaction was a singular event inflicting emotional damage. This false romantic stimulation is prolonged emotional manipulation."

"You're an adult. You agreed to this. You can end this if you want, but you haven't. Why? If our being together is 'torturous,' why are you here?"

"Because you asked me to be here," he snapped.

"I just asked you to turn around. You said no."

"Well, my eyes aren't actually hurting you. It may be annoying to you, but at the moment. I am enjoying your frustration," Eric smirked.

Stalemate.

A few moments lapsed in motionless silence. Some of his claims tumbled around my mind, nudging me for clarification.

"You didn't do this only because I asked."

"Is that a question, Rebecca?"

I said nothing but he answered anyway.

"After you stopped talking to me, it did occur to me that this charade would force us to interact, providing me with more time to convince you that our relationship is worth more than my mistakes. But primarily, I am here because this seems important to you. So, I agreed. I cannot say no to you when I know it will cause you distress—not after what I did."

With that, he started to undress, leaving me with two options: to get over it or to end this charade. Sill frustrated, I started undressing.

He didn't turn around, but he never looked at me. He was still completely respectful even while rebelling. I, on the other hand, was surprised as he started to undress. For a moment, my eyes lingered. He was nice to behold, like an Olympic swimmer, long, lean, yet firm. I caught myself and turned away from him. We dressed in our first selections and paraded out of the dressing room smiling and laughing, pretending to be us, concealing the resentment and tension that two and half months of lying had built.

Dressing room, change, model. Again and again, we repeated this process. Our diligent clerks kept our glasses filled, and it wasn't long before we were buzzed. Each reveal turned into jokes, dance parties, and a lot of wasted time and consumed alcohol. Sip by sip, champagne's influence crept in, and my walls came down. Nostalgia pulled me in, and I was enjoying myself, just hanging out with my best friends.

Encouraged by the liquor, Eric took my hand, twirled me around, and pulled me into a slow dance. He dipped me romantically, freezing in the pose, so Khadijah could capture the moment on her camera phone.

My heart sped up.

He smiled, returned me to a standing position, and kissed my forehead. Butterflies erupted in my belly. The moment felt wonderful but out of place, like an early chapter of a book placed near a tragic ending.

We returned to the dressing room for a wardrobe change. With my hands shaking, I rushed to change into the next dress, so we could leave. I needed a new strategy; this was not working anymore. This part of the charade was unraveling. I needed to go home to Christian.

My fingers were trembling, and I struggled to pull up the zipper. Eric tugged on the bottom of the dress and zipped it for me. I swallowed as his warmth crept up my spine. I looked up at the mirror to find him appraising the dress.

"Thank you." I turned to exit.

Eric said, "I think that is the one. You look astonishing."

"What did you say?" I'd heard him, but I couldn't process the words. This was the first dress he'd commented on all evening. A navy-blue backless dress, with straps that crisscrossed over my chest and wrapped around my neck.

"You look astonishing," he repeated firmly.

I walked out of the room to show Khadijah my maid of honor dress. He'd made up my mind. I joined Khadijah on the couch. We watched the boys through several rounds of dress-up, enjoying the free champagne and the silliness that bubbled up.

Jamie eventually decided. A gray fitted suit with accenting navy-blue bow ties. We made our purchases and stumbled out of the shop. All at once, we had the same epiphany: we couldn't drive. We stared around, silently questioning each other's sobriety.

"Nope," I said.

"I can't," Jamie added.

"I will not attempt it," Eric said. He shivered against the cold breeze. Cupping his mouth, he blew warm air into his hands.

The cold bit at our faces. Jamie and Eric's noses and ears were turning red. I buried my chin into the collar of my jacket.

We looked to Khadijah to get the affirmative that our cars would be parked for the night. Khadijah was facing the bridal shop, her green eyes glowing in the fluorescent lighting. She was pensive, lost in her thoughts. Nervousness crept over me. Had today rekindled her qualms about her wedding?

Jamie waved a hand in front of her face. "Khadijah?"

"How do they make money? They must spend as much on the amount of champagne we drank as we did on the dress," Khadijah drunkenly blurted.

"They embed the cost of the champagne into the final cost of the garments, along with fees for the service assistants. Not only did we pay for the champagne, but we also paid them to pour it. Intoxicated patrons are more inclined to loosen their budgets and spend more than anticipated. A more frugal option would have been to locate the dress you wanted at a boutique then order it directly from the manufacturer," Eric said, knowledgeable as always.

We all laughed. It had been a while since our friendship felt real and unburdened by deeper injuries.

"We need food," Jamie announced

"We can walk to my place. It is not far," Eric offered.

Everyone was too drunk to catch his slip. *My place.*

I glared at him.

He shrugged innocently.

What could I say to get out of this? You guys can't come over because my boyfriend is picking me up soon?

"Yes!" Khadijah sputtered out as she stumbled in place. Ever present, Jamie caught her before she lost her balance.

He kissed her briefly, then answered her question. "What we really need are seats, or else she's going to end

up a lawn gnome. She would be a cute gnome, though."
Jamie turned back to her. "Do you want a ride?"

Khadijah broke out in a huge smile. "You can't
drive."

Jamie tilted his head to the side and gave her a
challenging smirk. He turned around, leaned forward,
and bent down. After several failed attempts, he hoisted
her onto his back, then began to head toward Eric's
place.

A smile eased a crossed my face. Watching him
carry my drunk bestie so she wouldn't hurt herself was
sweet.

I texted Christian to explain that we'd gotten
drunk and needed time to sober up. He responded with
two steaming mad emojis. For now, they were directed at
Khadijah's last-minute plan. It had interrupted his plans
for us this weekend. Once I told him about the kiss, no
kisses I remembered. I'd planned to tell him about the
first kiss, but then the breaking promises fight happened.

Well, then, when I finally fessed up to both
kisses, he would rightfully be upset with me.

After we entered our apartment, force of habit
took over. My clothes were chilled from the walk, so I
changed into some warm clothes, leaving them on the
floor for Eric to put away. Then, I set off to the kitchen to
gather snacks and water. The sooner we were sober, the
sooner I could be picked up.

We snacked and decided to put on a movie. After
spending 35 minutes trying to pick a film to watch, we
decided on *The 5th Element*. Then, we spent two hours
talking over it, only stopping our gabbing to watch The
Diva perform, accompanied by our pathetic attempts to
recreate her grandeur.

Hours crept by and I was honestly having fun. Then, Khadijah and Jamie started to fall asleep on the sofa.

"Are you guys ready to go?" I asked.

Khadijah yawned and turned into Jamie's chest, "We will in the morning. It's too cold to walk back."

"That is fine." Eric stood and walked to the bedroom. "Are you coming to bed?" he asked me.

My eyes widened.

No. Shit. This wasn't the plan. New plan.

"Or is there something else you want to tell everyone?"

I looked at Khadijah. Her eyes were low. She was on the cusp of sleep, her body nestled against Jamie. Today, she'd been so happy. It was just a few more weeks. I could share a room, just for the night.

"No," I stood. I picked up a throw blanket and covered the couple. Then, I walked into my old room.

Eric gave me a look that meant *surprised.* He thought I'd confess. Maybe I should have. This plan was breaking down. Eric and Christian were tired of playing their parts.

New plan. Okay, I would sleep in his room to continue the charade. In the morning, I'd establish boundaries with Eric. No more kissing. Then, I'd go home and work it out with Christian. If the new boundaries weren't enough for Christian, I would end this charade.

Seeing our bed for the first time in weeks hit me hard. My breath hitched as dormant feelings swirled in me. I missed it, the couple that existed in those sheets. The morning smiles and the nightly snuggles.

Emotional Charades

No, I should leave this room. I should go into the living room and call off this charade. No good can come from spending the night here. That's what I should do.

That's what I should have done.

But a part of me didn't want to. That part of me, reminiscent and curious, climbed into our bed and he followed. This was the precipice of disaster, but it felt like the calm before the storm.

He stayed on his side of the bed. I turned away from him to face the wall. I shoved my head on the pillow and sighed quietly. Seven hours. I could sleep for seven hours, then get out of here.

I'd moved on.

I had Christian. This part of my life was a scheme…or. The thought of *or* shouted in my mind. I closed my eyes tightly and tried to think of something else. Or I still had feelings for Eric. I'd moved on. Or. Or now that the raw anger was subsiding, I'd stopped suppressing my feelings. Frustrated, I turned to my other side.

He was watching me. His brilliant smile was bright in the darkness.

We stared into each other's eyes. My heart sped up. I could hear it. It wasn't a question of *or* anymore. I still loved him, and he knew it. He grabbed my hand, and I didn't pull away.

He kissed me softly. Soft, warm tingles cascaded over my skin like a feather caressing me. My mind flashed *no* for a few seconds, then my body responded. I moved into him, kissing him back roughly because not all the anger had gone away.

On impulse, I straddled him. A pulse between my hips begged for something firm to press against. We tore off each other's clothes in between breathless kisses. I rocked my hips as the pulse of arousal made me wet.

He sat up, caging me in his arms and against his chest. He targeted the tender spot on my neck. I moaned and rocked against him. He grabbed my ass and pulled me into his hardness, rubbing my clit. I quivered as pleasant sensations echoed through my body.

I wanted him in a territorial way. Overcome with raw desire, I pushed him onto his back, crawled up his body, then rested myself onto his face. He grabbed the inside of my thighs and parted them more, pulling more of my weight onto him. His tongue and lips massaged my growing sensitivity. My legs jittered, and my eyes rolled to the back of my head. He held my hips, supporting my reign. I rode his face roughly, working my hips in search of my climax. He matched my energy.

"Oh my god!" I moaned as the wave of pleasure washed over me. He didn't stop. So, wave after wave riddled me. Overwhelmed, I jerked away.

He caught my leg and dragged me underneath him. He kissed me. His body pressed against mine. His arms cradled my head.

"What are you running for?" he whispered into my ear, then kissed down my neck.

I couldn't answer him. Words led to logic and sense, and right and wrong. I was operating on primal desire. I pulled his mouth back to mine. He reached to the nightstand, pulled back a condom, and sat back on his knees to put it on.

He crawled back over me. I felt him between my legs. He rocked his hips a little, rubbing himself between my lips. I tilted my hips up, inviting this reunion. I felt

Emotional Charades

the familiar glide of his girth. It was like riding a bike and he knew all my gears.

It wasn't long before I panted, "Yes!" into his ear. Near the edge, already contracting, pulsing, a few strokes from euphoria.

He smiled with satisfaction, "I'm going to win."

I couldn't let that happen. Our rivalry flared. I coaxed him onto his back, mounting him. I knew his gears, too. Like I had his playbook, I rode him to the rhythm that undid him.

"Rebecca, fuck," he gritted.

I could feel his nails dig into my hips. He was almost there, but this wasn't about making him cum. He needed to regret every day that he'd spent without me. I altered the pace again, denying him. He looked into my eyes, a question in his. I grinned in response and grabbed his hair again, pushing his mouth to my breast. He bit me, rubbing his hand up my chest until he found my throat. He squeezed the sides, just a little. I kissed him and returned to the pace he loved. He jerked, his body quaking beneath me. He pulled me tightly against him and held me. Lifting my hips, he pulled himself out of me. I whimpered a little. I wasn't done yet. In tune with my body, he pressed three fingers inside me. His fingers rocked. The internal tap sent syncopated pulses though me. Everything inside me tightened and clinched. My body started to convulse.

I tried to say his name. Only breathless moans escaped. My legs shook uncontrollably. I clung to him as his touch brought me to the edges and dropped me over. A serene explosive of pleasure radiated through me. From my fingertips to my toes, the orgasm racked me. In its wake, exhaustion infiltrated my limbs, and I couldn't move. Spent, I panted against him.

"I love you," he whispered, then laid back with me still in his arms.

I didn't answer. I was too busy processing the bevy of mistakes today held, along with the jealous wondering about when Eric had learned to choke his lovers. He'd never done that before. Did she teach him? Were they still lovers?

Chapter 19: Oops

My notification light flickered continuously as messages from Christian remained unread. An avalanche of guilt pinned me in place. Maybe if I stayed still enough, it wouldn't crush me.

Yesterday I was with Christian and only tolerating Eric. Today, I was the cheater. There were several names I could call myself, but *hypocrite* screamed the loudest in my head.

Then, there was the very real possibility that today was simpler. From one angle, I was just at home with my fiancé, reconciling after an estrangement. But that angle didn't capture the entire picture. Why was I still here? Did I want this? Was this just a stupid mistake?

Christian.

The bed shifted as Eric climbed out. "Would you like a cup of coffee?" Eric asked, interrupting my panic.

"Yes, thank you."

He returned, handed me the mug, and kissed me on the forehead. A cool calm rolled through me. At that moment, I realized I'd missed him and our life together, not just the perfect parts.

"Breakfast will be done in a little while. I have placed all your toiletries on the counter in the bathroom with fresh clothes. Join me when you are ready," Eric said and made for the door.

I glanced toward the bathroom. "When did you prepare the bathroom for me? You just got up."

He paused at the door, a telltale grin on his face. "Yesterday."

"So, you knew I was going to come home with you?

Eric leaned on the door frame, "Ever since that kiss at the fitting. I had hoped that under the right circumstances, we could really talk. I have just stayed prepared for that moment."

I smiled at his honesty.

He turned to leave.

"Are they still here?" I asked, remembering we had guests.

"No, they were gone when I woke up."

I took my time in the shower. My stomach tied itself in and out of knots. I was conflicted between wanting what I had in the past with Eric and wanting my present with Christian.

Fresh from the shower, I walked into a memory. The present reminded me so much of the past that I was whipped with *déjà vu*. All my favorite foods were waiting on the table, and he was sitting there, waiting to have a conversation. The kitchen was the same as the day he told me that it wasn't just a kiss. Everything seemed to turn gray and white.

Instantly, I felt defensive. I couldn't sit here and let him hurt me again.

"Last night didn't mean anything," I attacked first, ruining the possibility of a pleasant morning. "It was just an experiment, and I discovered that I don't love you anymore." We sat in the sharpness of my words for a few moments.

"Is that accurate?"

"It was just sex," I bluffed, calmly preparing my plate.

"No, it was not," he countered confidently between sips of tea.

"You can't fuck me into forgiveness."

Eric's forehead creased, "Your performance displayed an ulterior motivation. I cannot imagine how ramming yourself against my mouth could improve my performance or your pleasure."

"I was just working out some aggression."

"You are still here."

"Khadijah was my ride and she left."

"Rebecca, where would she have taken you? To Christian Taylor's? She believes you stay here." He paused for another second, breaking eye contact. "Uber is a very popular service currently. Had you wanted to leave, you could have." He continued before I had a chance. "Okay, I had hoped the civility shown last night was to last until today. I understand that there is nothing to be gained from dismissing one's actual problems. Would you like to begin?" He asked, resetting the conversation.

"I just don't want you to think that sex repaired anything." I softened after remembering that I didn't really have a point, just an attitude about the memories in this room.

He nodded his head. "First, I would like to assume responsibility for providing the catalyst for all the pain, discomfort, and loss of trust that has consumed us for the last few months."

"You can't just say sorry and make the pain go away—"

192

"I am not finished. Please refrain from interrupting me, as there is a great deal I need to convey to you." He sat straight up in his chair, staring at me. He waited in silence for me to acknowledge his statement.

I rolled my eyes, annoyed, "Fine."

"Rebecca, when you decided that Khadijah's relationship issues were more important than even a weeklong attempt to repair our 10-year relationship, when you orchestrated a farce to convince Khadijah that her trepidations about marrying Jamie were not valid, when you left me after making two mistakes in 10 years but allayed Khadijah's fears by encouraging her to latch on to our relationship as a role model, while also cohabitating with Christian Taylor, it made me feel like you are the most cold-hearted, inconsiderate person in the world."

"That is more than one problem," I said.

"It is a compound problem. I thought it would be best to explain the complete source for such a harsh statement. It is not every day that you tell the woman you love that she can be a terrible person when she is upset."

"So, you make a habit of sleeping with women you don't respect."

"No, just you, Rebecca," Eric exclaimed. "I never said I did not respect you. You suggested it in your attempt to bait me into defending or acknowledging my mistake. I did that already, and I gave you the opportunity to start the conversation from your perspective. You declined. This conversation is not going to go as you expected. I have anger and resentment towards you. I am not going to coddle your feelings. I might say something you do not like, and I expect that you will do the same. Please, if you would, could you address the statement I made?"

"What an interesting tactic for trying to win back your fiancée—hostility and insults."

"I do not have a fiancée. This conversation is not to win you back, but to determine whether our relationship is worth repairing. I did not insult you; I made an accusation, which you are welcome to refute. The hostility is coming from you."

"Of course I'm hostile. Do you remember the last conversation we had in this room, at this table? Let me remind you. You told me that you fucked your classmate for science. You were sitting in that goddamn chair, you'd made breakfast, and then you broke my heart. Now, you're suggesting that my reaction to that pain is worse than what you did." I shoved the table, tipping the beverages over. Eric righted the cups. He blotted the spill with napkins.

"Should we change rooms?" Eric suggested.

"What?"

"Since this location is aggravating you, should we relocate?" he clarified.

I blinked in awe at the simplicity of his logic.

"Rebecca, I am not suggesting that what you did was worse than what I did. This is not a comparison. You reacted to my betrayal in the way that you needed to heal. That reaction hurt me. I do not understand some of your choices and because of that, they seem vindictive. I want to be honest and discuss everything so that we can move forward. I know you still love me."

I thought about his words and my actions over the last few months. The silent treatment, Christian, the ruse, had all inflicted an emotional toll on Eric. I looked at him, wondering if I was ready to deal with his emotional journey. I could leave and continue to blame Khadijah for the resurgence of feelings for Eric since that kiss, continue to say that my time with Eric was all an act to please her.

But I was here, sitting at his breakfast table. I must have wanted something out of this conversation.

"The Newlyweds. Our relationship had this air of perfection and I loved it. I loved being the role model. I loved giving advice and being looked up to." I paused to try to figure out how to explain my actions. "When I told Khadijah about the kiss, she reacted like I had just told her Disney World had closed. She didn't see me in pain. She saw us. The next moment, she was calling off her wedding, and it seemed to have more to do with us than their relationship. I felt responsible. It just snowballed after that. "

"Thank you for responding." He smiled. "Why did you forgive Jamie for his mistakes but not me?"

"I didn't have a choice. I didn't forgive Jamie. Khadijah did, and trying to hate him through her forgiveness almost destroyed our friendship."

"Why were you unwilling to work on our relationship? You just left."

"Because I didn't want to work it out. I just wanted everything to get back to normal. I wanted to drop the subject and crawl back into our lives and pretend it didn't happen. I felt pathetic because I couldn't imagine leaving you. Then because of that stupid relationship status, I felt like everyone echoed that sentiment, that I shouldn't leave. The more I tried to get through it, the more anger and resentment built up."

Emotional Charades

"Why did you move in with a man you barely knew?"

"He made the pain stop." The bitter honesty left my lips. "He didn't know us, so he was on my side. He vindicated my anger."

The sentence brought a flush of tears to Eric's eyes, but he didn't cry. The sound of his finger tapping out his list echoed in the quiet that followed.

"I think I have enough information. Would you like to pose a question?"

I looked around the room. The questions I wanted to ask made me feel insecure, like I was showing my cards in a game of Texas Hold'em. "Why her? Do you have feelings for her?"

"She was in class with me when I developed the experiment, and she was willing. I have absolutely no romantic feelings for her."

A flame of jealousy flared in my stomach. "What type of feelings do you have for her?"

"Completely platonic feelings."

"Platonic?! Do you still talk to her?"

"Yes."

I pushed back from the table, eyeing the door. I wanted to jump to my feet, to leave. How could he still have her in his life? I sat still, willing myself not to move. I took a deep breath.

"Are you two still sleeping together?" I asked through gritted teeth.

"Rebecca!" Eric said firmly, "I have not touched her since the experiment. We have class together and sometimes we speak."

"So, nothing is going on with her?" I asked.

"No. Now, please, can we talk?"

196

Taylor Bianca B

I looked up. He looked distant.

"Rebecca, if I am honest…it is this type of reaction that I was afraid of. You reacted so quickly, and you left." He smoothed his hand on the table. His fingertips tapped his pattern lightly. "Like you don't want to try. Like you don't care." His voice was guarded.

"Eric, you cheated—"

He interrupted me gently, "I am referring to our first fight. We were 17. I accidentally embarrassed you during lunch in our high school cafeteria. You responded by not talking to me for two weeks. I was miserable, while you remained our school's social butterfly. I learned then that you could easily live without me. Concurrently, I learned that I did not want to try to live without you. Since then, I have had a seed of insecurity regarding it."

"Eric, I was miserable, too. I was just better at hiding it." Before all this, I thought we had no secrets. Now, I know that was a naïve belief. We all have parts of ourselves we don't believe deserve acknowledgment. "Why didn't you tell me you felt this way?"

"It was never constant. When we are together, it is easy to dismiss. We have spent more time apart this last year than ever before. You started scheduling me into your calendar. I felt like an obligation." He paused, then licked his lips, "Rationally, I knew you were just busy with the MCAT preparations and responsibilities as Khadijah's maid of honor. I know you scheduled couple's time so that we could see each other. Frustratingly, insecurities have a habit of ignoring logic."

I could tell he was hurt, but I was hurting, too, and I didn't know how to reconcile them both.

"I'm scared. I'm scared that this road leads to another folder, another heartbreak. When I'm scared, I run." My head dropped. That's what I'd been doing, running from this.

He leaned forward. "I would rather jump from the Blue Water Bridge into Lake Huron then break your heart again. I swear it," he said. His eyes were intense.

I looked at the ceiling, then back at him. I leaned toward him, "That seems a little extreme," I said. I gave a small smile.

He smiled. "I mean it." He interlocked our fingers. My thumb stroked the side of his hand.

We sat in our own discomfort and talked.

Chapter 20: Unread

An hour later, my phone played the melody to *Baby Got Back*. My alarm.

"Class?" he asked with a pleasant smile.

"Class. I need a ride."

Once inside his car, I basked in the precious feeling of a comfortable silence. It was soothing to get that load of emotion off my chest.

"Turn left here," I instructed.

"Why?" he responded, perplexed, as he changed lanes to follow my directions.

"I need to grab my laptop from—" then the fog cleared from my brain. "Shit! No, keep straight," I shouted as he started to turn.

He switched lanes at the last second. Several drivers honked to announce their disapproval.

"Sorry," I muttered.

My smile faded as the dopamine and nostalgia that flooded my senses last night dissipated. Reality hit me. Christian—not the idea. Christian the man, the person. *My* person.

How could I do this to him?

"Were you directing us to your boyfriend's house?" he asked, almost laughing.

"Eric, shut up. Take me to Khadijah's dorm," I said. I'd just blown up my healthy, happy relationship. For what? A life that was barely held together by a string of   lies.

"Is your boyfriend going to be mad that you slept over at your fiancé's house?" he teased.

"I don't have a fiancé." I stared straight ahead, the panic starting to radiate. I bit the inside of my cheek.

"I am working on that."

There it was again. The tiny flash of *or*.

"So, we are worth saving?" my voice cracked.

He looked at me with warm eyes but didn't answer. He drove the last few minutes to the dorm and parked the car.

"What are you thinking?" he asked calmly.

I sank into the bad mixture of emotions. I had just experienced euphoria, then the jealousy of a memory, now terror, and finally guilt. Is this what a relationship with Eric would amount to? An unpredictable variation of emotions? Worse, this would hurt Christian.

"I'm confused. What are we doing?"

"I am trying to redeem myself and earn you back because I love you. You, it seems, are having second thoughts."

He turned to look at me, making the expression that meant, *is that right?* I nodded my head.

He looked at the steering wheel and tapped a few times. "Rebecca, you have to talk to me. Even if you think I will not like it."

I let out a breath I hadn't realized I was holding. "Yesterday before the fitting, I considered ending this charade for Christian," I whispered. "Yet, 10 minutes ago, I considered rushing headfirst back into our relationship. Now, I'm mad and wavering on whether we should even be together."

"I understand that you are mad at me. I do not expect the disappointment to fade easily."

"No, I'm mad at myself, Eric. Our breakup has changed me in ways I hate. Lying to everyone, jealousy, now cheating…" I paused, ashamed to admit my betrayal. "Who am I?"

He sat back, pensive. Then, he turned towards me.

"The love of my life," he sighed. "Why are you wavering on the idea of reconciliation?"

"I don't know that I can trust you, and I don't want to spend the rest of our relationship jealous of every person I see you interact with." I took a breath, apprehensive about the rest of my answer, "And because of Christian. I care about him." Although I didn't know how I could convince him of that, not after the previous night.

He looked at me sagely. His hand found my chin and tilted my face towards him. I waited for the kiss to ease the tension.

"Trust is not an issue that can be resolved in a single conversation. We will need time to repair something as important as trust. We have made a large amount of progress in a short amount of time. 24 hours ago, you were pretending that you didn't love me." He reached for my hand. "Let us not rush into anything. We should start off slow, start over, date non-exclusively if that is what you need."

The *non-exclusively* caught my attention. "Are you dating someone else?" I snapped, jealousy showing its head again. Jealousy bypassing the fact that I was dating someone else.

He smiled a little, "No." He kissed my forehead, which set me at ease. "I am confident that if I pressure you to pick between us, it would eventually be detrimental to the restoration of our relationship. When you pick me, I want you to be certain."

My alarm sounded again. Distractedly, I dismissed Sir-mix-a-lot.

Then, my phone rang.

"Rebecca!"

"Christian!" I shouted into the speaker.

"Where the hell have you been and why haven't you answered your phone?" he demanded, his tone split between anger and concern.

"Oh, I'm at Khadijah's dorm now," I answered, dodging the other part of the question. "Could you meet me here with my laptop before my class? Thanks, baby…bye." I stuttered and coughed on the term of endearment. Eric's presence, after what I'd done, made every word feel dirty. I hung up the phone before I incriminated myself.

He stared out of the driver's side window, "You are sneaking your fiancé away before your boyfriend gets here," he quipped. He turned to face me, his smile forced.

"I do not have a fiancé," I restated.

"I am working on that." He grabbed my hand, pulled me towards him, and kissed me like he wanted me to think about it for the rest of the day.

Chapter 21: Where I need to be

Suddenly, I was doing the things for which I despised Jamie for: cheating and lying. I used to think he was among the worst people in the world for having the ability to lie so convincingly. Now, I understood. Lying was self-preservation in the presence of terror. But lying was a loan with a high-interest rate. You'd always pay for it later.

Cheating was as easy as proximity, desire, and availability. It was the people you loved that carried the burden of the hurt you created.

Christian took longer than I had expected to get to me. Sitting in my guilt was sickening, and I assumed the only remedy was honesty. I tried to arrange the words in an order that would inflict the least damage. All I ended up with were versions of my night that minimized my wrongdoing. Words like *champagne* and *inebriation* were being highlighted as the culprits. It was bullshit and I knew it.

There was a knock. The sound paralyzed me. A new lie came that would allow me to borrow more time without hurting anyone. I could stay in bed, pretend to be asleep. I didn't have to face this conversation today. He would call a few times and I would "sleep" through the ringing.

"Becca."

Emotional Charades

"Yes," I answered. Fuck! It was so hard not to respond to someone calling your name. "Here I come."

Unlocking the door, I felt like I was walking into a horror film, only I was the monster. I stood, afraid to face the consequences.

"Hello," he said, chipper. He stepped right into me, giving me a hug before he kissed my cheek. He entered the room like it was a normal day.

His presence filled the negative space. The room felt cramped.

"So, what happened to you yesterday?" he asked.

I was bewildered. There was no anger in his tone, just light-hearted concern.

Flustered, I answered. "Um, they served alcohol at the shop. We were too drunk to drive, so we all spent the night at Eric's apartment." I emphasized *all*. I listened to myself rearrange the truth. I tried to look casual, one arm wrapped around my waist, the other sitting on a jutted-out hip.

"Why didn't you text me back?" he asked in the same casual tone.

My heart raced; I didn't want to break his.

"Oh, well, um, Khadijah was watching." Then, without thinking it through, I dipped into the truth to give my story an honest ring. "Plus, after we were drunk, I was distracted and actually having fun with the gang. It was the first time in a while. Sorry, it just slipped my mind." Giving a sample of the truth seemed to do the trick. His shoulders relaxed.

"Huh, how inconsiderate." He wrapped his arms around me.

I scrunched my nose at his accusation. That adjective was starting to be applied too often to be inaccurate.

"I'll do better," I promised. I meant it. I wanted to protect Christian. He didn't deserve this.

I felt dirty, but kept my body language consistent with the lies. I winked at him in a flirty manner, and he giggled at my attempt. Could it be this easy? I could get away with it and not hurt anyone for now.

"Okay then, without the intent of arousing distress, may I dare to venture onto a topic that will inevitably cause you distress?" Maybe it wasn't that easy. I laid my head against his chest in case this was our last hug.

"What?"

He tightened the hug, "For your final project for Professor Lamb, you should expand your observation of Eric and Juliette at the café. The raw interplay of romance and heartbreak based so firmly in your truth gives you an advantage where you lack natural creativity. It would be a shame to not develop it," Christian explained.

His words didn't match his tone of voice. The words seemed vindictive, but his body language seemed calm, and his voice was casual, pensive even, like a timid kid asking to break their curfew. I pulled back from the hug, confused. I began searching his eyes for the motivation behind his statement. Christian's hands landed on my hips. He shook me a little.

"Hello, are you in there?"

Enough time had gone by for me to form an answer, but I was still trying to interpret this statement.

Genuine opinion or spiteful comment? Did he know I was lying? Did he know to what degree?

I raise my eyebrows. "'Lack of creativity?'" I asked to beat around the passive-aggressive bush.

"'No, not in a negative way. Some authors are skilled at creating epic worlds or characters out of thin air, like George R.R Martin, while others are amazing at picking moments out of their lives and relating them to audiences in an engulfing way, like Sylvia Plath. I've noticed your personal life is your inspiration. You're only a writer when your heart is in shambles." Again. The statement had teeth, but his tone was serene.

"What do you mean by that?"

"I'm just encouraging you to follow your talents. Even if the situation casts you in a pitiable light."

I understood now. We'd never had a real fight. This was what Christian was like when he was upset. My stomach turned. He was malicious.

I drew back. "Okay, I'm not interested. Thank you very much for your unsolicited suggestion." I glared at him.

"It could help you so you don't prove Professor Lamb right about your inability to write in color," he added with a charming smile that belied the venom in his words.

"No!" I snapped.

"Well, if you won't use it, may I?" His smile only grew, almost villainous. I started to wonder if he would add the wicked laugh to complete the character.

"What?" Where was he going with this question?

"The event, not your writing. I wouldn't plagiarize you," he chuckled a bit, digging the knife deeper. "I was there, too; I recall being inspired by your version of events. I would like to reread your work. I could write something from my perspective."

"Sure," I snapped in a moment of irritation, "why not?"

I strode past him to where he had placed my laptop. I started it, tapping my foot as it loaded. Locating the document, I then emailed it. He was trying to press my buttons, spitefulness at its best. I could just give him what he asked for instead of arguing about it.

"Are you okay?" he followed up sweetly.

"Yup. You?" I asked.

"Can you think of any reason why I wouldn't be?" he asked simply. His eyes searched mine.

I swallowed, then stared into his eyes. He was asking me for the truth. He was being an asshole and that wasn't okay, but what I had done was worse.

I heard my heart slow, trying to delay this moment. "I'm sorry for last night…I—" The truth sat on my tongue like poison. "It won't happen again."

I was too much of a coward to confess.

"Okay, then." He opened his arms and hugged me. I was stiff at first. Then, the air of hostility dissipated, and I settled into his arms. He dropped his head to mine. "Are you ready?"

"For what?" I asked.

"Your surprise. You remember we had plans before Khadijah kidnapped you?" He paused. "For a whole night."

I had forgotten, "You don't have to give me anything." Because he shouldn't. Because I didn't deserve it.

"It's already planned and it's time sensitive. Are you ready to go?" Christian asked as he opened the door.

Emotional Charades

Chapter 22: Road Trip

It was a romantic weekend getaway. I made every attempt to weasel out of the trip. Words like *finals*, *wedding plans*, *exhausted*, and *sick* had no bearing on him. Every attempt other than telling the truth, but I couldn't confess.

I didn't even know what exactly to confess. I'd cheated, obviously. But was I confessing, and begging him for forgiveness, or was I confessing and leaving him for Eric? Maybe Eric and I just needed closure, and last night was not about reconciliation. If I did break up with Christian for Eric, would it hurt him less to omit the cheating?

"Where are we going?" I asked. He glanced at me suspiciously, then reached for the glove compartment. He pulled out a stack of four-by-four note cards with a red bow tied around them. Millimeters separated our skin, but he was careful not to allow us to touch. He threw the cards in my lap without saying a word. I removed the tie and read the first note aloud.

The front read:

Clue: The tool used to appreciate the color in the world.

"Professor Lamb's criticism." I laughed alone. He cut his eyes towards me and twirled his finger in a circle, instructing me to turn the card over. It read:

Emotional Charades

Answer: Eyes - Collect your prize beneath your seat.

From beneath the seat, I retrieved a bottle of my favorite wine. These cards were remnants of a strategically planned romantic weekend. Only I'd ruined it.

Clue: A full-hearted desire, but nothing you need.

Answer: Want - Collect your prize from the center console. Several bags of chocolate were waiting there.

Clue: A word and a letter. Spell the word with the letter.

Answer: You - Collect your prize in the visor. I found two tickets for *The Nutcracker*.

The solved riddles read: *I want you to meet my family.*

My heart cracked. Not a sentiment. A physical ache radiating through my body.

"Yes, I would love to," I answered honestly, albeit selfishly.

We drove past evergreen covered hillsides until they changed into overlapping freeways, and then into the ghost of an industrial downtown.

As we parked in front of a modest brick house in Detroit, I put on the same mask I had worn for Khadijah. I could put aside my guilt and worry and make this a perfect weekend. I would be the perfect girlfriend. But there was one concern I had not addressed while we drove: Why would he want me to meet his family after last night?

"Are you sure you want me to be here?"

"Nothing happened, right?"

210

He got out and grabbed our bags. He didn't wait for an answer. He was trusting me—or trying to. Shame washed over me. I steadied myself, breathing in and out until the tension eased. I forgot about everything but the way I'd felt when we kissed yesterday. When I opened my eyes, I was her again.

All smiles, I followed him. I grabbed his hand and to my surprise, he didn't resist my touch. I couldn't let him down. I couldn't be anything less than perfect.

A tiny, brown-skinned woman with short-cut hair and beautiful cheekbones opened the door. Several faces darted from behind her as the rest of the family waited to greet us. Her four children all resembled her, but were similar in complexion to Christian. She and Christian embraced as soon as the door was wide enough to allow it.

"Mom, this is my girlfriend, Rebecca." He gestured to me. It was the first time he'd called me by a title. I opened my arms and in stepped his mother. Once she stepped out of the way, the four children encircled Christian, hugging several parts of his body. Chatter spilled out of them as they all tried to speak at once.

"Let's go inside; it's cold," Christian's mother said.

Her home was warm and meticulously clean, an accomplishment I thought was impossible with what appeared to be four kids under 12. I looked for the signs of a lived-in home as she led us to a bedroom.

"You guys settle in and come to the family room when you're ready," Mrs. Taylor told us. "You guys will stay in Christian's old room.

"Thank you very much, Mrs. Taylor," I responded graciously.

Emotional Charades

As I moved past her through the door, she grabbed my hand and squeezed it, giving me a last once-over. She looked at me like she already loved me. Like she was welcoming me into the family. My stomach tightened with unease.

Christian was already putting our belongings away. I dropped my coat on the floor and jumped into the bottom bunk of the bed. It was clear that someone had given up their place for the night; the blankets and pillows were missing from the top bunk. I studied the room like it was a museum dedicated to Christian.

The room was painted dark blue, pockmarked with the outlines of missing posters. The room had layers, details that indicated how it was once used and how it was being used now. The poster outlines and dark paint suggested teens, but the toy boxes on both sides of the room and the glow-in-the dark-stars tacked on the ceiling told me that young children slept here now.

"Is this the little boy's room?" I asked.

"It is now."

"Did you pick the color?"

"Carter did."

"The astronaut?" I recalled from our first day in the lounge.

He turned and looked at me tenderly for the first time today. I walked over and hugged him. He squeezed me tightly.

"Is there anything I should know? Any topics I should avoid?"

"My mom is silly and easy-going. She's religious, so don't take the Lord's name in vain. My dad is a goofball, but he won't be around much. He works a lot. It shouldn't be hard to win them over." He was giving me a cheat sheet.

"You're not religious, though."

"Yes, things like that…don't say that to her." He smiled just a little and looked at me.

I smiled back. His temper had lightened, and I wanted to make the best of it.

Hand in hand, we walked to the basement. The cleanliness of the top floor belied the lived-in family room in the basement. It was a mess, but a lovely one. I could tell that the time spent in that room was enjoyed. Toys, books, clothes, pillows, yarn, game consoles, and children filled the room. As messy as it was, it smelled of peppermint and fresh orange juice.

"What's on the agenda for tonight?" I asked, excited for a family night.

The kids stopped their activities and piled around the table, which held several board games. Each grabbed a game and pitched it as the best one ever. Ultimately, the choice was left to me. As a board game amateur, I picked *Clue* because I once watched the movie.

I was bad at it. Twice, I exposed my hand. Another time, I took the mystery cards. Everyone thought my lack of basic know-how on board games was hilarious. Christian's mom intentionally set me up to fail several times. The kids poked fun at my skills at every roll or draw. After *Clue*, *Taboo*, and even a failed attempt at *Skippo*, the family gave up on teaching me. It broke the ice. I loved it.

"I can't believe you've never played board games," his mom said, failing to hold in her amusement.

"I know it's weird. I didn't have any siblings."

They all laughed at my explanation. Christian fell into my lap while laughing at me. As he sat up, he kissed me on the cheek. This felt right, too. Being with him and with his family. I wasn't pretending. I enjoyed being his. I was in our bubble again. I couldn't fathom how I let the other night happen.

"I still love you." He smiled big and honest.

I stared at him in awe. I was looking for the moment of retraction. For the *oops, I didn't mean that* look. It didn't come. A giddy sensation started in my stomach. It raced to my chest as I stumbled into my own realization.

"I love you, too." Because I did. I planted a kiss on his cheek.

We stared at each other for the moment of confirmation where your eyes ask if you meant the words. Neither of us looked away.

We stayed in the moment, tickling, playing, and saying cute little nothings quietly. His mom laughed at us before pulling his arm so that he would lean to her side of the couch.

"I'm happy you met someone," she admitted, and then kissed him on the other cheek.

"Are there any games you know?" the oldest sister asked me.

"Yeah, charades, but with body language," I responded excitedly. I was looking forward to not being the worst at a game.

"Like...charades?" the twins asked, one slightly after the other.

I wanted to retract my statement. There wasn't a way I could explain this game without mentioning Eric. I tried to inhale all the air in the room to create time before

I had to answer. How could I tiptoe around the whole purpose of the game?

"It's um—it's—well, instead of movies or books, you act out an emotion, temperament, or mood. No words, just body language. Then, we all write–I mean, we all guess out loud." I had to edit out the portion where we wrote our guesses and discussed how we had figured it out. The whole game was designed to allow Eric to practice picking up social cues. Any second now they would start questioning me. I would be bringing Eric into Christian's home.

"Like this?"

One little body flew to the center of the room. Meghan had one hand on her hip, the other arm bent at a 90-degree angle with one finger pointing up. With pushed lips, she shook her head side to side a fraction of an inch, waving the extended finger in the air.

"Attitude?"

"Cursing someone out?"

"Mom?" the kids guessed.

Laughter erupted from everyone.

"Sassy?" I guessed.

Meghan screamed *yes* at the top of her lungs, ran, then jumped in my lap to give me a hug. I didn't deserve her affection.

"It's my turn," I announced, shifting her off of me, eager to break the contact. I jumped to my feet.

We played for a while, getting very creative with the rules. Once it had run its course, we picked a movie and settled in. The kids started to fall asleep one by one. Christian carried the sleeping babies to their beds, ignoring childish squeals of, "No, I'm not tired," or "I wasn't asleep." I followed their example, yawning and dozing, prompting Mrs. Taylor to excuse me to bed. Christian joined and we went to his room.

"I'm going to take a shower," he said.

Alone for the first time since I arrived, I checked my phone. I responded to a few updates from Khadijah. There were a few texts from Eric. Now, I was more confused than I'd ever been. I replied that I was at Christian's, and I would need a few days.

"Who are you talking to?" Christian asked. He crept into the room without a squeak.

"Khadi," I lied, surprised by his presence. He curled in on the bunk with me.

He frowned, "Tell her I say hi. Oh, wait, you can't," Christian said with his ever-casual tone. "Move over a little."

"Your parents are letting you sleep in here?"

"I have to make the couch look slept on and wake up before the little ones get up. You know, set a positive example. But yeah, it's fine."

He curled right into me and wrapped his arms around me. This part felt so confusing. This felt right, too. Being in his arms, in his world, and in love with him. Only this morning, I'd felt a similar *right* with Eric.

He kissed me, just a peck, but I wanted to give him so much more. I kissed him like we weren't down the hall from his parents' room. Then he behaved like we weren't.

You could feel guilty about something and still do it. Guilt could be overpowered by desire.

When my internal clock woke me, I was surprised. I expected to wake up throughout the night in a guilt-stoked panic, or to lie awake all night under deep self-scrutiny. But nope, I slept like a baby.

I wasn't the only one awake and enjoying the limited space in the bed.

"You are my unicorn," Christian whispered.

"Why am I a horse with horns?" I asked, an eyebrow raised. I lifted my head so that I could see his face.

"You are a mythical creature with the power to heal," he told me as if it were a typical statement. He rubbed my back, almost putting me to sleep.

"That was corny." My lips curled up in a grin. "But I liked it. Hey, thanks for the note cards. They were special."

He tilted his head down for a kiss. "I was really mad at you for staying out. I thought…that it was more. But one time, you stayed out with me all night. That was innocent but he overreacted. I did, too. I shouldn't have spoken to you like that."

My heart felt like it stopped. The room was suddenly 10 degrees. "Christian—" I almost confessed, but he interrupted.

"No, no listen. You, being here with us has been great. I don't want to be the person who overreacts. But if something is wrong, just tell me." His eyes searched mine.

I imagined it. If I confessed. If I broke his heart in his childhood bedroom, a few doors away from his mother. I'd lied for less. I could lie for another day.

"Nothing is wrong," I assured him, then moved the conversation along. "What are we doing today?"

"You get to meet my father."

"Yay."

We tiptoed out of bed to prevent waking anyone. Mrs. Taylor was already up and cooking in the kitchen.

Three pretty ceramic jars of saved cooking oil sat on her counter near her stove. They read *bacon, chicken.* and *fish.* The counters were tiled in white that also extended up the backsplash. The air in the room was filled with sweet and savory scents that made me salivate.

"Would you like some coffee, baby?"

"She doesn't like coffee," Christian answered as the confident boyfriend well aware of his girlfriend's preferences.

"Well, actually, I do. A lot of cream and sugar, please."

Christian looked at me, spellbound, while Mrs. Taylor started making me a cup of sugary coffee.

"What? But you never drink it. You told me you didn't like it the first day we hung out…"

I cheesed really hard, stuck between humor and a bit of embarrassment. "I know, I know, I hate ordering coffee in those really pretentious coffee shops. I was once berated for ordering a macchiato. So, I told you I didn't like coffee, but I waited too long to clarify." I vomited the words out, hoping that their haste would make it all make sense. "Forgive me?"

"Who are you? Mom, Dad, I don't know who this woman is," Christian joked. He massaged my shoulders while he spoke and then pulled me into a hug. He laughed in my ear, tickling me with his facial hair. I squirmed out of the hug, but kept a hold of Christian's hand.

"That makes two of us. I don't know her either." Mr. Taylor's statement was a sincere sentiment, but his tone indicated a joke. He had the same sense of incongruity as his son. Mr. Taylor was the missing piece of Christian's genetic puzzle. A stocky, fair-skinned man stood next to Mrs. Taylor, chopping vegetables for an omelet. He was an inch or two taller than Christian and had the same skin tone.

I marched over to him to make my introduction.

"Good morning. I'm Rebecca. Christian's girlfriend." It felt nice to say that.

We shook hands. His hands were rough and calloused. He was probably a hard worker in a physically demanding job. He had solid shoulders, with an extra 15 pounds around the midsection.

"Very nice to meet the girl living with our son," he responded in the same mismatched tone. Mr. Taylor wasn't going to be easy to win over.

"What would you like first?" Mrs. Taylor asked politely. She stepped towards her husband and bumped his hip with hers, throwing him a look. He tossed his hands up as if surrendering.

"Anything you have," I said.

She placed my plate and coffee on the table. I had a seat while they made their plates and joined me.

"So, we were expecting you earlier yesterday. I switched my work schedule around for this little visit," Mr. Taylor said. Christian and his mother both shot him concerned looks.

"Oh, it would have been nice to have spent more time getting to know you all better, and I'm sorry you were inconvenienced." I paused, waiting to see if my politeness would soften his directness. "I'm the maid of honor for my best friend's wedding, which is in a month. She calls me constantly for last-minute wedding preparations. Christian was trying to surprise me; I didn't know he was planning to bring me here."

Emotional Charades

Mr. Taylor returned my smile with inquisitive eyes. He could see right through me. I found comfort in his suspicious gaze. It was nice to know I wasn't an expert liar. Maybe it was that most people just didn't want to search for the truth.

I turned my attention to my breakfast to limit the conversation.

"Could I have another one?" I asked. I'd downed my coffee in a few gulps.

"Sure, sweetheart. Christian, could you?" Mrs. Taylor responded. Christian grabbed my cup and tried to recreate the concoction.

"If you waited this long, why tell me today?" Christian asked.

"I'm super tired. I didn't sleep the night before, and last night, we stayed up late. Caffeine is the only way I would make it through today."

"You stayed up all night doing maid-of-honor duties? What were you doing, looking for the groom?" Again, he spoke like it was a joke, but I understood the real question.

Christian and his mom looked at me. My palms started to sweat. I wiped them against my pajama bottoms under the table. I took a large gulp of my coffee to give myself a moment to think through my response. If I said anything vague, he would ask more questions.

"Oh, uh, we went to a bridal shop to get her a new dress and to find me a maid-of-honor dress. The groom's party had to find their attire, too."

"A new dress? Is she wearing two?" Mrs. Taylor asked, taking the bait that would lead the conversation away from me.

Taylor Bianca B

"No, she burned the first one," I stated the information calmly, so it could settle in. Then, I let the nonsensical words paint the story in their heads.

The whole table gasped out loud. Christian and his mom asked follow-up questions. They were intrigued by the dramatics. Mr. Taylor leaned back into his chair and let the story play out. He listened and laughed at the appropriate moments. It was a draw—he still didn't seem to like me, but for the moment, I hadn't given him a reason not to.

Christian had a full day planned, so we showered and left before the children were awake. He showed me the highlights of Detroit. Belle Isle, The African American History Museum, and the Detroit Institute of Art.

We went to *The Nutcracker,* enjoying some wine before we entered the venue. Today, I was a happy girlfriend, genuinely enjoying my surprise.

When we returned, the family was playing my version of charades. Samuel or Emanuel, I couldn't tell the difference yet, was wrapping up his turn. His hand rubbed imaginary hairs on his chin, while the other squeezed the skin between his eyes.

"Fool. Clown. Dwarf!" the family yelled, calling out wrong answers on purpose.

"Ugly?" offered Emanuel or Samuel. He was the comedian of the family. He was playing to the crowd and soaking in the laughter.

"Thinking," I interjected.

"Yes," Samuel or Emanuel clapped his hands and then pointed at me. The room booed at me for ruining the joke.

Emotional Charades

Still laughing, Mrs. Taylor asked, "How did you start playing charades this way?"

"My best friend used to have a hard time recognizing non-verbal cues. This game was a skill builder," I answered.

"Oh, Khadijah, the bride?" Mrs. Taylor concluded.

"Eric," I answered reflexively.

Mr. Taylor perked up at the name. "Her ex-boyfriend, right, Chris?" He spoke past me.

Mr. Taylor's tone and questions made sense now. Christian had talked with his father about our relationship. Before I walked into this house, Mr. Taylor was concerned about my dedication to his son. Concerned about my attachment to my ex.

"Yup, and apparently her best friend, too. Although, a week ago, she wouldn't even say his name," Christian added. His hand, which had been in mine the entire day, slipped out. He released me and walked away without a word, look, or an indication of whether he wanted me to follow.

The children shot looks around. They were aware that something was wrong, but they couldn't understand the complex issues swimming around this conversation. They watched me, and I stood in the middle of the room, stuck in the quickness of that moment.

Christian's parents exchanged looks.

"I'm sorry," I spoke to the whole room.

No one responded.

The floor felt like it was falling as I walked away. I had no ground to stand on. I went to Christian's room. He was gathering our belongings. We'd been planning on spending another night, but I could tell from Christian's focus that we wouldn't be sleeping here again. I strolled past him and sat on his bed, waiting for him to finish.

"Can we talk about this?"

"Not here, Rebecca. I don't want to fight at my parent's house. I'm already embarrassed enough."

He opened the door and walked away, completely ignoring me. I followed, tracking his slow, purposeful steps to his car. He didn't bother to say goodbye to his family. We just pulled off like strangers.

The drive began and then it ended. The time in-between expired in what felt like seconds. He parked, and with hesitation, asked the questions he should have asked Friday.

"What aren't you telling me?" he asked solemnly.

"Nothing," I responded. After a 45-minute ride, I still wasn't prepared to be honest.

He sighed with disappointment. "Rebecca, you haven't referred to Eric in friendly terms in months. What suddenly changed?"

"You couldn't have expected that I would stay mad at him forever. He was a huge part of my life and not every memory is bad," I said, side-stepping the question like a politician, flipping the script like a coward.

"Yes, I did expect you to get over the anger, but not all at once, and not after you spent the night with him," he said calmly.

I raised my eyes from the floor. I wanted to be completely honest, but honesty at this moment felt pivotal. Who to give up and who to stick it out with? I don't know. At the same time, I couldn't keep Christian with lies. But the thought of losing him felt monumental.

Emotional Charades

I didn't know which words to string together. "Eric and I... we talked. We fought and it led to—"

"Did you sleep with him?"

"No," I said quickly.

Relief eased its way through Christian. His shoulders dropped, and his head rolled back to his headrest.

I couldn't tell him the truth, but I didn't want to tell him a lie. I knew there wasn't a compromise between the two, but I tried anyway.

"Christian, we did talk a lot. Eric and I addressed the animosity and the hurt. We made some headway."

"Towards what, Rebecca? Headway towards getting back together? Inconvenient considering you have a boyfriend!"

"It's not like that. It's complicated. I just—"

"Ha," the first syllable of a loud laugh cut me off. I heard the tone. The indication that his next words wouldn't be kind.

"You know that day you stormed out of class, I only followed you because I thought it would make a good story. I never meant to get trapped in your drama. Here I am the fucking fool." He turned towards me, "You should find somewhere else to sleep tonight," he suggested emotionlessly.

I felt like I'd swallowed coal. My throat was dry and irritated. I knew he was just trying to hurt me, trying to protect himself with venom-laced words. Still, silent tears slid down my face.

He exited the car without another word. He hadn't told me I couldn't come into the house, but it was clear that I wasn't welcome. I requested an Uber and

224

Taylor Bianca B

waited in the car. The Uber dropped me off, and I was in bed asleep before my bedmate could ask a question.

Chapter 23: Pajama Party

This morning, my alarm was unique: Khadijah singing the *Barney* theme song. It was her passive-aggressive method of waking me.

Buried beneath several blankets, I pretended I was asleep. I could hear the floorboards creak in rhythm with the music, but I couldn't picture the scene Khadijah was making. Peeking out, there she was break-dancing. Sort of.

"You're a goof!" I answered her early morning performance.

"You're a bear!" Khadijah rebutted.

"What?"

"Hibernation, like you sleep a lot."

"Wow, that was a terrible joke."

"Don't hate, that was comedic gold." She waved a hand. "Now that I have your attention," she announced like she was the ringleader of a circus. "We have finals in a few weeks. If we want to graduate Summa Cum Laude, we must…" She paused, waiting for me to fill in the blank.

"Not run away from school, which I'm now considering."

"Study." She struck a victorious pose, flexing her lean muscles.

"Coffee first," I said, too tired to take her alertness. It was only 6:30 am. Far too early for this.

From her last awkward pose, she retrieved a lidded cup with steam escaping the spout. Khadijah was always prepared.

Reluctantly, I shoved off the blanket, grabbed the cup, and took a sip.

"Tea!" A question and an accusation.

"It's better for you—healthier," she said while passing me another lidded cup. I removed the lid, distrustfully.

"Thank you," I said with friendly resentment in my voice.

"Better to ask for forgiveness than to ask for permission."

"I despise you."

"Gasp!" Khadijah reacted with all the drama in the world, fainting on the mattress near my feet. She tilted her head towards me and winked. "Love you, too. Also, we aren't going to graduate Summa Cum Laude if we don't study for finals. Then you have the MCAT."

The smile that spread across her cheeks was radiant, one I hadn't seen in…years. There was no worry or trepidation behind it. Her smile didn't fold in on itself. Her head didn't drop with despair. This was my best friend. A woman I hadn't seen since the day I hurt her. Even before that, the real her had been faltering. Reappearing in the spaces between her heartbreaks.

"I've missed you."

"I know," she said. "We've both been busy with school and preparing for the wedding. Plus, they increased my hours at work."

I smiled in response and wrapped my arms around her.

"I really missed you," she whispered in my ear as we hugged. It seemed like she meant it in the same way I had, that I haven't been myself for a while.

We were skirting around serious topics. I couldn't tell another convincing lie. If she asked the right question, I might break down.

I released her. "What's on the agenda, Madam Studies-Too-Hard?" I asked. She read through the agenda, and I nodded at the appropriate times.

We followed the agenda to a T. At the end of an eight-hour study day, I felt assured of my knowledge. I was even confident with my final assignment for my creative writing class.

"Good. If we keep this up for the rest of the week, prioritizing by exam date, we will annihilate our exams." Her hand shot up and lingered in the air. A request for a high five, which I stared at in amusement. She brought her hand down, high-fiving my face instead.

I nodded my head. "I have to annihilate my finals. I have a B+ in creative writing now. If I nail my final, I'll have an A for the course. Maybe an A-." My foot started to tap. What if my final assignment wasn't good enough? I could retake the class. I started to bite my thumb.

Khadijah knocked on my forehead. "Hey, what's going on in there?"

"I just have to ace this class. A 4.0 will help show admission boards that I'm a perfect student."

228

Her eyebrows drew together. "You have to stop putting so much pressure on yourself," Khadijah said.

I gawked at her. Had she looked in the mirror lately? Plus, I wasn't pressuring myself. My parents…supported my plans to go to med school. Eric, Khadijah, they were all supporting my efforts. No one had told me I had to do anything. Had I placed weight on my own shoulders?

She nodded her head. "I know pot, kettle, black. But listen, in the history of med school, has a student been admitted without a perfect 4.0?"

"Of course."

She grabbed my hands. "Then that's what you'll do. Maybe this class will be your admission essay. You can title it, *There's No Such Thing as an Easy A: How I learned Not to Underestimate the Seemingly Simple.*" She shrugged with a pretty smile.

My mouth fell open. My eyes drifted down. I had created this pass or fail scenario, but I had options.

And I wasn't the only one with too much on their plate. "Are you going to start taking your own advice?" I asked.

"Ah." She leaned back and ran her fingers through her hair, "I will right after I finish everything on my to-do list. Next up, make us updated study schedules.

"I'm already tired just thinking about all of that. Let's do something fun tonight," I begged.

Khadijah scrunched her whole face. I recognized the look; she was preparing to deliver bad news.

"I'm meeting Jamie at 6:00."

"No." I pouted like a child about to throw a tantrum. "But we haven't hung out without the wedding plans or the boys in forever." I was not above guilting my best friend into spending time with me.

"I have to."

"All you have to do is stay black and die," I joked.

"But I'm not Black,"

"Stay brown?"

"That'll work."

We chuckled.

I sulked and tried to hold her hostage with a hug. Okay, it was more of a wrestling pin than a hug. Despite my efforts, she freed herself and prepared to leave.

"Jamie is outside; I'll see you…I'm not sure, are you spending the night again?"

"Probably. I don't feel like going home." Because I didn't have a clear definition of where home was.

"Last time we spent a few nights together, I tried to call off my wedding," she quipped.

"Who needs men?"

"I wish I could stay. But we should do something next weekend. I can cancel one of the wedding events, and it can just be us for a night, okay?"

"Sounds like a plan." I accepted defeat.

At the door, she paused, "I did want to tell you to—"

"I know. I'll look for an email."

"No. Not that. I can tell that something is going on with you and," she paused, the space between her words filling me with dread. What if she said Christian? I was not ready for her to acknowledge the hypocrite I had become. My jaw clinched as I waited for her to find her words.

"Eric. I'm not going to make accusations; you only spend the night when something has happened. I just wanted to say watch yourself. I know you're angry, but don't ruin everything you've built out of pain."

"We're fine. I just needed a little space," I reassured her, reprising my role as her role model.

She sighed and walked out, hunchbacked. For a moment, I was insulted. Was she, of all people, giving me relationship advice? Petty thoughts circled my mind, then reality grabbed me in the form of a text. The alert went off and panic set in. I knew it was one of them, but I didn't have answers for either.

If I chose Eric, we would continue until our inevitable wedding and the rest of our lives together. Was jumping directly back into a long-term relationship what I wanted? I still didn't trust us yet. It would never be the same. I understood that now. We'd become new people. Loving Eric was not the same as being comfortable with spending the rest of my life with the lingering resentment.

Plus, how much of me wanted this to please others?

If I chose Christian…could he ever forgive me? Maybe I could fix the damage. I would remove Eric from the picture, give up this whole fiasco, bring him into my life, introduce him to my friends, and my family.

We'd fight. I could grovel at his feet. I didn't know how to fix it. I just knew that Christian was the place where I felt safe. Why would I give that up? Then, there was an answer to my question. The passively-aggressively way he sometimes berated me. His anger was justified. His execution was vicious. He would have to learn a better way to communicate.

Emotional Charades

My text alert sounded again. I was panic-stricken. I was in love with two men, and I'd made colossal mistakes with both. What could I say? I grabbed my phone, still unsure of what conversation would ensue.

It was Khadijah.

Khadijah: *We should include GRE and MCAT prep time with our study prep.* (Sunday 7:46 pm)

Khadijah: *I'll add it to the agenda that I'll email you. Love you, goodnight.* (Sun 7:47pm)

The relief helped me decide. I couldn't give them both what they wanted, so I decided to give them the same thing.

Rebecca: *I'm spending a few nights at Khadijah's. I have to think about what I want.* (Sunday 7:50 pm)

Eric: *I will see you soon. I love you.* (Sunday 7:51pm)

Christian: *Whatever Rebecca.* (Sunday 10:35 pm)

I laid there, feeling awkward in my own presence. I used the silence, the aloneness, to isolate my feelings from everyone's expectations. I tossed and turned, uncomfortable with the self-evaluation. What did I want? Maybe I needed to be single. Maybe I didn't deserve either of them. What did I love about them?

Chapter 24: What I Needed to Say

The morning came with a clear answer. I had to go to Christian.

I would have one chance to do this right, so I moved deliberately slow. I needed the time to prepare my words. I couldn't just offer an apology. He deserved more than that.

Then, time was up. I was on his doorstep unannounced and unsure of how he would react. The door key sat idle in my hand as I stood there, debating whether to use it or to knock. The choice was taken away from me as Christian pulled the door open and blocked the entryway. He read my face, discerning my intentions.

"Come in and get your shit, Rebecca," he stated flatly. He stared at me for a second, then stood aside to allow me to enter.

Nothing happened the way I had planned. I thought I would walk in, and we'd have a seat. After a heartbreaking conversation, we'd end on civil terms. From the moment he opened the door, my plan failed and failed again.

I shifted past him to enter the house. I tried to remember my apology, but my vocal cords froze. I'd chosen this, but it still felt tragic.

"Well?!" he shouted. He stood holding the door open, giving a limited timeframe for this visit.

"Can we sit down and—"

"Why? Aren't you here to get your shit and leave me?"

"I came to talk."

"Talk? Is this talking like you and Eric did the other night?"

"I just wanted to explain." My eyes welled up and my voice cracked.

"Today, you give a fuck. Wednesday night, when you stayed out all night but couldn't call or text, did you care? Did you want to talk then?

"Christian, you know I care about you."

"Really? Name a time when you considered my feelings? I'll wait." He posed a question he thought I couldn't answer.

"When I almost cancelled meeting your friends at the club. I think you know that I care. Shit, did you see the look on my face when you told me that you only started seeing me for writing material?"

"Did you see the look on *my* face when I found out that you fucked your ex the night before you met my mother?"

I walked into that one like it was a glass door. I looked down. "Christian, I just want to talk."

"About how you're the slut that stole Christmas? At least The Grinch had a heart."

"Christian."

"You could be the heartless scarecrow, but you're more of the cowardly liar. I bet you won't tell Khadijah you've been fucking some guy for a warm bed."

"Christian, you're not just some guy to me." He couldn't think that. He had to know.

He winced a smile, "Did I satisfy your *what-ifs*? Was I a good candidate?"

The conversation got trapped in a rhetorical stalemate. Any word I uttered led him to pose a demeaning question or a flat-out insult. I didn't bother to track the amount of time we spent on the useless portion of the argument. I'd learned that the length of an argument was meaningless. Only words mattered, and I let him have as many angry words as I could take.

I deserved them.

Being insulted by a writer was a little more jarring. He'd managed to call me a slut in nine distinctive ways. It was while he was circling the 10th slut-related insult that I spoke up.

"Christian, do you want me to leave?"

"No, say what you came here to say so that you can feel better about this bullshit."

I wanted to give him some solace in a complicated situation. I needed to reset this conversation. I moved to the couch, then I gestured for him to join me. He stood in the same spot near the door and only crossed his arms. He didn't look like Christian. He looked like his father, which removed any optimism I had about the outcome of the conversation.

"Christian, I love you—"

"You love me? I guess you and Eric learned how to love in the same fucking way. You both just cheat on the people who love you."

"It's not like that, Christian!"

"How isn't it? I was there, remember? I saw them, too."

"We have ten years of history."

"Yes, and he shat on that when he fucked his classmate for science." He heaved the statement at me like it was a weapon. A pronounced vein on his forehead throbbed.

We stalled there for a few minutes. He paced in front of me, but let me simmer over his words. My pulse quickened and anxiety set in. I had no retort for his words. They were true. I sat there a little less confident in my future with Eric. When it came down to fight or flight, my instinct was to flee the emotional danger.

It was a part of myself that I was working on. My tendency to react to my emotional whims, to not completely consider the situation or the aftermath. That tendency had pulled Christian into my life and me into his bed.

Composed, I gave my retort. "You're right about him. But this isn't about him. It's about us. I can't offer you what you want—what you deserve."

"Wow, a couple of days ago, everything was fine. We were happy."

"We were," I admitted, and it pulled at the chords of my heart. "But I've been an emotional wreck, selfish, and barely present for you."

"And your solution was to go back to the person who broke you."

"I still have feelings for him," I confessed. "I don't know whether we'll work it out or end it for good, but I have to find out."

"So, I was just a convenient distraction. What? To make him jealous?"

I whispered because I knew that this bit of honesty wouldn't help anything, "Inconvenient, actually. Who expects to fall in love with a guy they meet immediately after a breakup?" I gave a weak smile, then added, "The rebound is supposed to be short and callous."

"I'm not your rebound."

"That's the problem. You aren't. I wasn't supposed to meet you now."

"What the fuck does that mean, Rebecca?"

"I fucked up and I'm sorry! I really am. I still have feelings for him, and I don't want to string you along while I deal with them."

He rolled his eyes and turned his back to me. "Anymore." He peered at me over his shoulder. "You don't want to string me along *anymore*."

"I—" my mouth opened, but my explanation seemed meaningless now. Once the anger subsided, my feelings for Eric were still there. A little worse for wear, but intact. The fact that I had strung him along unintentionally didn't change the result.

"Rebecca, be honest with me. Did you sleep with him?" he asked. I knew why he wanted the answer. I could tell that he was divided. A part of him knew that I was guilty, and the other part needed me to admit it.

"Yes." My jaw shook, but I held back my tears. I sat back on the couch in silence to give him the time he needed.

Christian turned to face me. "I understand. I hope he takes the shattered remains of your love and decimates it."

Apparently, he didn't need that much time to process. My tears were back, although I didn't feel they had a right to be there. I ambled toward the door in silence. Everything that needed to be said had been.

"Rebecca," Christian called.

I turned.

Emotional Charades

"Get your shit before you leave," he said in an infuriatingly polite note.

Chapter 25: Butterflies

I unlocked the door with the key I never gave up and dropped the only bag I'd ever packed. I was back at Ground Zero, not exactly where it started, but where the damage was done.

The jingle of keys stole my attention. I stared at the door, nervous.

"Rebecca?" Eric gasped, dropping his keys. "Have you made a decision?"

I had.

When I'd thought of who I wanted to be with on their worst day, it was Eric. I wanted his worst day and his best. I wanted to share mine with him. I waited a few moments, re-gathering my thoughts, deciding again to say what I came here to say.

"It's over with Christian." There was a sharp twinge in my chest, but it faded.

The slightest nod was the only sign that he had understood me. "Are you certain about that decision? I did tell you that I did not mind if you continued to see Christian Taylor."

"I know what you told me. But it would be wrong to hold Christian hostage for you."

He hastened towards me. "That is not what I meant."

I weaved between the furniture, wanting to keep my distance. There was a lot that I wanted to say. I didn't want our chemistry to take over and for us to move too fast, like we had the other night.

"If I want to give you another chance to break my heart, I shouldn't bargain with his."

He made his way to me awkwardly, like he had forgotten where the furniture had been placed. "I am only seeking clari—"

"This isn't about research," I said. Rushing, trying to work through my list.

"That is not what I—"

"You can't treat our relationship like a project anymore," I said, weaving around the furniture.

"Rebecca, that is not what—"

"I'm willing to try to work it out, but on my terms." I turned abruptly to confront him.

Just then, he caught his foot on the coffee table. His arms flew over his head, followed by the thud of his body hitting the floor.

"Are you okay?" I gasped.

He shot up and smoothed out his clothes. "Ow. Yes."

Surprised, I slapped my hands over my mouth. My eyes watered as I tried to tamp down the childish amusement that followed a fall.

"Are we back together?" he asked like a kid earning back his allowance, overly eager for the answer.

"Yes."

"Thank you," he said, his voice cracking like he could cry. He closed the few feet between us and wrapped his arms around me. He then rested his head on my shoulder. He felt like a jigsaw puzzle being snapped into place. Comfortable and familiar, I had no desire to end our embrace or to mention the parameters I had come here to set.

When I woke up that morning, I hadn't only decided to end ties with Christian, I had also some revelations about Eric and where our relationship should restart.

Eric was having revelations of his own. His lips brushed the top of my shoulder, moving up my neck and beneath my ear as his hand made its way underneath my shirt. The other hand slid into my hair and gently pulled my head back. He kissed me. My blood raced and sang with desire. I lifted my leg to hook around his hip. He grabbed my thigh, hoisted me up, and I wrapped my legs around his waist. It was everything I wanted. A simple, pleasant way to reconnect. But it was not what we needed.

I broke the kiss, "Stop!"

He put me down, and I took a much-needed step back. I exhaled the sigh of sexual frustration.

He looked at me in perfect confusion, "Rebecca?"

I threw one finger up, the international sign for *give me a second*. I had to find my resolve again. Should I give in to temptation or do what I thought was best for our relationship?

"I think we rushed the physical part." I paused to correct myself, "*I* rushed us back into that part of our relationship after that night at Khadijah's. I think we need to work exclusively with the emotional part. On building back trust. We've thoroughly proven that the physical part isn't the problem." I looked down at the bulge in his sweatpants.

He was listening, leaning on the back of the couch. One hand pulled his collar like he was hot.

"How do you suggest we do that?"

"We are going to take it slow. You sleep in your room, and I sleep in here." I pointed to the master suite. "We have the lease for this apartment for a few more months. If it doesn't work out, we get separate apartments and we move on. Do you agree?"

"Yes! I would do anything for you," he said, like it was a foregone conclusion.

"Okay. I will see you in the morning." I walked into my bedroom alone.

***

"Rebecca, your breakfast is ready," Eric called.

"Reaaally?" I teased.

Pleasant scents tickled my stomach. Following them, I opened the bedroom door. Food covered the coffee table in our living room. I kissed his cheek as I passed him and sat in the middle of the couch so that I could reach all the food. He stayed standing, apparently lost in thought.

"Eric," I called.

"It is clear that this breakfast is for you," he said, confused. "I do not require this much diversity in my morning meal. Have your favorite foods changed? Should I prepare something else?"

"Eric, I was kidding," I responded while walking towards him. I planted another kiss on his cheek, then grabbed his hand and pulled him to the couch.

He remained standing, un-puzzling something I had said. He paced back and forth, arms crossed, arranging the words he would need to solve the puzzle. I dug into the food while I waited for the question he was forming.

"Okay, what exactly was the joke?" he asked sternly.

"Eric, what joke?"

"Ree-aa-ly," he mimicked. "You said you were kidding, but about what?"

"Breakfast."

"Breakfast is funny?"

"Is that a question?" I teased. "I only meant that it was obvious that the layout was for me," I explained to end his deliberation.

He shrugged his shoulders then sat with me. "Okay. Why did you not just say that?"

"I'm out of practice." I turned to him, a slight smile on my lips. I was trying to smooth the communication gap with calm gestures.

He stared at me, and I could see him deliberating on whether to ask another question.

"Out of practice for what?"

"Effective communication," I joked.

"Are you teasing me?"

"No!" I shouted in surprise.

Eric was visibly stunned. He shifted uncomfortably.

"I'm sorry. I didn't mean to raise my voice."

"It is okay."

It wasn't. Eric had retreated into himself, obviously analyzing the morning with a mental microscope. Several times during his internal debate, he paused and looked at me like he was going to ask me something. I answered with my attention, but he shook his head and continued musing. It hurt me a little. It was like watching him with a stranger. This was the pain that growing apart had created.

Emotional Charades

After eating, I escaped to the kitchen to clean the dishes. The space eased the tension. I watched Eric settle his internal debate.

"Rebecca, would you like to watch TV with me?

"Sure, be there in a second." I finished the dishes, then joined him. I laid down on the couch, my head resting in his lap.

Maybe we would just never be able to do breakfast again. The third time was not the charm.

He had a show called *Impractical Jokers* queued with a mid-season episode. It was a reality show about four frenemies who tortured each other and blamed it on humor.

Eric was hooting and chuckling throughout the episode. His lap jerked and disturbed my resting head. I ended up watching him enjoy the show more than I watched the screen. The humor escaped me, but I enjoyed his levity. After a few episodes, I grabbed a book from my overnight bag.

I laid back in his lap because sometimes, you want to be near someone more than you want to be comfortable. I opened it where I had left off, and the moment after I reached the page, the TV switched off. I looked up to see Eric beaming down at me. His eyes were my favorite thing to look at.

"What are you reading?" he asked.

"Oh, I'm reading *Ocean at the End of the Lane* by Neil Gaiman."

"Is it as good as *Neverwhere*?"

"So far. I'm really enjoying it."

"Would you like to read aloud or lay it down between us?"

"Umm, I'm pretty far into the book. You can watch your show. You seem to really enjoy it."

"We always read books together," he stated matter-of-factly.

"I'm already in the middle of the book." It was happening again, the awkward misunderstandings.

"It does not appear to be a large book. Would starting over bother you?" he asked.

I felt like the question was a trap. No matter what I said, I would have to start over or endure another spur of questioning.

"I don't want to. I'm really eager to finish," I said as nicely as I could, trying to keep the fleeting peace.

"You could read from where you are," he suggested.

"The story is complex; you'll have to read the whole thing to follow."

That look was back, the one that indicated I was now a stranger. My resting place became uncomfortable again. Now, his body felt rigid like his muscles were flexed.

"Could you sit up, please?" he asked. I obeyed. He jumped up, making his way toward his private space. The spontaneous reunion was reaching the un-fairytale-like portion.

I finished my book in silence, hoping that a short time apart would undo this tiff. By the two-hour mark, my irritation was unruly.

I just wanted to finish my book. On the other hand, starting over a 260-page book wasn't a big deal. My brain debated itself about whose fault it was. His? Mine? Both of ours? After sitting in the discomfort of his absence, I concluded the fault was probably not important. Responsibility was important. It would always be someone's responsibility to mend the damage.

I nominated myself today.

I pulled the Nintendo 64 from behind the TV stand. Following tradition, I blew the dust out of the gray, plastic cartridge. Then, I shoved it into the oval slot. I turned the volume all the way up.

I let the *Super Mario Bros* theme music be my invitation to Eric. I let the music play a few times, but he still didn't abandon his shelter. I finished the first board before I heard his door crack. Then, the floor creaked as he made his way towards me and took his place on the floor.

The second joystick stretched out to his position. I paused the game to restart it in two-player mode. We sat there for a few hours reacquainting ourselves. The fear of another fight kept our words to a minimum. We just stayed in each other's company.

"What is your evaluation of today's events?" he asked a few hours later.

"Honestly, I haven't evaluated anything yet. This is new for the both of us." I smiled.

"I allowed myself to extrapolate a possible conclusion from today's disagreements, if they continue to occur. I am afraid of that projection." He paused. "I am afraid of losing you."

I bent my head to catch his downcast eyes, "Tell me why you're afraid."

"I am afraid...in the time that we have spent apart, you have changed. Your personality is notably different. If your personality has changed, so could your preferences in men."

Taylor Bianca B

I pulled back a little, wrapping my arms across my belly. A similar fear had kept me up before.

"You choked me without asking," I said, darting my gaze away from him.

"Come again?" It was the most fragmented sentence I had ever heard him say.

"The last time we had sex, you put your hand to my throat and applied pressure." I tried to joke, "You altered our sexual routine without discussing it with me first. You have always discussed your desires. Then, you changed."

"I am truly sorry if I crossed the line. It was not my intention."

"No. It shocked me a little. Not because I didn't like it," and here was the sore part, "Juliette must have shown you that. She told you not to ask. She changed you."

"Rebecca." He said my name with grief. "She did not teach me that."

"I just wanted to highlight that we have both changed, and now we just need to get to know one another again," I blurted in a rush. I didn't want any more indirect information about their time together.

I slid my hand over his. He interlaced our fingers. I gave him an expression that meant *go on.*

"I am afraid that our reconciliation is your martyristic sacrifice so that Khadijah doesn't burn down the steeple."

"Eric," I said sternly. "Martyristic is not a word."

He chuckled, and I watched his shoulders relax. "I am serious. I struggle with your sense of responsibility to others. I need to know you are here because you want to be."

"I want to be. Even if that means we have a few awkward breakfasts or reread a couple books."

He grinned and huffed a little laugh.

"What?"

"I was a little annoyed about that book. You probably did not notice. Well, I downloaded, and speed-read it while I was de-stimulating. It was very engaging," he said, a bit of bitterness to his tone.

I erupted into laughter. I laughed so hard that I pitched forward into him. My head rested on his shoulder. He vibrated with laughter, too. He wrapped his arm around my waist to keep me in place. His other hand touched my chin. Gently, he tilted my face towards his. My laugh snuffed out.

"With respect to getting to know one another again, may I kiss you?" he asked.

My heart fluttered. I nodded.

His lips delicately brushed mine. A whisper of pleasure hummed through me. I pulled back. I knew better than to linger in his kiss.

"I'm gonna head to bed. I'll see you tomorrow."

"Goodnight."

***

My eyes fluttered open at the sound of knocking on my bedroom door.

"What?" I grunted.

"Rebecca, are you awake?" Eric asked.

"It's too early." I turned over, repositioning myself to fall back asleep.

"I want you to come to class with me."

I shot up to study him. He was standing at the door, wide awake, and holding a mug of coffee that I assumed was for me. I reached for it. He brought it to me and took a seat on the edge of the bed.

I squinted my eyes in almost a flutter motion, silently asking for answers.

"I would like for you to attend a lecture from Professor Rogers."

I choked on the first sip of the coffee. Eric patted my back, and I spent the next few seconds nursing a wet cough.

"You want me to go see the professor who told you to cheat on me?"

"No, Rebecca, that is ridiculous. He did not tell me to cheat. He presented case studies and research, which I extrapolated into an experiment. The cheating was my fault alone."

"Eric." I paused, waiting for him to look me in the eyes, "semantics."

He looked down then started chewing on his cheek. I could see his wheels turning. After a minute, his head jerked up. "I want you to go for my credibility. I need you to know for certain that I am being honest about how this started. I am aware it does not change what I did."

"I believe you," I asserted.

"I do not want you to have to believe me. I want you to know," he countered.

This felt like a bad idea, intentionally stepping onto an emotional landmine.

"I'm not sure."

"Please. Just one class." He grabbed my hand. "Please."

Emotional Charades

I sighed. It was just one class, just an hour. He'd kept up my ridiculous charade for weeks, after all. "Alright."

***

Professor Rogers stood in the center front of a whitewashed lecture hall. The room angled upward, so every seat faced down to the podium and board. He was wearing tan pants and a tweed jacket. He was middle-aged and stout.

The current slide read: *The lack of interpersonal communication skills, a byproduct of web-based social interaction.*

AKA - the internet makes us assholes.

"Why do you think 'asshole behavior' is more prominent online?" he asked the class. His words echoed slightly as he projected his voice. Even close to the back row, I heard him clearly.

A few hands shot up to offer answers.

"Put your hands down. This is my class. I want to tell you what I think." He smiled.

A short round of laughter travelled through the class.

"I'm here to explain a particular cause. With social interfaces, you're missing non-verbal reactions. Thus, you are missing the context that indicates you are an asshole. Without that knowledge, you become a bigger asshole, scientifically speaking." He started his lecture.

I could see why Eric liked him. He layered his lecture with jokes and relatable examples like verbal abuse in gamer culture.

After class, Eric insisted that we speak with the professor. He wanted Professor Rogers to summarize the

250

lecture that had inspired him. They chatted for a moment, and then Professor Rogers started the cliff-notes version of the lecture.

Eric gave me our expression for *see.*

I nodded.

"I recall your thesis and proposed experiment you turned in," Professor Rogers said.

Eric's neck snapped back towards Professor Rogers, and he turned pale.

Professor Rogers continued, "It could have considerable implications in relationship development research. Lifelong monogamy is antiquated, and this could be a bridge to more realistic relationship goals. You should continue the project. You could organize a trial for graduate research."

"I would have to reframe the parameters to create a clearer protocol," Eric responded, grabbing the back of his neck nervously. He placed his hand on my lower back, "This is my fiancée, Rebecca."

"Nice to meet you, Miss."

"Same."

"Engaged, really? You two could be participants," he joked.

Does he know? I shot the question to Eric with a look. His eyes widened for a second to answer *no.*

Eric started, "We should go."

"Have you two been together long?" Professor Rogers asked.

My eyes narrowed into slits. I peered at him with all the non-verbal communication I could muster, but he ignored it.

"10 years," Eric answered.

His brows raised, "Oh. Something like this might be useful to your relationship."

"No!" I shot. No longer depending on my non-verbal skills, I said, "Something like that could destroy a relationship."

"It's likely that you will break up anyway. Young couples, like you, typically outgrow one another before they ever wed. If they marry, they're likely to divorce within the first two years of marriage," he offered with a sarcastic smile.

I could tell he was evaluating our relationship, not just speaking in the statistical sense.

"Fuck you!"

"Excuse me?" Eric and Professor Rogers said in unison. Not as a question, but as an opportunity for me to amend my words.

"Fuck you and your shallow reliance on science to be an asshole. We are real people. You can't just suggest that we ruin our relationship for a poorly conceived experiment."

"You are a dramatic one," Professor Rogers said, then smiled at Eric in a *sorry for you* manner. "I'm sure you would be capable of recovering from your childhood romance," he condescended.

"Professor," Eric admonished.

I placed my hand on the podium and leaned into the professor. "You're probably bad at sex."

"Young lady!" he gasped.

Eric laughed nervously. He grabbed my hand and pulled me toward the door, apologizing and excusing us.

A few steps from the door, I planted my feet.

"You've probably never made a person cum. You probably say you're celibate but you're an incel." I felt

Eric's hands around my waist. He picked me up and put me over his shoulder. "It's just that no one wants to have sex with a person-shaped platypus," I continued as he carried me out of the room.

Later, we sat at our table in silence, sharing a tub of Moose Tracks ice cream. Sunlight bounced off the inch of snow we'd gotten. The glinting light twinkled on all the surfaces in our apartment.

Eric sat bones straight. His spoon lazily dragged across the surface of the ice cream. His eyes were locked on me. There was an expression plastered on his face that meant *so?*

"I'm sorry that my behavior might have ruined a relationship with a potential mentor." I deliberately apologized for the consequences of my actions, not for my outburst. It wasn't a slip of the tongue.

"Okay."

"I don't think I have tolerance for anyone trying to interfere with our relationship."

"It's okay, Rebecca. I understand." He stopped. "Actually, I do not, but I am not concerned that you bullied my professor."

"He was an asshole," I added.

His eyes darted to the left, then refocused on me. He leaned across the table until we were face to face.

"Ree-aaally?" he asked, impersonating me. He planted a small kiss on my cheek before righting himself in his chair. The saying was true, a kiss could make everything better.

"Person-shaped platypus," Eric said, shaking his head. We both laughed.

Emotional Charades

I placed my hand on top of his on the table. He curled his hand underneath mine and stroked my ring finger with his thumb.

I smiled at the touch. My chest felt light. I wanted this all again. Not a carbon copy of what we had before. I wanted this new relationship we were building.

I looked up to see Eric's lips curled downward in a frown. "What's wrong?"

He shifted in his seat, "From our conversation yesterday, I have been wondering…whether it is or is not okay to try new things in the bedroom without a proper discussion."

I thought for a second, then leaned towards him. "Discussion is awesome, and I like it; I feel more prepared to make the experience enjoyable. But it's not necessary if there's respect and trust in the relationship. Learning on the fly is fun and exciting."

"You trusted Christian that much in under 100 days?" he asked.

My mouth dropped open. I wanted to give him the comfortable answer, the painless answer. I took a deep breath." I did," I answered honestly.

He tensed, released my hand, then stood. He paced for a moment with his hands on the back of his head.

Our reunion was littered with emotional landmines. We'd been trying to avoid them. Maybe we needed to trigger them. We needed to disarm them before they could harm our new foundation. There was a huge one we needed to address.

"I think we need to tell our families the truth."

He turned. His eyes pierced me. "Why?"

"We can't pretend we didn't break up for the rest of our lives. It's a lie. Another facade. It will breed more lies."

"Is this about him? You need our family to know he existed? You wanted to hide everything before."

"This isn't about him, and I know I asked you to lie. I shouldn't have. Lying didn't work. It made everything worse."

He looked at me, his eyes screaming, *I told you so*. I could only respond with an eye roll of *I know*.

He rubbed his knuckles on his lips. "What if they pressure you again? Disregard your feelings or use moralistic excuses to justify us staying together? I do not want you staying with me to please them."

I grabbed his hand and placed it against my cheek, "I'm here because I want to be. I want to tell them, so you don't have to live in that uncertainty. And to answer your question, if they try to pressure me, I will call them person-shaped platypuses."

His eyes shimmered as his shoulders rocked with low laughter. He encased me in a hug. My favorite hoodie, my sense of warmth, the feeling of being insulated, the comfort only he could provide rushed over me.

I tightened my grip on him. The tension brought his right ear close to my lips.

"It doesn't even mean anything. Platypus is just a funny word." We both laughed.

We held each other while our laughter died.

He spoke into my hair, "You are right. I want to know that your presence here isn't an obligation."

We called. We weren't explicit. We didn't go into details. Just the high-level facts: infidelity, a lie, our breakup, living apart, Christian, and getting back together. Respectfully, we told them we didn't want unsolicited advice.

I leaned toward the speaker. Their response could go one of two ways. I was prepared for both. They expressed their hurt feelings about the secrecy. We acknowledged their feelings.

"Maybe if you had been open with us, we could have helped you navigate through this without all the drama," my mom said.

There it was. The second act.

I picked up the phone and put the receiver end close to my mouth. I took a deep breath. It wasn't every day that you cut into your parents, especially not Black parents.

"The last time I tried to talk to you, most of you didn't listen. You invalidated my feelings and pressured me to just forgive. It's the reason I didn't tell you. I didn't trust you." I let the statement sit there, waiting to dismantle any rebuttal they offered. Stone silence. "And we are adults. We will make mistakes, but they are ours. You have to respect that."

It was as silent as a crypt. I could hear my heartbeat.

"Sweetie, I didn't know we made you feel that way. I'm sorry," my mom offered. I eased back on the couch. The tight tension all over me started to ease.

Then, there was an echo of apologies. Our beloved parents taking accountability for that day. I hadn't known I needed this acknowledgement. Maybe I just didn't believe it would happen. But my body softened. Hurt feelings I hadn't acknowledged were exonerated. I felt lighter.

I accepted their apologies. Shortly after, the call came to a polite end.

After the call ended, Eric laid his head on my stomach and I ran my fingers through his hair. For the first time in a while, there weren't several overlapping lists of lies and half-truths circulating in my mind. No plans or contingencies to keep my life whole. I felt free.

Well, almost free.

Chapter 26: Wedding Party

Christian refused to downplay the tension and hurt engulfing us. For the last few weeks, he was the first to volunteer to read his latest works. He explicitly wrote about our experiences under the guise that his stories were pure fiction.

There was one about the time *I lied* to his mother about being in love with him. Today, it was about the spontaneous time we had sex in an empty movie theater.

I cringed in my seat as students raised their hands to ask questions.

"Is that about Rebecca?" one student asked.

"Of course not. It's just a story," he answered while grinning sardonically, looking right at me.

My head dropped. A low hum of chatter eased around the room. This class now felt like a torture chamber.

"Who wants to read their story?" Professor Lamb asked, trying to move the conversation along. She told me she'd tried to speak with him about his topic selection, but he claimed it was complete fiction.

Class was uncomfortable at best and toxic at worst. He was taking his revenge too far. Still, I suffered through it. My guilt made me loyal to Christian's pain. I'd caused it. There were only a few more weeks of class left.

258

After class, Christian lingered in the hall, discussing his works with whoever would listen. So, I stayed in the classroom until the hall cleared, using headphones to ignore his vindictive comments.

"Girlfriend, that was the most savagely awkward moment," Ambrosia exclaimed as she gently pulled out one of my earbuds.

I wiped a tear away before I glanced up at Ambrosia.

"Like, I could die. Like dead, like not recover from the amount of awkward in class today." She clenched her chest, then fell limp on her desk.

I giggled at her antics.

"Girl? Girl, girl, girrrrl," she repeated the word several times, but each "girl" made a slightly different implication.

"I know; it's crazy."

"No, babe, it's craaaaazy," she said soberly. "When are you going to shut this shit down?"

"I hurt him."

"So! The world is not fair. People don't actually get what they deserve."

"I really fucked up, Ambrosia. I met his family and—"

"Yeah, we all know you're a bona fide asshole. But there's venting, Rebecca, and then there's the fact that I now know your labia's color pallet. Listen, I like Christian, but he's crossing lines."

"Lines?"

"Yeah, several of them."

"How is your final project going?" I asked, changing the subject.

Ambrosia turned her head and gave me a very deliberate side-eye. "Okay, we can pivot to another topic. My story is the bomb! Despite Professor Lamb's protest, my final project is about my overweight superhero. Commander Lard. I'm working on that name. Don't judge. I think I'm going to turn it into a short series about…" Ambrosia stopped, her head craning towards the door. I waited for her to continue talking, thinking she needed a moment to recall some details.

"Re-Bec-ca." It wasn't exactly a shout, but it had the same commanding effect.

"Khadijah. Hi," I stammered, a little taken aback by her presence.

She crossed her arms and tapped her foot, visibly irritated. "We have make-up and hair today."

"We're supposed to meet at 10:30. It's 9:45 am," I offered, confused.

"Well, you haven't answered your phone. I thought you might have forgotten or got distracted by someone."

"Hi, I'm Ambrosia. Her distraction." Ambrosia gave her a weak wave.

"Hi, I'm…"

"Khadijah. I got it, girl," Ambrosia's body language was speaking volumes. She was studying Khadijah, her eyes running up and down her frame, her lips pursed. Her expression said, *I don't like this bitch,* as clearly as any words could. But instead of verbalizing it, she settled on a curt exit, "I'm going to get going. See you Wednesday."

"Bye, girl. Hugs."

260

She raised her arms like a toddler asking to be picked up. I fell into her embrace and let her rock a little bit of comfort into me.

I followed Khadijah begrudgingly. Every step was heavy-footed and echoed in the empty hall.

Eric and I had decided not to tell her. We just didn't see a healthy outcome, but this was getting out of hand. She was. She was mean, demanding, and stressing me the hell out.

Deep breaths. Deep breaths. Temporary. This is just temporary. After her wedding, she'd return to my well-meaning, bossy best friend, not a tyrant ambushing me in class because I missed a call.

The salon was fancy but outdated. It was seemly designed in the 90s with black and gold decor. Rows of old, hooded dryers sat in rows down the center of the room. New modern driers with wheels were tucked in corners. The wash bowls were in the back, meaning stylists and clients tracked back and forth. The driers were loud, so conversations were polite shouting matches. It gave the space a hectic vibe.

Today, it was packed with the whole bridal party, plus a few aunties. Her mom insisted that all maids do a hair and make-up test. Mrs. Fawaz had a rogue bridesmaid ruin her wedding pictures. She didn't mind footing this bill to make sure everyone understood the aesthetic.

Not paying for the wedding had always been a power play to encourage Khadijah to wait until she graduated. Now that it was clear Khadijah was going to get married no matter what, they'd loosened their purse strings. There was a casual competitiveness about family weddings, and she couldn't let her daughter be outdone.

Emotional Charades

A light cheer floated around the room as we all caught up and enjoyed the company. My irritation dissipated while watching Khadijah in her element. She was taking pictures of each party member and creating a look book for each member. Their hair, makeup, and nails. Every detail. This level of perfection had to be exhausting. I couldn't help but respect her drive.

I scanned the room to see what Amara was doing. When I found her, she was under a drier, swiping through something on her phone. An aunty, Dada I think, stood over her shoulder, agonizing over Amara's every swipe.

Good. If an aunty was preoccupying Amara, Khadijah could be the star of the show today.

Once my hair was washed, I was placed in a chair facing a mirror. Most of my hair curled into a tight afro, but a few pieces hung limp and loose, a result of heat damage from the last time I'd straightened my hair, despite the heat protector.

The stylist began to section my hair to blow dry it. I stared at the loose sections. I felt flush and my pulse quickened. Christian's voice saying, *'You don't like straightening your hair'* came back to me. He was right. I didn't.

My pulse started racing as I watched her prepare her station. The blow-dryer with the attached comb, the pressing comb, and the flat iron.

"Could we do this style without straightening my hair?" I asked the stylist.

"I could," she shrugged. She looked around the salon for the decision-makers and waved her hand.

Khadijah and her mom drew towards us.

"She wants a curly version of the style. Are you okay with that?" the stylist asked, pulling my curly hair back, demonstrating how the style would look. It was a half-up half-down look.

"Why?!" Khadijah shot.

Mrs. Fawaz spoke over her. "That's fine. I love curly hair."

She raised her hand and walked towards me. I braced for her hands to sink in my hair, but instead, they came to rest on my shoulders.

"You will look so beautiful," Mrs. Fawaz said. Then, she walked off. My heart filled with cheer at her simple compliment and inaction. She didn't touch my hair like I was a pet.

"That's okay with me." Khadijah addressed the stylist, then walked to me, "But why?"

She flipped through her binder to find the notes on my styling.

"I'm scared of heat damage. I have a few loose sections from the last time."

Her eyes widened in understanding, "Yes, of course." Not needing to look at her binder, she turned toward the stylist, "When you lay her hair for the half up part, use a soft brush and her preferred gel or mousse. Sanek strips and low heat with the dryer."

I smiled at her, and she nodded.

"Oh, I still have to ask my mom about our girls ' night," Khadijah said, then bustled off to find her mother.

See, her reaction wasn't bad. I should tell Christian about—

I didn't let myself finish the thought. Occasionally, I had the stray desire to talk to him as a friend, to continue a debate or laugh about an inside joke.

I quickly shut down the impulse. I couldn't have my cake and eat it, too. I blocked him on everything. It would be too easy to like a post or leave a comment.

Khadijah was talking to her mother. She glanced at me like she needed help. I joined her, sure that I could assuage the situation.

Khadijah started, "My mother wants—"

"I was thinking we could all use a day off. So, I will plan an event," Mrs. Fawaz said in a clear, crisp voice. She looked regal. Her head was held high, her shoulders were back. As a queen, this was her decree. Instantly, I knew she wouldn't brook any objections. Still, Khadijah and I, the mere subjects that we were, tried.

We failed. Now, our girls' night out was family affair.

Our ride from the salon was split into different ventures. Khadijah was talking a mile a minute, excited about the sudden addition to our already packed wedding festivities. I plotted out a tactic to tell Eric.

"What are you going to wear? What am I going to wear?" she questioned. She beamed at me, her eyes bright green, the corners creasing from her smile.

"I predict…clothing," I stated anticlimactically.

"Don't be pessimistic. It's going to be fun!"

"Eric isn't going to like this," I explained. Eric had a final on Monday.

"Oh, he'll get over it. What's one more party?" She clamored on, and I let her, still pondering the effects of adding another straw to the camel's back.

We'd reached my house and I still didn't have the pitch prepared. Eric was sitting innocently on the couch, greeting us with a smile, not knowing we were the bearers of inconvenient news.

"Hello, Khadijah. Hello, sweetheart, You girls look..." He paused with what seemed like a struggle for the right words.

"We just left the hair and make-up trial for the wedding," Khadijah explained.

"Oh, you girls look nice." He managed to pull together a polite lie.

By Khadijah's request, the stylist dismantled our pinned-up hairdos, leaving our hair in directionless curls that we maneuvered into ponytails. Our skin was dry and pale from the application and removal of several layers of make-up. Stripes of the stuff still lingered in odd places around our eyes. We looked like the morning after a bachelorette party.

"Khadijah is leaving out that she had the make-up and hairstyle undone so no one would know what to expect."

"Thank goodness!" Eric exclaimed, "I mean, that is good to know. Being aware of the day's agenda, I had prepared to compliment you." He smiled while wrapping his arms around my waist. "I lied well, though, right?" he asked like we were alone.

"You did great, baby."

"Hey, that's rude!" Khadijah stated, half-offended.

Eric glanced at me for clarity. I gave him the expression he would understand as *not really*. He shrugged his shoulders at Khadijah, a little too late to be in response to her comment.

Emotional Charades

"I have something funny to tell you," I said with a giggle. This moment seemed as good a place if any to slide in bad news.

"What?" He locked his eyes on me.

"Have you ever watched a comment get taken the wrong way?" I asked.

"Of course, I have. I am normally the commenter."

"Okay. A few weeks ago, Khadijah and I decided to hang out alone without any wedding or relationships. Just the two of us."

I glanced at her, and she nodded solemnly.

"Okay, that is a great idea." Eric looked at me, then to Khadijah, missing the apprehension in my voice.

"Yeah, it was. So, at the shop today, Khadijah was asking her mother if we could skip the dress fitting for the mothers' of the bride and groom. She told her we just needed to blow off some steam."

"Okay…" He creased his brows.

"Khadijah's mom thought that was a great idea, too. So great, since it turned out that everyone involved in the wedding party needed to relieve stress. We were super excited. She called and canceled the fitting, then called a restaurant to host us. See, she thought that we wanted to blow off steam *with her*. Now, we're having a pre-wedding cocktail party. "

I said the whole tale with a smile on my face and the air of a joke.

"That is funny. That whole conversation got away from you guys, huh?" He chuckled at our expense. "Now you're obligated to attend a highfalutin evening?"

I smiled and cocked my head to the side. "*We* are."

His chuckles stopped. "Wait, are you telling me that I am expected to attend another formal event?" he asked, finally understanding.

Timidly, I nodded my head. His hands started to tap lightly on my hips. I hated that I had caused it.

"An additional event during finals week?"

"And our parents are invited." I slid in the last caveat.

"What? Why would our parents be invited?"

"I tried to avoid the party by saying that we were planning to have dinner with our parents. That snowballed, too. Both pairs accepted and are coming. Also, they are going to stay here, and we are going to stay at Khadijah's."

Khadijah had worked out the sleeping arrangements on the drive here. She felt bad that our parents would have to rent a hotel room on such short notice.

"I would not like to attend," he said quietly. "I am already dealing with the stress of the wedding and the speech. All those people I don't want to speak with…and us. And finals…"

The honesty in his words stung me.

"You don't have to go. It's okay."

"No, we need our wedding party at a pre-wedding event," Khadijah interrupted.

"Khadijah, it's not even a real thing. Your mother made it up."

Speaking past me and directly to him, she pressured, "Eric, it would be considered rude if you don't come. You're the best man. You have an obligation!"

"Khadijah!" I shouted.

"What?"

"Don't," was all the explanation I could garner.

"What? I should just let Eric ruin my wedding?"

"You should be concerned about your marriage and not a meaningless consumer-driven ceremony that shows no correlation with marriage longevity," Eric responded.

"Did you look that up in a textbook, huh, the same one that told you to kiss Juliette?"

He looked at her with trepidation, his hands tensed against my back. Then, his eyes locked on mine. I could tell that he wanted me to tell him what to do. Give him the sign to apologize or to explain his intention. The muscles in my face gave no instruction, too focused on staring at her. Waiting for her to apologize, to explain her intention. But she was staring at Eric.

The standoff lasted until Eric removed himself from the equation. He went into his private room. He closed the door calmly, although I wished he'd slammed it.

"Don't ever bring that up again," I commanded, staring her down, daring her to say the wrong thing. Of all the despicable things that Jamie had done to her, I'd never thrown it in her face like that.

"Oh, alright," she said amicably. She waved a careful hand in the air and sat on the couch as if she couldn't feel the animosity in the room.

I stared at her, tension keeping us speechless for a beat.

"My bad. I'm just worked up. I shouldn't have said that," Khadijah apologized.

I took a beat, trying to force myself to calm down, then said, "Oh, well, guess we'll just be one Eric short."

"Make him do it," she commanded, iron in her tone.

"What?" I asked kindly, trying to misunderstand her.

"You can make him do it. You have that like control over him. Like how you tell him when he is talking too much or being rude."

Her words made my blood ripple, "If he doesn't want to go, I'm not going to force him."

"Rebeca, it's important."

"No, it's not."

"How can you tell me that my wedding isn't important?" Her cracking voice and wet eyes appeared so quickly. When had she become emotional?

"That's not what I'm saying…"

"He has to go!" she shouted, her eyes focused on his door, speaking at him.

"Khadijah! He said no."

"No, he has to go!"

"I'm sure we'll have a great time without him," I offered, trying—really trying—not to lose my shit.

"But—" she shouted.

"No, Khadijah!" I snapped, tired of the back and forth.

"He'll get over it."

Just like that, she was an animated character again, green eyes ablaze with the irritation of tears. She dislodged her already disheveled ponytail, making her look manic. An epiphany struck me: this moment was not original.

Like *déjà vu*, we had been here before. The dorm room, with Jamie and burning the dress, the bakery. I was sure that the moment she got her way, the tears would vanish like a mirage.

"Sometimes, you can be really manipulative!" I told her, honestly.

I could think back to every outburst, every emotional tangent Khadijah had thrown over the last few months. They all seemed to have a purpose. The instant she got what she wanted, the tears disappeared. I had never seen her from this perspective. All her stunts, they were manufactured.

And they worked.

I sat in my thoughts, trying to recall how many times I had gone against my own will to please her. Most of the time, it was for a good cause, like getting me to study more or organize my schedule. Now, she was abusing it. I was just Khadijah's little sheep.

"You're kind of being a bitch today," I added.

"Oh!" she gasped. Her tears froze before they could leave her eyes. Her huffing gave way to silence, and her drooping shoulders squared as she stared at me in disbelief. Her mouth parted. The breakdown that was imminent a moment ago vanished. For the first time, I'd called her bluff and the meek, tearful character disappeared.

"Did you call me a bitch?" she asked with a grain of animosity.

"You need to leave," I said calmly, anger building inside me.

"You just called me a bitch, and now you're kicking me out!"

I crossed my arms and stared her down as she waited for me to retract my statement.

"I'm gonna go," Khadijah said it as if it were a choice.

"Good...um. Okay." I fumbled with my word choice. I almost said, *'Good riddance.'*

I walked her to the door, only to slam it behind her.

The audacity for her to think she, of all people, had a right to bring up cheating! Her future husband had fucked the whole volleyball team, and what? She couldn't accept *no* as an answer without having a tantrum? Who the fuck did she think she was? I was not her marionette. She wasn't the puppet master. Fuck her party and her wedding if she was going to act this way, the way I had always allowed her to behave.

The logical side of my brain kicked in, interrupting my rage.

How could she talk to Eric like that? I raged in my mind on her behavior, on her choices, but it all kept leading back to me. My actions made her think I controlled Eric and that she controlled me.

Not anymore. I wouldn't let that stand.

His door opened a decimal and I jumped to intercept Eric at his door.

"We aren't going. We don't have to, and she was wrong for trying to guilt you into it," I said before the door was fully open.

"We can go. What is one more dinner?" he offered.

I stared at him in bewilderment. "But you don't want to."

"Definitely, I do not want to go."

"Then you don't have to."

"I am aware that I am not obligated to go. After consideration, I concluded that if I do not attend, Khadijah will be insufferable towards you."

"We shouldn't respond to her mood swings. She has to grow up sometime."

"No, that is not my true motivation. If she is irritating you, you will complain to me. I do not wish to hear those spats."

I smiled. "So, this decision is about you."

"Profoundly selfish."

I hugged him, delighted that we had maneuvered this tense moment without fighting. He wrapped his arms around me and kissed my forehead.

***

He made the decision, and I went along with it. After informing Khadijah, she apologized for her words, and we moved on tending to the last few wedding preparations. We made sure to obey our study schedule alongside them.

The busy week passed quickly, and it was Sunday in a blink. The cocktail party had started ten minutes ago. I'd just finished getting dressed when I got Eric's text that he was outside waiting. Next to his messages were three texts from Khadijah that I hadn't bothered to read, but I was sure were about tardiness.

Ever the pragmatist, he had gotten dressed for dinner this morning and went on with his day dressed like a Ken Doll.

I rushed to the car.

"Okay, we can't stay out too late. I have class at 8am and a final fitting right after." When I noticed that Eric hadn't started to drive, I said, "Eric, we are going to be even later."

272

I glanced up to see him staring. His eye shimmered.

"What?" I smiled.

"I just realized you are going to keep getting more beautiful with time. I keep thinking I have witnessed you at your most beautiful. When we went to prom, then graduation, and homecoming a few years back. You continue to impress me with how beautiful you are. One day, I will get to see you in a wedding dress. I look forward to that."

Can a heart glow? Mine felt like it could. "You saw me in my wedding dress."

"I saw you in a dress. It was not our wedding." His eyes lit up. "I look forward to seeing you walking towards me, promising to try this for the rest of our lives."

He was musing, not really trying to compliment me. Finished, he started the car, not noticing that I was staring at him with adoration. I'd fallen in love with him all over again.

I walked into the pre-wedding party. I was light as a feather, hugging his arm like I would collapse without it. So focused on him, I barely took in the fancy restaurant that Mrs. Fawaz had picked. Gold and red accents decorated a brightly lit cream room. Citrus scents filled the air and made my stomach stir in anticipation.

My perfunctory scan of the room stopped when my eyes settled on this pretty, blonde woman with a pixie haircut. I exhaled in slight amazement as I walked up to the host.

"Hello, Juliette." I tried to make my tone as even and casual as possible. "We're with the Fawaz party.

"Hi, Rebecca, right this way." Her voice gave way to a bit of nervousness.

She didn't speak to Eric, and I thought that it was a good choice. Eric wrapped his arm around my waist.

She led us to a private section of the restaurant. Most of the guests were already eating. We joined Khadijah and Jamie at a round table.

"I was not aware she worked here. I am sorry." He apologized the moment she walked away.

I looked down at my hands. I needed a beat to compose myself. There would always be a pinprick of pain in our love story. Seeing her brought it front and center. But this, being with him, was what I wanted. I wasn't afraid of history repeating itself.

"It's fine. You couldn't have known she worked here."

I looked across the table. The bride and groom were already engaged in an uncomfortable back and forth. Since our argument, I'd reduced my role in managing Khadijah's outbursts. I deferred to Jamie and time for healing her tantrums.

"Should we leave?" he asked.

"Would you like a drink?" I countered.

"Sure." He paused. "Are you upset?"

"Would you like several?" I asked, smiling eagerly.

"Are you upset? Should we leave?"

"I want to dance, like at the fitting. If you're buzzed, you won't feel nervous." I tilted my head to the dance floor.

He leaned his head towards me. Resting his forehead on mine.

Taylor Bianca B

"Are you okay?" he asked. His voice was serious. I could tell he wanted to make sure I wasn't pretending again, that I wasn't trying to fix this situation by suppressing my feelings.

"Yes!" I answered honestly. "I want to dance with you."

He took a deep breath and relaxed back in his chair. He waved over the waiter. "May I have two shots of tequila and a tequila sunrise?"

"I'll have water," I smiled. "I'll be the designated driver."

I leaned in and kissed him. What was supposed to be a peck wasn't. His hand slid to the back of my neck. He pulled me into a deeper kiss. His lips were firm and forceful. His tongue parted my lips. I felt like I could sink into him.

I moaned into his kiss. He pulled back, a dirty smirk on his face. His eyes danced.

He leaned forward and whispered in my ear, "I miss hearing you moan."

I crossed my legs, squeezing them tightly. All sorts of desire started to stir between them.

The waiter returned and placed the drinks in front of him.

"How is it that you can kiss me like that in public, but dancing makes you nervous?"

"I am experienced and confident in one of the two areas," Eric explained quickly.

A fork clinked against glass.

"Thank you all for coming tonight. I wanted to let everyone know how grateful we are for all the love and support you're giving my baby girl. As a father, you're never ready to see your daughter as a wife. I wanted to thank Jamie, knowing you makes this process special. I hope the love you have shown her will continue throughout your marriage."

I tapped Eric so that he would look at me. I made the face that meant *don't say that.*

He frowned and shrugged his shoulders, confused because he hadn't said anything. I tilted my head towards Khadijah's father. He looked back and forth from Mr. Fawaz to me.

"B-ha-ha-ha," Eric's laugh roared through the quiet room. He had gotten my joke, that Mr. Fawaz shouldn't hope that.

The room stared at us, most of them with pleasant smiles on their faces, waiting for us to share the joke.

"Sorry, inside joke," I announced to the room. The other guests chuckled awkwardly.

But not Jamie and Khadijah. For them, the timing was clear. They stared at us, faces tight with anger. Eric looked at me, waiting for me to instruct him on proper protocol. I just shrugged my shoulders. I wouldn't use our language as social reins anymore.

There were pictures and toasts and Khadijah and Jamie bickering in the background. I was completely denouncing my role as her peacekeeper. When she stormed off the floor, I didn't follow, and to no one's surprise, neither did the other bridesmaids.

Instead, Eric and I danced and kissed and hugged, and I found myself incapable of sitting in my own chair. We were in a new wave of infatuation.

"May I have this dance?" Mr. Bridgeport asked. I'd half-forgotten our parents were here.

"Of course," I answered happily. I took his hand, and he led me to the dance floor.

Taylor Bianca B

"You look beautiful, dear."

"Thanks." He led me in a waltz. He was a much more confident dancer than his son.

He smiled at me like I was the bride."

"You and Eric both have that stare," I told him.

"What stare?" he asked, smiling.

"Like you're about to say something beautifully complimentary, and I'm going to cry."

Mr. Bridgeport stopped the waltz and took a step back. "You got me." He raised my hand and spun me once, then pulled me back into his frame. "You know you changed my life, right?"

"What?"

"When he was diagnosed, they told us that he would have trouble making connections, making friends. For a while, it was playing out that way. As a father, I was so afraid that he was going to have a shit time in the world. Then, you ran across the street and changed that. You befriended him, and that lifted a fear from my life." He choked on the words.

Tears appeared as I predicted, and I laid my head on his chest, just as happy that our lives had intersected that day.

"Ahh!" he exclaimed, clearing his voice. "I'm happy you guys worked it out. I would have been salty to anyone else he managed to bring home."

"Salty?"

"Yeah, Landon has been teaching me. I told him I would call any girl he brought home by your name."

"Can I cut in?" my father asked.

Mr. Bridgeport stepped back, and my father took his place.

"Daddy!" I hugged him.

Emotional Charades

"Baby girl, you look so beautiful."

"Thanks." I smiled and hugged him harder. "Dad?"

"Yes, baby girl?"

"Am I going to have two daddy-daughter dances?" I asked with a chuckle.

"Ha-ha, have you met your mother? Do you think Eric is going to leave the dance floor without giving her a mother-son dance? So, yep. Just start the song over."

Warm fingers wrapped around my wrist and pulled my attention.

"I am ready to go," Eric announced. His cheeks were flushed, and he was tapping on his thigh. I glanced around the room looking for what had triggered Eric.

Khadijah's eyes were overflowing with tears. Jamie was standing in front of her, his lips moving a mile a minute, spewing words I couldn't hear. He was likely talking Khadijah down from whatever emotional ledge she was currently standing on.

Eric must have gotten stuck in the middle of their feud. Consciously, I peered toward the door to make sure Juliette was at her station and not the cause of this emotional break. She was still at the host stand.

"Okay, let me say bye to Khadijah and I need to get her room keys since we're staying at her dorm tonight. Can you make sure our parents have our keys?"

"I already gave them a pair. I will wait in the car." He walked out.

Khadijah and Jamie politely paused their tiff as I approached. I managed to get her keys without getting entangled in their drama. I said bye to both pairs of parents and the Fawaz's, not bothering to explain Eric's sudden departure.

The night air nipped at me as I pulled on my coat at the door. I crossed the parking lot to peer into an empty car. Eric was seated on a bench not far from it.

"Eric, it's cold. Why aren't you in the car?" I asked, walking toward him, suddenly afraid I had made him ill. "Are you alright? Did you drink too much?"

I was in front of him before he responded, and I had to call his name a few more times.

"Eric, are you okay?"

"Yes." His head shot up, almost surprised by my proximity.

"Why are you sitting in the cold?"

"You have the keys. You took them when you decided to be the designated driver," he responded, answering the question but not providing the details I was after like why he hadn't just come back in. Or why he'd left so suddenly in the first place.

His hand wrapped around my waist so suddenly that I almost pulled back. "Rebecca, I am sorry that I did something that could have broken your spirit. I would never want to be the cause of you feeling inadequate. I love you more than I think I am supposed to, but if I ever become the source of your anguish, leave me."

I frowned at the seriousness in his tone. Whatever fight Jamie and Khadijah had involved Eric in, it had struck a chord.

"Okay." He looked up. "I will leave if you ever become my source of anguish, but you have to promise to never become my source of anguish," I countered. I reached for his hand, and he took mine.

We shook on it.

Emotional Charades

He pulled my hand to his lips. He kissed my hand, and then my wrist. My body flushed with heat as I imagined the other places I wanted his lips.

"Let's get going." I pulled his hand and he stood. We ambled to the car and drove to Khadijah's dorm. When I opened the door, the single bed inspired a question.

"Am I sleeping on the floor tonight?" Eric asked, his hands on my hips, his mouth a breath away from my neck.

I grinned. "If you want, we can sleep on the floor together?"

I bit my bottom lip and stepped backward toward the bed, towing him with me. When my knees hit the edge, I eased down slowly onto the bed, then made my way toward the head.

Eric stood there a moment, admiring. He walked to the side of the bed, his jacket and tie falling to the floor. He crawled in bed beside me, and we laid face to face.

"I love you," he said, caressing my cheek.

"I love you, too."

"I am nervous," he admitted.

"Me too."

"If you are not ready to reintroduce sex into our relationship, I can—"

I silenced him with a finger to his lips.

"I'm excited," I whispered, dropping my hand.

My hand crawled underneath the tail of his shirt. I pulled him towards me; his lips brushed my neck. I needed to feel his flesh. I wanted all barriers between us to vanish. My fingers skated across his lower back and pulled him closer to me. I touched something on his lower back that was moist and ridged.

"Ah," he moaned, wrenching away from me for a second. Then, he dove back into our kiss like the pain didn't matter.

I laughed into his kiss. "What is that? Did you scrape yourself on something?"

"I—don't—know," he said breathlessly as he attended to his kissing single-mindedly.

From beneath him, I craned my torso to the side to see what I had stroked. I yanked his shirt completely from his pants, then bunched it up towards his arms.

"Rebecca, I need to unbutton this shirt," he laughed, his shirt wrapped around his back and arms.

I didn't answer. Instead, I stared at the reddened trails that led from his side down to his back and beneath his pant line. His laugh still echoed in the room, but all humor had been snatched from me.

Shifting from beneath him, I righted my dress. Then, I rushed to my feet, backing away from the bed.

"Eric, what is that?"

"What?" He stood, coming toward me.

"What is that on your back?"

"I do not know what you are referring to," he said with such clear eyes that I doubted myself.

"Look," I pointed toward the mirror.

He pulled his shirt up and stepped toward the mirror, freezing as he saw the lines and welts drawn on his back. He twisted so that he could see the claw marks without the mirror. He stared at them, bewildered.

"It is nothing, Rebecca." He spoke like he was trying to keep a wild animal calm.

"Wrong answer. Those are scratches—nail scratches. Ones you didn't have this morning." I could feel the tears begging to escape, and I tried to hold them in.

"Rebecca, it is nothing to worry about."

I thought back to all the fights we'd had. I wasn't going to waste words or time by asking the wrong questions.

"Who scratched your back, Eric?"

"Rebecca?"

"No, it wasn't me. So, what were you doing for your back to get scratched?

"I promise…"

"Not an answer. Did you cheat on me, again?

"Rebecca, no!"

I felt myself becoming irrational. Why? Why was he lying? There was one way to get those types of scratches.

"How did you get the scratches on your back, Eric?" I yelled.

"I did not cheat on you."

"How?"

"I can't explain the scratches." He said it like it was a fact.

"Unbelievable," I shot. "Not true. You're just choosing not to tell me."

"I promise, I did not do anything."

"You're avoiding the question." Suddenly, my imagination started to spiral. "Do you love her? You see her one night and you what, you had to have her? At a dinner party with our parents? Or did it happen before the dinner? Have you been sleeping with her this whole time?" My chest tightened as I rambled out the possibilities.

"Who?"

"Juliette!"

"No, Rebecca," he struggled for words. "I haven't touched her since the café."

The mention of the café brought back the image of them that day.

"She clearly influenced you, got you into choking." I was ranting now, resolution out the window. I was on the verge of tears, holding them back by sheer willpower. My voice strained.

"Rebecca, I have already told you, she didn't teach me that," he spat.

His words hit me with a new meaning, like they sat in the air and re-ordered themselves.

"Someone else did?"

A defeated look coated his face. He nodded sheepishly.

"You   slept   with   someone   else?"

"While you were living with Christian Taylor, I did engage with women sexually."

"You bastard."

"Did you expect me to wait while you were with another man?"

"Yes," I answered honestly. "Leave! Get out."

"Rebecca, you can't be mad about that. We were not together. "

"You aren't mad about Christian?"

"That's different."

"Why? Because you wrote a thesis about it?"

"No, because you fell in love with him. I am mad that I pushed you into his arms, that my choices fueled your attachment to him. I am mad at myself," he shouted. "I have only loved you, but now you have that attachment. And yes, it is distressing to me."

My eyes fluttered a few times, then, I turned away from him. I was supposed to deny it, but it was true.

He massaged his temples, "Rebecca, could we talk this out in the morning when I am sober?"

"Sure, answer one question now. What happened to your back?"

He froze, mouth half-open; I saw the strain on his face.

"You don't want to talk. You want time to come up with an argument. You want to organize your words so that you can feel righteous."

"Is that what you think?"

"Yes."

"It is not like that. Give me a little time and it will all make sense."

"How can you expect me to trust you?"

"I am not lying," he pleaded.

"Well, you're not telling the truth."

"Rebecca."

"Please leave before I say something I can't take back. Before I say something you can't forgive me for," I warned.

His eyes sobered for a moment, then he complied, walking to the threshold, defeated. He stopped and turned.

"I cannot leave you while you are upset," Eric protested.

"Leave!" I screamed.

Eric just stared, hurt apparent on his face. He still didn't.

"I need you to leave," I repeated, gaining control over my voice.

"Rebecca, please!" He dropped to his knees. His fingers interlocked like he was praying.

"Okay."

His head fell forward like his prayers had been answered. I skirted him, grabbing my keys and my purse.

"Then I will," I said as I let the door shut behind me.

I needed to clear my head. I wasn't running from a hard conversation this time. I was pressing pause before shallow words tried to vindicate my hurt feelings.

I heard him scrambling to his feet. Then, the door snatched open. I rushed into the stairwell. No patience for the elevator. He was a flight behind me, charging down the stairs and still calling my name.

Suddenly, I heard a thud and a grunt of pain. Then, something small skidded past me and smacked the wall. I jumped, startled, then turned.

Eric was sprawled across the top few stairs. He started to sit up, holding his ribs on the right side.

My heart raced for a moment. *Shit, is he okay?* I started up the stairs, rage momentarily frozen by worry. Then, I paused and considered leaving him. Maybe he deserved a little pain.

"Are you okay?" I said, settling on the middle ground of being angry and concerned.

He nodded but scrunched his face in pain. He rubbed his side and winched at a tender spot. "Rebecca, I really…"

Emotional Charades

"Eric," I said, shaking my head, "Please stay here tonight. I need to clear my head. Khadijah has some extra strength Tylenol in the top drawer of her desk. We can finish this tomorrow."

He looked resigned and gave me the look for *I understand.*

I turned, grabbed his phone from the floor, and handed it to him. He looked up with big, dilated eyes.

Could your heart get whiplash? 10 minutes ago, I adored those eyes; now, I could feel vitriol pushing up my throat like vomit at the sight of them. I swallowed, choking back the words. I turned and left.

I drove for a while to clear my mind, then pulled in front of my apartment. My parents' car was there, but the lights inside were off. I crept in quietly. I changed into light sweats and slept on the couch.

Chapter 27: A Difficult Day for Lying

I slept on the night's events like the princess with the pea under her mattress. I couldn't get comfortable, not on the couch or with the answers he had given me. Even the answers I tried to piece together didn't make sense.

Initially, I was more upset with the revelation that he hadn't suffered in abstinent pining. By morning, it was a mild annoyance. The scratches were my primary irritant now. I could picture Juliette putting them there. All in all, the details didn't feel cohesive.

1.   The speech outside the restaurant, was he talking about himself?
He must have been.

2.   But if he had known he had scratches on his back, why not avoid sex?
He was drunk. He could have forgotten.
3.   He probably cheated on me while our entire family was dancing in the same room.
I just couldn't believe it.
4.   He said he wasn't lying.
How could I believe that?

That point had held me there, stuck in re-evaluation. He had withheld the truth, but never lied to my face. Then again, she was there. Maybe he loved her. I let out a breathless sigh. My chest hurt. It was so clear; she was there, and he had been nervous. He'd wanted to leave.

I walked into class with that thought process looping. The voices of my classmates reading their final stories barely registered to me.

"Any more suggestions or comments, class?" Professor Lamb asked, her voice pulling my attention from my notebook.

Christian scoffed so loudly that Professor Lamb asked if he wanted to add a comment.

"No, but I'm ready to read."

"Christian, you may begin."

"Love has a look in the lustful eyes of secret lovers. The health of their attachment, stoked by their public secret."

Every word sounded like nails against a chalkboard. "Not to-fucking-day," I interrupted, jumping to my feet and stuffing my belongings in my backpack.

It was my poem from the café, of Eric and her. My patience for Christian's retaliation broke.

"Christian, you are a fucking ass!" Ambrosia exclaimed like she had been holding it in for weeks. She jumped to her feet, and packed her things, joining in my protest.

"Mr. Taylor, I'd like to have a word," admonished Professor Lamb.

"Here's my project. It was nice having a class with you." I dropped my final assignment on the desk. Ambrosia fished her assignment from her bag and did the same.

Taylor Bianca B

We stormed out, our footsteps echoing in the hallway.

"Oh, fuck this! What? I can't write a story about an event I witnessed?" he yelled, following us into the hall.

"You don't have to dignify this with a response, but if you do, call him a bitch. In your own words, of course. You wouldn't want to plagiarize someone else's work," Ambrosia scoffed.

"Listen, Christian, you can write whatever you want, but I don't have to listen to it. I don't have to put up with your twisted revenge." My eyes stung.

The class mobbed the door as if there were a force field holding them in the classroom.

"Revenge? I'm just telling a story."

"Sure, just an innocent story. You know, I'm so tired of you guys playing with words. You're furious with me; fine, I deserve that, but don't piss on me and tell me it's rain. You have said every hurtful thing you could think up for weeks, and you know, Christian, I'm sorry I hurt you, but I'm happy I never have to see you again."

My voice had reined in a crowd now. Students from other classes were peering out their doors or stepping into the hallway. I looked around, trying to feel justified instead of embarrassed.

"Us *guys*?" He paused for an instant. Concern lined the corners of his eyes, his brow furrowed. His lines smoothed, replaced by a devilish grin, as he asked, "Did he hurt you again?"

I tried to look unbothered while he studied me, then I dropped the charade. "What do you want from me?"

Emotional Charades

His sick smile faded. His eyes darted down and then back to mine.

"Closure! One conversation and it's over. You just fucking stopped talking to me like I was nobody. Was it that easy?" His brows shot up. He looked surprised, like he hadn't planned to say it.

I felt my heart constrict, "Christian—"

"Rebecca!" Khadijah called.

My body went rigid with irritation. The crowd parted. Khadijah stood at the end of the hall, disheveled and winded.

"Of course, you again," Ambrosia muttered.

Khadijah ran the remaining length of the hall, stopping directly in front of Christian. She stared at him like she had come here to wage war against him.

"What, Khadijah?" Christian asked sardonically.

"Khadijah, why are you here?" I asked, annoyed that she had popped up again. There weren't any appointments, study sessions, or errands to run.

She turned towards me with red eyes. I inhaled, waiting for whatever manipulation was accompanying her tears. I stared back, impervious to her histrionics.

"Why haven't you been answering your phone?" she sobbed.

I rolled my eyes, "I didn't feel like talking to anyone. What is it this time?"

"I've been calling you for hours!" she shouted hysterically.

Frustrated, I shouted. "What do you want?"

"No one has been able to reach you or Eric."

"Eric's in your dorm," I shot, exasperated.

"He's not. I went there first. No one answered."

"He is…" the statement died in my throat; a ringing drowned out my thoughts. He'd fallen on the stairs. *No, no, he is fine. It was just a fall. But he was holding his ribs. If he broke a rib, he could be in serious pain or having trouble breathing.*

I called Eric and paced while the phone rang. No answer. Something had to be wrong; he'd answer for me. I called again with no success.

"This is why you didn't answer. Because you're with him!" Khadijah yelled. "You're the cheater, You turned your phone off so you could be with him," she accused me, a trembling finger pointed toward Christian.

Christian glared at Khadijah, then turned to me, "And you tried to defend her to me?" he asked, shaking his head.

Khadijah gasped like she was center stage in a murder mystery. His familiarity was all the confirmation she needed. I glanced at Christian, shrugged my shoulders, and gave him an exasperated look. Because there was no defense for her at this moment. She'd come on the pretense that she was concerned about me and Eric, but here she was, making a scene over a conversation.

I couldn't be bothered by her dramatics right now. My phone weighed too much in my hand. I didn't have any missed calls from Eric.

No text. Nothing.

I closed my eyes and the worst possibilities flashed. I still had her room keys. What if he was in her room but passed out from the pain? Or struggling to breathe or speak? Fear made my chest hot. I felt like my bones were quivering, sending deep ripples of panic coursing through me.

Emotional Charades

I stormed off, racing to Khadijah's dorm.

I had to be sure he wasn't in there alone. Unable to stop myself from imagining how scared or how alone he might feel.

Key in hand, I unlocked the door, then burst in. He wasn't there. But still, the room felt wrong. The bed wasn't made. He would have made it. The Tylenol sat open on her desk. He would have put it away. Unless he wasn't okay.

I turned, finding Khadijah on my heels.

"You're a cheater. You're just like Jamie. You don't deserve Eric," she declared.

She was right and wrong at the same time. Mostly, she was in the wrong place at the wrong time. She was blocking my way to the door. I needed to rush home to see if he was there. I tried to sidestep her, ignoring her rant. She side-stepped to stay in front of me.

I saw red, My eyes focused in on her. I couldn't hold back my frustration.

"Khadijah, you don't care about me or Eric. You only care about how we affected you. We don't know where he is, but you are talking about Jamie! About cheating. He could be hurt!" I spat.

She took a step back, her eyelids fluttered. She regained her righteous footing, "Maybe you would know if you weren't with that man."

It always came back to the lies. The lies I'd built my life on for the last two and half months.

I licked my lips, "Eric and I were broken up for two months. I convinced Eric not to tell anyone. At that time, I was with Christian. So, I'm a no-good cheater. I cheated on Christian when I realized I still loved Eric."

292

She sputtered out fragments of disbelief. Then, she stalled and her eyes fluttered. She was putting it together.

I rolled my eyes and stepped around her now that she was distracted. She pivoted when I reached the door.

"Why didn't you tell me?" she asked solemnly.

I looked over my shoulder. "It seemed like you couldn't handle another crack in your image of love. And selfishly, I wanted to believe in the couple you looked up to."

I left her with the whole truth.

Chapter 28: Placing all the Pieces

I raced home. Panic overtook my rational brain. Only terrible thoughts permeated. I called, texted, messengered him, and still no response. Images of him coughing up blood or choking raced through my mind.

I burst through the door. He was there. My heart skipped a beat, and my hands shook. I wiped my hands down my face. It was coated in tears.

He was okay, sitting at the kitchen table.

My panic started to subside, and the details of the room started to fill in. His shirt was open. Mr. Bridgeport was examining a dark purple bruise on his ribs. My parents and Mrs. Bridgeport stared. My mother walked towards me.

The sound cut back in, and I realized my mother was asking a question.

"Sweetheart, are you okay?" She placed her hand on my shoulder.

"Yes, Mom. I'm okay." I turned to address Eric. "You weren't answering your phone, and you'd fallen."

Eric gave me the expression of *I'm alright.* "My screen cracked when I fell."

He held up his phone and clicked a button so the screen would illuminate. The glass had layers of webbing cracks. I couldn't even make out the screensaver, which I knew was a picture of us. His thumb swiped the screen, but it didn't react.

"I was worried." I swallowed.

"I only made it here a few minutes ago. I walked. Dad insisted…"

"I insisted that he let me look at him. He was holding his side and his breaths seemed labored."

"Is he okay?" I stepped forward.

Mr. Bridgeport looked from Eric to me. "I think so. I think it's a contusion. A bruised rib. It's going to feel sore. Worse when he laughs, coughs, bends, or walks a mile from campus."

Mr. Bridgeport's eyes were on me. Then, the rest of the parents' eyes were, too.

"We got into an argument last night. He stayed on campus, and I came here to cool off." I pointed to the dress I'd worn last night. It was still on the couch. Eric took a deep breath. He winced as it agitated his ribs. Still, he looked more at ease now. I realized where he thought I'd slept.

Mrs. Bridgeport started, "Are you guys still—"

"Mrs. Bridgeport, I know you mean well, but this is between us." She looked taken aback. "We'll let you know about anything important. I promise," I stated firmly, setting a boundary.

My heart raced. I clasped my hands together to hide my nervousness.

"We're just concerned that you two are making a mistake," she said, my mother was nodding with her words. She looked kind.

"Okay, sweetheart." Mrs. Bridgeport glanced at the other parents in the room and nodded.

Emotional Charades

"Maybe we should all get going," my dad suggested. He corralled the other parents.

I was grateful to him for it.

They left in a swarm of hugs and well-wishes. Mr. Bridgeport stopped at the door, "He's going to need a little help for the next couple of days. Alternate Motrin and Tylenol to manage the pain."

"And follow up with a doctor if his symptoms get worse," I finished.

Mrs. Bridgeport hugged me, "You two take care."

I waved them off, closed the door, and rested my forehead against it, my hands still shaking. I clenched and unclenched my fists a few times to relax them. I turned to see Eric coming out of his private room. One hand on his ribs and the other holding a stack of folders.

"Eric, you should be sitting."

He chucked a stack of folders onto the table. I heard them, the weight of the folders hitting the table. I eyed them curiously.

"This is every sexual interaction I have had outside our relationship. It covers when I cheated," he admitted without a disclaimer, "as well as the intercourse that happened while we were separated."

"Eric, right now?" I snapped, surprised. I was being ambushed with information I hadn't requested.

"This is every sexual deed I have ever done without you." He spread the files across the coffee table. Their titles jumped at me.

Experiment 1: Promiscuous partner
Experiment 2: Mature partner
Experiment 3: Athletic partner

I peeled my eyes from the covers, from the part of me that wanted to devour the research, to review it with a fine-tooth comb, hoping that I could find her. The one he wanted, the one that scratched his back.

"Eric, I don't want to see that."

"I'm showing you this as an offer of goodwill. I have nothing to hide from you. I would not lie to you. Please, talk to me," he pleaded. I didn't feel like he was trying to win the conversation. He just wanted to have one.

"Then tell me," I whispered in desperation. "I don't understand. I thought we had made it through this." I stared at him, searching for the truth.

He looked tormented, but he didn't look away. He reached for one of the folders on the table, then yelped when his ribs reminded him of his limitation.

"Fuck!" I exclaimed, kicking the side of the couch. "Eric, I don't want to fight. You're hurt. Let's handle that first."

"I do not want to avoid a fight. I would rather have you rip apart this apartment. Shout at me and say hurtful things. It is better than you staying here in self-assigned duty while closing me out."

My jaw flexed, "Then tell me, why did you do it?"

"I promise, I did not do anything."

What was this? Was this a game? Some type of long-term revenge? Why was he doing this to me? Why did I want to believe him? I sank onto the couch. Since last night, nothing was right. I should have been in class taking my…Class!

Oh, crap. I pulled out my phone. It was 10:30 am. My exam started at 10:40 am.

I shot up, frantically grabbing my bag and the keys. Eric watched me, moving towards me slowly. He probably thought I was bolting again. I turned to him; his expression was a beg.

Please, repeated.

"I'm just going to class," I explained. I tucked my chin and cast my eyes down.

"I know you are. I trust you," Eric told me. The word smooth and even.

I whipped my head up, now I was studying his beg. He trusted me not to run away this time. So, if he wasn't begging me not to flee, what did he want?

Chapter 29: The Pre-Party

Mind over heartache, I focused completely on my test. I wasn't going to drop the ball on myself, again. But just as soon as it ended, my mind continued to recycle the same internal argument. Repeatedly, it came to the same conclusion: This didn't make any sense.

But then again, cheating didn't have to, right?

Ambrosia texted me, checking on me after the grand finale of our creative writing class. We decided to meet for tea.

I caught her up on what happened after I stormed off, about telling off Khadijah, to which she responded with an enthusiastic, '*About damn time.*'

She was the most supportive friend I'd ever made. She never said a word against Khadijah. She never applied any pressure or judgement about my friendship with Khadijah. She was supporting me without the need to be cruel or right.

It was so easy to be open with her.

So, I told her about Eric, the scratches, Juliette's proximity, and setting boundaries with my parents. She listened and, as always, was able to lighten the mood while keeping it straight with me.

"What's going on with you? I know you're tired of hearing my mass," I asked.

"Girl, nothing in my life is as interesting as this right now. We can catch up on me tomorrow." She leaned towards me, "Do you know what you want to do?"

I sat back in my seat, shaking my head. "I want answers. So that I can decide…I want closure."

Christian's words snaked through me. The unfinished conversation. His anger, his hurt. From Christian, my mind drew a direct link to Juliette. She might have the information I needed. She might be my closure. A brilliantly bad plan started to develop.

"I can ask Juliette," I said under my breath, "I know where she works." I cocked my head, waiting for her to tell me it was a bad idea, and desperate.

Ambrosia didn't bat an eye. She was on her feet in an instant, "I'll drive."

I followed her, "You don't need to go."

"Have you ever confronted a side chick before?"

"No."

Ambrosia tilted her head and looked up at me through her eyelashes. "You need backup. What if she and her coworkers try to jump you? What if you find out something difficult to hear? Are you going to want to be alone?"

I imagined the worst, Juliette telling me that she and Eric were having a child. I shook my head, "I wouldn't want to be alone."

"Okay, then," Ambrosia said. She walked toward the parking lot. I watched her for a moment. My eyes watered. This was what a healthy friend felt like. I followed her to her car.

Adrenaline rushed through me; I could hear my heart pounding. Ambrosia laid out a plan as she drove.

She would go in first and sit at the bar so she could watch, just a precaution.

I mounted a list of questions, all the while holding onto the caveat that Juliette probably wouldn't be there, that this was a fool's errand.

Then, I stepped into the restaurant. Adrenaline faded as anxiety crept in. There she was, Juliette, pixie cut and pretty. I stood behind a couple, impatiently waiting for my chance. I tapped my foot and angled around the couple to see her, to gauge her reaction. She rushed to assign the couple in front of me to a table.

I stepped toward her podium like a contestant on a game show. Nervous and eager, I could win or lose an emotional fortune based on the outcome of our interaction.

"Rebecca…um…"

"I need to talk with you." I tried to say it with confidence, my head held high, my tone level, while swallowing back the nervousness swishing in my stomach.

"Um, ah okay, but I'm not off for two hours so you can wait, or…" She paused for what looked like a moment of indecision. "You can call me later. I could give you my number," she finished meekly.

Like a balloon popping, my raw nerve deflated.

I returned to reality. She was at work. Even now, patrons and her co-workers eyed me suspiciously. This was altogether embarrassing. Plus, I felt a little stupid with the *coming to you as a woman* cliché.

Flustered, I fiddled with my phone. "Oh, of course, alright." I held it out to her before snatching it back. "Actually, I'll wait."

Emotional Charades

I wanted this to be a confrontation. She'd slept with my man. I wanted to see her expression as she confessed.

I sat at the bar and fidgeted with the napkins. I'd updated Ambrosia and was waiting on her response. The bar was lowlight with dark brown stained wood. My phone chimed. Ambrosia had decided to stay and wait with me.

She sat in a booth across the bar from me. For two hours I waited, feeling stupid but determined. I ordered a couple of drinks to pass the time, and to pad my confidence.

Juliette joined me at the bar with ease and a benevolence I didn't expect. All smiles, she rested a gentle hand on my back to alert me to her presence.

"Hello, Rebecca," she greeted as she squeezed into the stool beside me.

Tipsy, I had almost forgotten my list, forgotten my goal.

"Oh…h-hi," I stammered. I shook my head to clear it from the booze, but only accomplished stirring it. "Are you and Eric still sleeping together?"

"No!" she responded without delay. She leaned towards me, her hand on my shoulder, her eyes locked on mine, and firmly shook her head.

"Don't lie to me, please," I said, desperate. My entire list of questions re-ordered themselves. They'd revolved around her admitting guilt.

"Sounds like you already decided that we are?" she asked. "Why ask me then? It's not like you'd be able to tell whether I'm lying." She turned to the bartender. "Lemon drop, please."

Through my hazy perception, I understood her point. So, I resolved to ask a question where the truth was already established. "Why did you sleep with him in the first place?"

"What? You aren't just deciding that my slutty nature compels me to only sleep with other women's boyfriends?" She downed the shot.

I scoffed at karma for bringing my words back to me, "That wasn't my best moment, but you did live up to it."

She huffed and ran her tongue over her teeth, "Can I have three more lemon drop shots?"

The bartender supplied us with more libations. I thought she'd get up and leave. Or I would need Ambrosia's backup after I got slapped out of my chair.

I stared at the yellowish liquid still rippling. She downed the first shot, set the second one in front of me, and slowly sipped from the other. It seemed she knew exactly how drunk she needed to be to bear the awkwardness of this conversation. This probably wasn't her first confrontation.

I chugged mine, preparing to wince from the burn of the vodka, but it was smooth.

"He was gung-ho about this experiment. Convinced it was the key to keeping you from leaving him eventually. I told him it was *stupid*," she said the word heavily. "He convinced himself that it had merit. He started talking to other classmates, which surprised the hell out of me. He's never been super social."

"And why was he comfortable striking up a conversation with you?" I asked, noting the casual way she spoke about him, like they were friends.

"Because of you." She clapped her hand on the bar top to emphasize her point, her tone, and body language never crossing the line from assertiveness to aggression.

Her accusation struck my pride.

"Me?" I asked, befuddled as to how she'd come to that outrageous conclusion.

"Yes," she said defiantly. "After you read me for being a colossal whore for standing in a bar, Eric felt the compulsion to apologize. We became acquaintances."

"Oh." I shrunk into my seat. It sounded too familiar. Classmates becoming friends, then becoming more. "So, that's how you ended up sleeping with him?

"No. Look, Eric started asking for volunteers. Asking random girls in our class." She slowed the sentence down to emphasize her point. "I only volunteered to stop him from asking strangers so he wouldn't get kicked out of school for sexual misconduct. And to prevent rumors from making their way back to you that he was prowling for every girl that crossed his path."

"So, you were doing me a solid?"

"No." She paused, picking up her drink and finishing it. "Doing him a solid, I guess. Honestly, I never believed he would go through with it. I volunteered, and he didn't bring it up for months. Then later, out of the blue, he scheduled it like it was a doctor's appointment."

"That sounds like him. That's essentially how I lost my virginity."

"Yeah?"

"Pretty much. He didn't go around asking other girls, but…"

We chuckled awkwardly.

"Rebecca, I thought he would back down when it came time to…" She paused, dancing around the words 'having sex' as if they were off-limits. "I shouldn't have gone through with it."

It probably hadn't helped that I'd called her the campus trollop. I swallowed; I know I didn't make it happen, that I didn't deserve to be cheated on, but I'd wondered if my vicious words had given her motivation to participate in his experiment. I looked down, my chest felt heavy.

"Was this payback for what I said that day?"

Her eyes widened and she leaned back in her chair. "No. With the reputation I have, I've heard worse."

I believed her—or I wanted to, at least. There was a pity for her there, too. Most of that vengeful energy should have been directed towards the cheater, but she'd been the scapegoat.

"And you're sure you didn't scratch his back at the dinner the other night?" I asked one last time.

"Honey, I have never been accused of that." She laid her hands on the bar to display her nails. They were worn down to the nub. She raised a short nail to her teeth, peeling off a tiny sliver.

Evidence.

It wasn't her. Or…that fucking. Or she'd bitten them down today. Or maybe it wasn't her. She was the only one that fit. Or he could have another girl.

I exhaled at that real possibility.

This time, I could imagine a breakup. I'd leave knowing this wasn't meant to be. Understanding that long-standing relationships changed and that I'd adjust.

Emotional Charades

She was right about one thing. I didn't know her. I couldn't tell if she was telling the truth. She could be a great liar.

But I knew Eric. If I caught him off guard, I could definitely tell if he was lying.

"Can I ask you a ridiculous favor?"

She peered at me confused. "Sure. You can ask."

"Would you come home with me?"

Her head slumped forward like it would fall off her shoulders. I maintained eye contact. Assuring her that I meant what I said.

"Barkeep, can I get four shots of anything?" He quickly set four shots filled to the brim in front of her. She passed me two. She downed hers immediately, slamming the empty glass on the counter. "You want me to do what?"

Chapter 30: Full Disclosure

I faltered at the door of my apartment, unsure if my hastily made plan would amount to anything. But, just maybe, I could get the closure I needed. Since closure felt like a need, maybe everyone deserved it.

I texted Christian.

From Rebecca: My place in 20 if you want to talk. (10:40 pm)

He didn't respond.

I turned the knob, preparing to lock eyes on Eric, to read the truth before he could disguise it. I walked in, Juliette trailing me.

Eric, Jamie, and Khadijah's faces scrunched up in surprise. What were they doing here? I focused on Eric's face. His eyes pinched, his head tilted, and his mouth dropped open. Then, his brows rose, and his mouth closed. His expression shifted to understanding.

No shame, no guilt, and nothing that screamed I just slept with her behind your back.

Eric was seated on the couch. Jamie and Khadijah were standing to the right of him.

Jamie stepped toward me, peering at us with bemusement. He froze when he recognized her.

"Hi… Juliette?" Jamie shot awkwardly.

Emotional Charades

"Hi," Juliette responded flatly. She flashed me a look that I took as, *are you satisfied?*

I shrugged. I didn't think it was her. He'd brushed off the anxiety of seeing her here in an instance.

Khadijah did a double take like she couldn't trust her eyes.

"Juliette." Eric greeted my guest.

"Hi, Eric."

My skin crawled at the slight exchange. I bristled for a second, then recovered.

Khadijah and Jamie were standing between me and Eric, glancing back and forth at us. They were trying to piece together the details. Neither of us said anything. I was still trying to process Eric's lack of guilt.

I was sure it wasn't her.

"What is she doing here?" Khadijah asked.

"What are you doing here?" I retorted. She was the uninvited guest.

She walked over, keeping her eyes on Juliette. She grabbed my hand and pulled me to the side.

"I came to apologize," she said in hushed tones. "What is she doing here?"

"I brought her here to see if they slept together."

Khadijah's face looked ashen. She shook her head in disbelief.

"What is going on?" she asked in a far more level tone than I expected from her.

I paused, waiting for the tears, for the anguish in her voice, for her eventual breakdown that would steal the show. The only sound was the whistle of the heating vent.

"Rebecca needed confirmation that I didn't have intercourse with Juliette the night of your dinner," he

308

answered in the same solemn tone. "I feel confident that she obtained sufficient intelligence to dissuade herself of the notion, since they now appear to be friends."

Juliette and I looked at each other. *Friends* was not the right word. She'd explained during the ride here that she'd only come because she felt guilty for being with Eric.

"It was just a kiss. Eric would never sleep with her," Khadijah said, disgusted.

By the time she had surveyed the room, her eyes had connected the dots. "It was her. He cheated with her?" She stared at me in horror.

I stared at her in undeserved bemusement. I felt like she was eavesdropping on a private conversation, that her caring questions were somehow inappropriate. She, of all people, didn't need to know what Eric and I were going through. She couldn't handle it, but here we were.

Voices clambered over each other.

"Yes," Eric answered.

"But I was not the one who scratched his back at the reception dinner," Juliette said.

"Yes, he slept with her then blamed it on an ill-conceived experiment," I added

Khadijah and Jamie looked at each other like they needed to confirm what they'd heard.

Eric's eyes shot up and he stopped breathing.

I followed his gaze. Christian was standing in the doorway. The hallway light outlined his silhouette. *Oh, fuck.* When I had made this plan, I thought I had time to explain that I'd invited him. Time without Khadijah and Jamie. I thought it would be just the four of us.

I heard the tapping first.

"Rebecca, is there something you would like to explain," Eric said through gritted teeth.

"Yes," I pivoted to face him. "About an hour ago, I had the stupid idea that the four of us needed some closure."

"Is that Juliette?" Christian asked, staring at me with disbelief and concern. He'd only seen her the one time. He took a step inside as if curiosity were towing forward.

I shut my eyes tightly, then opened them. This was real.

"Yeah, that's her," I answered.

"Wow," he muttered. His eyes flickered with inquisitiveness.

The awkwardness was so palpable, my stomach clenched. The room lurched, maybe from the liquor, or the blood that was rushing to my head. My heart was pumping erratically.

"You didn't respond. So, I didn't think you were coming."

"Neither did I," he said, looking around the room. "Is this a public trial. Are they the jury?" He gestured towards Jamie and Khadijah.

"This," I said, twirling my pointer finger, "this is a shitshow."

The corner of his lip rose the slightest bit. A glimmer of my friend passed. He quickly ran his hand over his mouth and the almost smile was gone.

"So, he cheated on you with her again?" Christian asked, stepping back into his Mr. Hyde character. A grin pinched his dimples.

"You told him I cheated on you?" Eric asked.

"Clea-rly," Christian answered.

310

Eric's jaw clenched, his eyes narrowed, and his nose flared. He must have been wondering when I told Christian. Wondering why I had, and wondering whether there was still something going on with us.

Christian crossed his arms and looked smug.

"No, he guessed that something happened," I explained. I turned to glare at Christian.

"It's none of his business," Eric said through gritted teeth.

Christian looked at me like he was disappointed, "You're right about that."

He turned to leave. This was too much. Too messy. Before I could get my bearings, Ambrosia was at the door.

"Oh, I'm too late." She made eye contact with me.

Everyone stared waiting. "Too late for what?" I asked.

"I saw Christian pull in as I was pulling out. I was trying to warn you." She was shaking her phone and glancing at me.

I need to get an Apple Watch after today. No more missed messages.

I dropped my face in my hand, and sighed, "Does anyone want a shot?"

"We brought booze!" Juliette exclaimed, lifting the bottles of tequila for everyone to see.

"Me?" Ambrosia asked, raising her hand in the air to volunteer, "but I need two." She took the bottles, found her way to the kitchen, and searched the cabinets.

"The blue cabinet above the dishwasher if you are looking for shot glasses. I would like one as well," Eric said, his voice sounding grim and depleted. "Stay, Christian. I am sure we all have things we want to say."

Christian glanced over his shoulder at Eric, then at me. He stood holding the door, teetering on indecision. My stomach tightened. This surprise relationship intervention was the worst idea I'd ever had.

Christian sighed audibly, then closed the door. He went into the kitchen and helped Ambrosia prepare the drinks.

Juliette and I sat on the love seat. Jamie and Khadijah joined Eric on the couch. After scanning the room, Jamie jumped up and pulled two chairs from the dining room table into the living room. Now, there was enough seating for everyone.

After a quiet beat, Ambrosia announced, "I've made enough for all of us."

She walked around the room with a tray full of shots. We only had a few shot glasses, so she improvised and took every glass, coffee mug, and condiment cup, filling it with an ounce and a half of tequila.

Ambrosia set the tray on the coffee table and took the chair closest to me.

Christian had taken limes from the kitchen table and sliced them into wedges. He lingered in the kitchen a few moments after Ambrosia. I peered in after him, trying to gauge which Christian would rejoin us. There was a smirk on his face while he texted someone, probably telling his friends about this unbearable situation or writing another sonnet.

Christian brought the limes to the table. He grabbed the last chair that sat between Khadijah and Ambrosia.

Everyone took a shot. Then, Jamie took two more, shaking his head profusely. We all looked at each other, then back at him. He picked up another shot and pulled it to his lips, but froze.

"You cheated as recently as our dinner?"

"No," Eric stated plainly.

"Rebecca seems to think he did," Christian instigated. He retrieved a shot, a sly sneer on his lips. Christian seemed to enjoy stirring the tension. He'd told me that he hoped Eric would break my heart again. Now, he was getting a front-row seat.

Jamie stared at Christian, then scanned me and Eric. He shook his head again roughly, like he was trying to dislodge the truth.

"How?" he asked, seemingly stuck in a daze. His nostrils flared like he was a little angry.

"Jamie, what is the question? How what?" Eric asked.

"You didn't learn from my mistakes? You didn't witness all the damage I did?" Eric was still catching up, but I understood. Khadijah wasn't the only one who looked up to us. He'd thought Eric was better than him.

Khadijah's demeanor shifted. A quiver rolled down her body, and her eyes locked on the floor. I could feel her embarrassment so similar to my own at the moment.

"Really! None of you knew this?" Christian asked in astonishment.

"I knew that he kissed another girl." Khadijah looked down and fidgeted with her nails.

Christian shook his head and rubbed his hair in the direction of his waves.

Emotional Charades

"I've always figured that it was one of those openly kept secrets. Like you all knew, but you didn't care." He spoke to the group, but his eyes narrowed in on Khadijah.

She and I understood that the trajectory was meant for her. She rolled her eyes then shot a glance at me. Purposefully, I shifted my gaze, not wanting her to ask me to back up her character.

"I was an incredible fool regarding that line of thinking," Eric answered Jamie's question, ignoring Christian interjection. He grabbed another shot.

The tension in the room was easing the more we drank, for all except Eric.

He looked uncomfortable. He scanned the room repetitively, his eyes moving rapidly, returning his gaze to the ground then repeating the action. He didn't look at me, though, not for cues on how to deal with the situation or to regulate the irate emotions I was sure he was feeling.

His eyes locked on Jamie. "Recent marriage rates show that marriages are failing at a slower rate when individuals marry later in life. The summation is that the experience gained through dating, promiscuity, financial stability, and establishing and obtaining personal goals is significant when predicting marriage longevity. There is also the cultural shift in the role marriage plays. It is no longer a need for survival, but more of an agreed partnership. My theory was to manufacture those experiences without dissolving the current relationship."

I watched as his reasoning settled on them and as their pensive faces analyzed the data, trying to reach a conclusion. Some heads nodded in general acceptance, while others looked stuck completely.

"That's not how Rebecca explained your experiment to me. She said you wanted to see what you liked that she didn't let you do," Christian revealed, confronting Eric's P.R. version of events.

"No fault of hers," Eric interjected. "You rethink your delivery when your fiancé moves out. You have the time to ponder a lot of things in that kind of isolation. Corresponding conditions explain why couples who marry young are divorcing at a higher rate. I led with the 'lacking elements' originally—an egregious oversimplification."

I cringed. Hearing Christian and Eric talk about me was like being stripped naked in public.

"Nah, horse shit," Jamie announced. "Like, I get the premise, but you cheated, plain and simple. The actions don't become something else because you thought about it. How many times have I talked with you about what I did? The damage is so evident." He choked on his words, then pushed through. "I just don't know how you could have reached *sex with another person* as a logical solution to whatever this is. You saw it first-hand. I just don't..." He lost the words, shaking his head.

He grabbed Khadijah's hand. I could tell he was trying to squeeze an apology into it.

"I understand that now." Eric looked at me, an apology lingering in the space between us. He gestured to the table where those folders still sat, "As evidence of my prior earnest belief in my theory, here are the research, notes, and essays I wrote."

"You don't have to show this to everyone," I spat. I wished I had the ability to smite them from existence.

Emotional Charades

"I want you to know that I am not intentionally hiding anything from you. I want to be transparent so that you do not have any reason to lie or cover up for me."

I wanted to point out the obvious flaw in his actions, but the fight that would follow didn't need an audience.

Everyone stared at them, embarrassment, and curiosity swirling.

"I don't know. That just seems like a lot of extra homework. Maybe the sex just got boring. It's been like 10 years," Ambrosia suggested, looking at the folders like they were contaminated.

"No, that was not it," Eric and I said in unison. An awkward smirk crested at the corner of both of our mouths.

"Oh, alright, you two are some little freaks, got it," Ambrosia added, giving the crowd a much-needed chuckle.

Christian's demeanor retreated a little. Where before he was sitting forward, engaged in the conversation, he now sat back against the couch, his phone an inch from his face. Ambrosia's curiosity won her over, and she was the first to reach for the folders. She fanned them out, displaying their titles. *Promiscuous partner, overweight partner, mature partner, and athletic partner.*

I watched, both curious and horrified. I knew which one she would opt for the instant I saw the titles.

"That one is calling my name." She reached and pulled the folder entitled *overweight*. I looked at her, shocked that she hadn't just ignored them like the rest of us.

"What? We're all wondering what scientific porn looks like." She lifted the folder and skimmed the contents.

"Okay, well damn." Abruptly, she looked up. "You seemed so surprised with your findings. Was your premise based on some depraved notion that overweight women can't be sexual or sexually gratifying?"

"No," Eric answered.

Ambrosia gawked at him. I assumed, for the simplicity of his reply. "Then what was the purpose of singling out fat girls?"

"The object of the experiment was to select archetypes of desired sexual interactions. I am attracted to women who are classified as overweight. Her specifically because she agreed to have intercourse. The outline in the binder should have explained."

Ambrosia flipped back to the first page and reviewed something.

"Oh, well," she added with a grin, seemingly taking his comment as a compliment to her. Still giggling like she was the ambassador for big girl appreciation, she grabbed her phone then started to fiddle with it.

The lyrics, *"Fuck it up for the big girl,"* played while she bobbed to the beat.

I threw a pillow at her. Christian sang the words to the song, air fanning Ambrosia to encourage her antics.

Khadijah quickly swiped a folder from the table.

Jamie stopped her hand. "You don't really want to read that. "

"Yeah, I want to know what spell she has over men," she whispered in an attempt at a hushed conversation. They went back and forth debating about the folder.

Juliette stared at Khadijah, a clear challenge.

To avoid the altercation, Jamie and Khadijah buried themselves into the folder.

"This one is empty." Juliette flopped open the folder.

I shrugged. "I never looked through them."

"He showed you these before?" Juliette asked.

"He tried to show me yours," I smirked. "As evidence that he didn't cheat." I air quoted that part.

"Eric, you didn't?"

My attention drew to Eric. Agitation radiated from him, causing me to evaluate the room from his perspective. In the last few minutes, the room was filled with chatter and music, Ambrosia and Christian singing, Jamie and Khadijah having a hushed argument, and Juliette and I reviewing the oddness of our acquaintance.

He was the odd man out in a sea of stimulation. Our history told me where to look and what his behaviors meant. His thumb touched his fingers, lightly repeating his pattern, soothing himself.

His other hand started to massage his temple. This impromptu gathering was my creation; I didn't have to allow the room to overstimulate him.

"Ambrosia, would you mind turning the music down?" Eric asked before I could form the words. Before I could step in to protect him.

"No problem, sweetie." She paused the music.

I stared in awe. I had always inserted myself between him and confrontation, assuming he needed me to. But I was cutting him off at the pass, effectively preventing his growth. Our division had gotten him accustomed to fixing his own problems.

Eric caught my eyes, giving me a look asking, *are you alright?*

"Oh, I'm okay. Just lost in thought," I responded to his look.

"That. Is that it? So, you two actually do that emotional charade game?" Christian asked after our exchange.

Eric looked at me, a question of concern on his face.

I blinked the look that meant *sorry, but yes*. He dropped his head and bit his bottom lip. My heart sank a bit.

"That! What was that?" Christian asked.

"She confirmed that she told you about our game."

"So, you two can communicate, like with telepathy?" Ambrosia asked.

"They can. I've seen it," Khadijah confirmed.

"No, we can relate like basic stuff with expressions. More like a sign language specific to us."

"How though?" Ambrosia asked.

"Have you ever practiced something for 10 years?" Eric explained.

"What does that mean?" Ambrosia asked.

"When we were younger, our families played a game to help Eric distinguish body language. His therapist suggested it. We sort of adapted it for our relationship, as like signals."

"Signals for what?"

Emotional Charades

"For when I'm behaving socially unacceptable. Signals to stop talking, apologize, leave, stop being myself in public, etcetera."

I glanced at him; he had never expressed it like that before. All at once, I felt bad for the 10 years of queues. I used our love language as a social leash.

"Ah!" Ambrosia gasped, "Rebecca, is that why you sometimes hold odd faces? Girl, I thought you had gas."

She was the link that made this awkward evening pliable. We laughed like she had the mic at a comedy special.

"Let's get a demonstration," she suggested, and suddenly, I didn't find her so amusing. She eyed everyone in the room, getting their confirmation that a demonstration was in order.

I looked at Eric with a question in my expression. *Is this okay?*

He nodded. I stared at him for a beat, trying to make sure he was comfortable with this. I repeated that same expression again. He responded with a series of expressions that meant *I'm sure.*

"Okay." I got up and grabbed a few notecards from my desk.

" I'll write a list of words we have signals for then show everyone but Eric and we'll see if he can guess them. Okay, everyone?" I explained.

My lips pursed together in a hard line.

"I said something rude," Eric said.

"Just rude, but I'll give it to you," Khadijah announced as the unofficial scorekeeper.

We played, scoring a perfect hundred on our nonverbal communication skills.

"That's kind of impressive," Juliette admitted. "Seems like you two were made for each other."

"Yep, I'm his personal build-a-bear to suit his needs," I said.

Eric's attention snapped to me, "Are these your factual sentiments about our relationship?"

I thought about it for a moment. "Well, sort of."

"Well, if you have been trained to control me, then I am the marionette. I take your cues on everything. I have an array of cardigans and matching slacks, even though I prefer sweats. I allow you to lead my interactions because it pleases you. I am just happy that I get to be with you."

"So, why did you put up with all of this? Why did you put up with being trapped by my needs?"

"Because then when we come home, you drop all of that. I can say or not say anything. I can be rude or unproductive. I just get to be with my best friend." He said it flatly, like it was a fact I should have known, like the effects of gravity or the color red.

And maybe I did. It was my favorite part of us. The us that existed in this house. Hearing him say it felt like a revelation. I wish we were alone. The moment felt so intimate.

"So, you both feel trapped. Sounds perfect." Christian smirked, "What else would be different if you weren't trapped?" Christian asked, stirring up the conversation.

Eric looked at Christian, causing nerves in my stomach to pull like a ripcord. I didn't know where this was going.

"I would not be friends with Khadijah," Eric answered.

Emotional Charades

The room roared at his admission. Like the audience of a slimy talk show, we all shouted our reactions. Cacophony ensued for a few moments until Khadijah shushed us.

"No, let him finish," Khadijah insisted. She gave a little head nod for him to continue.

"Over the years, I have developed a friendship with you and I do love you as a friend, but I definitely do not like you as a person. You do terrible, rude, inconsiderate things, and you never apologize. I resent that I am expected to account for my mistakes that I do not always understand, but you get to burn dresses and throw tantrums like a toddler." There was no tension in his tone.

The room didn't hush. No gradual lowering of decibels. Just silence. The sound of crickets chirped in the distance. Tonight was going to be filled with awkward truths. I had a burning question, too.

"Why did you cheat, Jamie?"

"Ah…" He sat back, putting his hands to his face like a mask, then shook his head until they came free. "I never wanted a future with any of those girls. I thought I was entitled to fool around. I was so young. I met you so young." He paused, looking at Khadijah like she were a work of art. "You don't think you'll meet the person, ya know? The person you can see yourself walking down the aisle with at 18. I thought it was the thing to do. Men cheat." He rubbed her cheek, wiping away a tear that had broken free. "She forgave me the first time. I thought I had it all figured out. I would do my little side thing and one day, I would grow out of it. We'd move on with a clean slate. What I didn't figure is that it would change her. I damaged a part of her and legitimately, I am trying to make it up to her. I ruined her confidence. Imagine such a smart, beautiful person seeing something else in the mirror."

We all listened acutely to his prospective heart-wrenching. I could almost feel the weight of the pain he'd burdened Khadijah with. And why? For some toxic notion of manhood.

" I've found lists she'd written, where she tried to work out what those flings had over her. Eric, I've talked to you about this. How could you make my mistake?"

"I didn't do what you did," Eric said ardently.

"Bullshit! I don't buy it. You saw our struggle. You know the damage. You did what I did," Jamie shot back.

"He's right," Christian said, throwing a shot of his own. "I was there for the aftermath. I was there for the rebuild." Christian was staring into my eyes. That shared experience was irrefutable.

"How did you get so involved?" Jamie blurted.

"An inconvenient rebound," Christian said.

"You weren't a rebound," I insisted.

"Clearly. Since he is in our living room," Eric snapped.

I sighed. There were too many hearts in the room to appease. "The truth is that it was all bad timing. I needed to vent and to break down a little, but it was so close to the wedding, and Khadijah seemed like she would fall apart if I did. I didn't feel like I could trust my feelings to my other friends. But I could talk to Christian. He became my friend. Then more."

"The really bad timing was that dress fitting," Christian added, a twinge in his eye.

"Would this be the one where she kissed me and found her wedding dress, or the one when she came home with me to cheat on you?" Eric asked.

"What?" Christian looked at me incredulously. He stood and walked to the balcony.

My heart constricted. I looked at Eric, expressionless.

"What?" Eric said defiantly. "You can expose my indiscretions, but I have to be discreet about yours?"

"I hadn't told him about that kiss," I said sheepishly, angry but hyper-aware that this moment was born from my bed of lies.

I followed Christian to the balcony of my apartment. "Christian, I'm..." My apology died off, distracted by the amber ash glowing in the darkness. "Christian, you don't smoke."

"Just because you've never seen me do it, doesn't mean I don't."

"I'm sorry, you and I got in a fight when I got home." I pause, hearing how hard I was trying to position myself into the best light. "I should have told you when it happened."

He exhaled, the smoke mixing with the cloud of his breath in the cold night air." Do you know when I figured it out? When I was sure you'd cheated?"

"It was obvious when I stayed out all night."

He flashed his contagious smile. It wobbled then disappeared. "No, it wasn't when you stayed out," he admitted, and my stomach clenched. "I trusted you. I was mad, but..." he paused for what I anticipated was going to be an uncomfortable truth. "I believed your drunk night story. It was when you were lying in bed at my parent's house. I asked you who you were texting. You said Khadi."

I stood there shaking my head in the dark, knowing that I must have been nearly invisible against the night. "I don't understand."

"It was the tiniest detail, but it was an anvil dropped from a rooftop. I knew you were lying about something right then. You never shorten anyone's name. You never call me Chris, or her Khadi. And what else would you have had to lie about?"

"But you didn't say anything."

"I was in denial. I hated knowing." He took a deep drag.

"Christian, if being here is too much."

"And miss this traffic accident?" He pointed inside. He smiled, but it didn't reach his eyes. "Plus, you know Khadijah has hated me for months. I'm delighted to rub her face in the fact that I'm the good guy."

I dropped my head. "*Was* the good guy," I corrected. "Christian, the way you behaved in class was too much. I don't deserve your sympathy, but that was cruel."

He flicked his cigarette stub into the darkness. He looked at me with consideration.

"I know," he looked down and shook his head, "but I'm not sorry yet."

I took a step towards the door.

"So, you kissed him at the first dress fitting?" he asked.

"I did." That single omission had placed me on this path. If I'd told Christian that night, he would have put his guard up, and I never would have gone home with Eric after the next fitting.

Emotional Charades

"Asshole." He grimaced, "After tonight, I never want to see or hear from you again."

I nodded.

He pushed the door open and allowed me to walk in, then followed.

The conversation was flowing between our guests. Ambrosia was now sitting next to Eric, seemingly intrigued by whatever he was saying. Khadijah, Jamie, and Juliette remained in their original seats but were leaning toward Ambrosia and Eric.

"I first asked her out when I was 13," Eric answered.

His eyes focused on me as I walked in. They said *I told you so.* I recalled a conversation we'd had. He told me if he pressured me to pick between them, it would eventually be detrimental to our relationship. Now, his petty statement had me tending to Christian's needs in front of him. His eyes flickered to the only two open seats, placing Christian and me next to each other. Ambrosia had shifted seats.

"But when did you guys get serious?" Ambrosia asked Eric, continuing their conversation. Ambrosia looked from Eric to me, her brows were pinched.

"I apologize, Ambrosia, I was distracted. Could you restate your question?"

"When did you guys get serious?" she asked, but her focus was on the tension in the room.

"When we were 13. I already explained that. Have I misinterpreted your question?"

"You can't be serious at 13," she said, laughing at the implication.

"Rebecca, what am I missing?" he asked, a tiny bit of frustration in his tone. "Ambrosia has asked me the

326

same question three times but is expecting a different answer."

"She doesn't think we could have been serious at 13. Effectively, she is asking you when we fell in love because she thinks it's different from when we became a couple," I explained.

"Is that accurate?" he asked.

Ambrosia cocked her head to the side. "Real shit, I didn't know that was what I meant, but yeah, that was what I meant."

"Then the answer is when I was eight years old. She came over to play kickball with me. I had been playing alone. I could not keep up, but I did not want to tell her that I couldn't. I was afraid she would leave. I fell, I fall a lot. I fell, and I was expecting her to run away or tease me. That had been my experience up until that point in life. She stood there until I could calm down. Later, she played games with me." He looked at me like I was that same girl. "It was the first time I had a friend. I loved her then."

There were tears in my eyes. The room listened to him in quiet contemplation. Eyes darted around, the listeners looking for confirmation that they understood him.

"What?!" Jamie asked.

Then a hiss of chuckles spread through the room starting with Jamie, slowly creeping into Khadijah, then traversing the room, until I was infected. All except for Eric, who stared in disbelief at our reactions. He started tapping his pattern again, just his fingertips, against his thumb.

"What is funny?" This time, he asked the room, not just me.

Emotional Charades

"Romantic love. Not friendship love. They want to know when you...I don't know, first thought Rebecca would be the woman you would marry," Khadijah offered.

He stopped tapping.

"My answer is the same. When I was eight." He looked around. "Like my parents, they were best friends and in love. The two concepts always intersected to me."

"Ah, he was never jaded. The first girl he had a crush on, he grew to love. He never experienced the *it's just puppy love stage*. He is an anomaly." I defended his response to a room of snickers.

"We are anomalies," he said.

"We are." My heart hummed a little. Nothing was perfect right now, but that part had been.

"So, we're just going to ignore that look he gave her when we walked back in?" Christian asked.

"I think that was our plan," Juliette answered.

Everyone shrugged.

"What did you...communicate to her?" Christian asked.

I looked at Eric. His response was to look at the table that was holding his sexual deeds as reading material for our guests. He shrugged one shoulder.

I giggled at his implication that our dirty laundry already covered the table.

"You guys did that thing again," Juliette said, "Let us in on this joke."

"She wanted to know if it was okay to disclose what my expression meant. I thought the question was unneeded considering the information laying on the coffee table."

"You two can read each other's minds," Jamie observed.

"What did it mean?" Christian asked with no mirth in his tone.

"After our night together, Eric offered to be non-exclusive. He thought I should date both of you. Gradually growing apart from you, instead of sudden separation. He thought that it was the safest way to get me back." I tried to keep the information light, but informing Christian that Eric and I had discussed his place in my life made me want to vomit.

The weight of the comment pushed him back in his seat, "Damn."

Christian looked away from me and the group. Facing the kitchen, he took a few moments to himself. Self-loathing leaked from my pores. Though it seemed like this was what he wanted. He was asking questions and driving the conversation. Likely collecting the dirt and the details to add to the mountain of reasons he should hate me.

Christian walked to the door and left without a word. I heard the door close, and so had that chapter of my life.

"So, you just live your life with no fucking idea of how people are perceiving you?" Ambrosia asked, too intrigued by our communication style to focus on anything else.

His eyes cut to Ambrosia, a smirk on his face. I could tell he was interested in her questions.

"A portion of the time. Once I get to know people, I encourage them to tell me directly, which helps me set gauges, or I at least feel comfortable asking if I did something…" He looked around the room. "Outside of that, there are techniques I can use to cope." No longer tapping his finger, he felt at ease with this conversation.

"Techniques, like what?"

"Like, proximity is two feet. 1 to 1 conversation structure—I speak, you speak. These rules make me seem like you all," he said, a slight distaste in his tone.

"You all?" Juliette asked.

"Yes."

"I meant to ask what you mean by that.'"

"Thousands of words exist so that concepts can be relayed in detail, but somehow, the collective masses decided that nondescript gestures serve as 80% of communication. In our society, I am forced to dismiss the logical layout of language for the subjective idea of non-verbal communication. To spend my energy imitating the nonsensical communication style of the majority. Society's preference for non-verbal communication confounds me." He looked up, starting to address us instead of his internal musing. "So, every interaction I have with a new person is a pop quiz in non-verbal communication."

"Eric, you seem so—"

"If you say normal, I will have to ask you to leave."

"Comfortable, I was going to say comfortable. Earlier, you were doing that tapping thing. You looked uneasy as fuck. It's stupid, but I guess I thought you were always like that."

"I understand that. No, I am not stuck on one setting all the time like a…" He paused to find the punch line to his joke. "…an analog game." His smile was bright, clearly dazed by his own humor. "I was overstimulated before. The noise, the unexpected company. That tapping thing is called stimming. My stim is repeating a list. It calms me."

"His list is the anatomy and function of the human brain," I added.

"Rebecca, that isn't my list anymore."

"Since when? I've seen the list written in your room."

"Since I was about 14. I started to become an expert on another topic." He winked at me.

Me. I was his list now. My eyes swelled. Our company seemed to miss the admission.

"I'm sorry if my questions were rude. I'm ignorant about the topic," Ambrosia said.

"Ask. I prefer it." He rambled on a bit. He shared great insight, but the night and the intoxication had stolen his audience. Khadijah and Jamie were fast asleep. Juliette and Ambrosia were still awake and listening. But they were yawning and resting their heads on their hands.

"Should we call it a night?" I intervened.

Both ladies looked at one another, as if practicing their own secret language, and decided to call it a night.

Ambrosia offered to drop Juliette off. I insisted on giving her gas money for her trouble.

Chapter 31: The Aftermath

Cinnamon and toast—the smells of Eric's apology—woke me. A mixture of hunger and nausea strangled me. Teeter-tottering, I made my way towards the food, only for the scene to baffle me. Khadijah was cooking in my kitchen.

"Khadijah."

She peered over her shoulder, "Oh, morning, Rebecca." She turned back to the stove and stirred something in a pan.

Taken aback, I just stared at her. Was this a dream? Or a nightmare? Why was she making me breakfast?

She ignored my stunned silence. Before I'd figured out what she was doing here, she'd prepared two plates, two mugs, and took a seat at the table.

"You still need to study for three finals, but Eric shouldn't be alone for a few days. To help you balance everything, I've created a schedule. Jamie and I will take shifts with Eric while you study," Khadijah explained. She pointed to a yellow legal pad. Her neat script stained the page.

I joined her at the table, smiling at her pragmatic apology.

She flipped the page on the legal pad. "I called your phone carriers about Eric's phone. I had to pretend I was you. They said they can fix the screen under your insurance for $50, but they'd need to send it off. It might take a week or more. The other option would be to upgrade, which would cost $200 out of pocket, but you'd have a new phone today."

"Thank you. I'll let Eric know." I picked up my mug but paused before taking a sip. I eyed her suspiciously.

She rolled her eyes, "It's coffee, geez. I can't teabag assault you when I'm already on best friend thin ice." Her voice cracked.

She dragged her knuckle under her eyes. She sipped from her mug and grimaced.

"Are you drinking coffee?" I asked, noticing the dark hue.

"I have been up most of the night." She took a deep breath, peering into the cup. "I have been self-involved, self-centered, a drama queen, and apologies don't fix anything. So, here are my acts of service until you can forgive me."

The resentment I'd been guarding eased, easing the blame I'd assigned her for this whole situation. The fault wasn't important. Just the desire to repair the issue.

I grabbed a fork and started to eat the scrambled eggs and cinnamon toast. "This is good. Thank you."

I ate while she reviewed the schedule. Jamie had gone home to shower and shave, but he'd be back to cover the morning shift. She would stop by later for a check-in, and I was to spend the whole day studying. She wanted me to leave the apartment, so I wasn't distracted.

I went to the library and followed Khadijah's lesson plan. Once I reached the point where information seemed like Klingon, I conceded that I had absorbed as much as I would before the test.

Emotional Charades

With nothing left to review, I wrote. I wrote for myself. I wrote to myself.

What I liked, what I didn't like, what I wanted, why I was going to medical school, who I wanted to be with, and whether I wanted to be with anyone at all. My own guidebook to self-discovery. Writing it gave me a sense of ease after last night's conversations.

I stayed until they kicked me out. Even though it was late, I walked home, desiring the tranquility of solitude, hoping to maintain the contentment I had reached.

I felt a twinge of panic as I entered my apartment. Eric was on his feet, stiffly walking around cleaning up the kitchen, all alone. The Florence Nightingale in me wanted to drop my bags, rush to his side, and make him sit down. The maid in me wanted to clean up the apartment. I froze for a minute, trusting him with himself, firing myself from all the self-assigned roles.

"I thought Khadijah was supposed to stay until I got home?" I asked, a little thrown that Khadijah hadn't followed the schedule she created.

"Hello, Rebecca. Jamie already got me dinner." He pointed to a pizza box on the table. "I explained to her that I did not require additional assistance this evening."

"Do you need anything now?" I offered, instead of assuming.

"No, I am fine. How was studying?"

"My brain feels like it'll melt." I leaned onto the counter in the kitchen. His fingertips found my temple. Gentle massages coaxed me into his arms.

I flashed back to my list. It helped me identify this part of me. How I leaned toward the good times and into the moment and even our future, neglecting the present. I had to stay present. There were things I wanted to get off my chest. I pulled back and sat down across the counter.

"I have a few theories I want to run by you."

He sat down at the table. His eyes widened, "Proceed."

Then, there was an opportunity to start a conversation, not a spiel or expectations, just a question I had written down at the library and the realization it led to.

"After you reviewed the marriage statistics, the experiment you enacted wasn't your first conclusion."

"Correct," he responded solemnly, an old sadness revisited.

"You initially concluded that the best course of action was to break up?"

"Correct."

"Then you tried to concoct this experiment, to gather those experiences without breaking up?

"Inaccurate! Then I became fixated on it. I was researching my biggest fear. Our entire relationship, I have been scared that you would make a connection with someone else. That you would learn that relationships didn't have to be like ours, waiting for you to move on from the novelty of your first crush. I thought I could manufacture those experiences, trick the odds. A miscalculation of monumental importance." His eyes gleamed, the tears sparkling in the light.

"In our time apart, I learned relationships can feel fixed. It's hard to introduce a new side of yourself when you're living up to another identity. I learned I couldn't forgive you at first because we were *The Newlyweds*.

Emotional Charades

Now, I realize we are just two people who hurt each other. I came to the realization that we didn't give each other room to grow. At least not out of our expectation of each other and ourselves. To me, I was just a daughter, a student, a friend, and a half of The Newlyweds."

His eyes wandered around the room, processing. "I never meant to hold you in place. I have always felt like the luckier one. Grateful that you saw something in me," Eric explained.

He looked at me. His eyes intent and intense with the honesty of that statement. My eyes flashed; I looked up to hold back the pressure of tears.

"You really feel that way? Have you felt that way this whole time?" The words started to choke me. "That doesn't flatter me. I don't want you to feel uneven in love."

"70% of polled couples say that one loves the other more. It feels very factual to me."

That pulled at the fibers of my heart, "Did I tell you what my final project was about?"

"No, you did not."

"For my final project, I expanded my hero story."

"What was it about?"

"It was about a brave boy, who risked the terrors of a bowling alley to impress a girl."

"Is that true? I know you do not have a reason to lie, but I...need reassurance," he said insecurely.

I pulled out my laptop. "I wrote it when I couldn't say your name out loud. When I was positive that I hated you." I opened the story I'd recently reread. I placed it on his lap. He browsed through the story with urgency.

"I want you to know that up until…this…I never wanted to be with anyone else. If I were the one polled, we'd be in that 30%."

This thin line of misunderstanding had fractured our relationship. A fissure of insecurity that I'd never seen.

"Rebecca!" He closed his eyes and took a breath, "You cannot make your decision today."

"Why?" I stared at him. I wanted to have the hard conversation.

He looked pained, but he didn't answer.

My head dropped. "Goodnight."

I pushed off the counter and walked to my bedroom.

Chapter 32: My Hero

The next two weeks happened in an instant, flying by like the timer during an MCAT practice test. I blinked four times, completed three tests, then it was time to attend the Mehndi.

The Fawaz's house was gorgeous. It was a prairie style house built on a grassy hill. Basically, a mansion. Though, it didn't feel imposing.

Entering the house was like traveling from winter into spring. Vibrate yellows, oranges, and pinks warmed the room. Family and friends clad in yellow bustled around the room. There was chatter, laughter, and the enticing aroma of delicious food.

Khadijah was already getting her henna done. The artist had completed both of her feet and was working on her right hand. There were two other henna artists there to service everyone else.

I lapped the room to greet everyone. When I saw Mrs. Fawaz, she said I looked hungry, and there was a plate of food in my hand within seconds. I topped everything off with a mango lassi. I had no complaints.

After I ate, I sat for my henna application. The henna left an earthy and lemon scent in the air. The artist free handed a beautiful and simple tattoo that ran to my wrist.

When Khadijah's was done, we hovered around her to admire it. Her's was intricate. It ran from her fingertip to her forearm.

"It's so pretty, Khadijah," I said. Amara and I were in a small group huddled around Khadijah. We were searching the tattoo for the groom's initials. They were hidden within the design.

"It's everything I wanted." Khadijah turned to the artist, "Thank you again. It's perfect."

"You're welcome," the henna artist said.

"They are so elegant," said an aunty, admiring the tattoos. "Too bad you're not wearing a traditional gown to properly display them."

Khadijah blinked slowly. I'm sure she was fighting to not roll her eyes.

"Aunty Dada, you know her dress is cut to show them off. Khadijah's going to be a beautiful bride," Amara interjected. Her eyes gleamed as she looked at her sister.

Aunty Dada gave a plastic smile, "That will have to do." She turned to Amara, "I am so happy you decided to be more traditional. You're going to make an even more beautiful bride."

Amara's jaw went slack. I did a double take. She hadn't really said that.

Aunt Dada looked benevolent, casually returning her gaze to the tattoo. A small grin tugged at her lips.

Khadijah's lips were pressed, and her jaw clenched. Her eyes started to redden. Her tears were seconds away.

"Excuse me," Khadijah said softly, her head held high as she walked away.

Emotional Charades

I stayed a second longer to glare at Aunty Dada. Then, I followed Khadijah. Amara stepped into auntie's line of sight and crossed her arms.

I caught up to Khadijah in the foyer. She was fanning her eyes and taking deep breaths. I wanted to touch her, but our henna was still setting.

"I am so sorry. That was rude."

"What's a wedding without a little shade?" she shrugged. "Honestly, I knew someone was going to compare me to Ms. Perfect. Why does she always try to overshadow me?"

"What?" Amara said, as she rounded the corner. "Didi, is that what you think?" Her brows pinched and she tilted her head to the side.

I felt bashful at the tone of her question. It reeked with hurt. I wanted to squirm away and let them have this conversation in private. But I stayed because I didn't want to it to turn into an argument at Khadijah's Mehndi.

Khadijah looked from me to Amara. Her eyes started to glisten. She sighed and her shoulders dropped.

"Why else would you announce your plans to consider an arranged marriage now?" she asked earnestly.

Amara looked taken aback. She stared at her sister. She sighed then walked to Khadijah. "I want our kids to be best friends. You're likely to have kids in the next three to five years. I have always wanted our kids to grow up together. That's why I agreed to consider an arrangement now. I want to start a family…dating hasn't worked for me. I'm tired of being ghosted. I am tired of investing in a relationship only for them to be a dead end. So, I told Amma that I would try it. I didn't mean for it to come out now."

This was why I couldn't reconcile Amara's obvious affection for her sister and her sudden decision to marry. They were directly connected, just not in a malicious way.

Khadijah's chin tucked in. "So, you weren't trying to make me look bad?" Khadijah's voice was earnest, like she'd stepped into her childhood insecurities. This might be the moment she got to dismantle them.

Khadijah was in tears. They were slow, quiet tears. She fanned her eyes.

Amara lowered her head and rested it on Khadijah's forehead. "I love you. I would never try to hurt you."

A sense of peace washed over me. This rivalry had burdened Khadijah. Maybe in its absence, she could take better stock of her needs. Now, maybe therapy wouldn't be off the table.

I felt like an intruder. Like I'd invaded this healing moment. I slipped away to give them privacy.

They stayed close to one another for the rest of the party. Amara ran defense. Any questionable comments were stopped in their tracks. It was nice watching them kindle a sisterly bond.

A couple of hours later, I was headed home with a container of leftovers and a vow to get a good night of sleep.

***

The next day, I woke up to an empty house on the morning of the Nikkah. My only company was a menacing maid of honor dress that I hadn't tried on in a month.

Also, grades were in today.

Emotional Charades

Okay, they'd been in for a week.

Today was just the day I had gotten the nerve to check them. I sat at my computer and opened the grade book.

Four *A*s, and a *B* in creative writing. I smiled, then clasped my hand on my mouth. I did that. Pride radiated through me. My chest felt full like an inflated balloon. I'd worked hard, stepped outside my comfort zone, and learned the value of a story. That *B* was a shining achievement.

It was perfect.

My phone chimed, making sure I was awake, that I hadn't abandoned the day for the comforts of my warm bed. There was a single text from Eric.

He'd spent the night with the groom's party. I hadn't been avoiding Eric or offering him sickening silence. Our schedules were so busy that they were keeping us distant. I'd been approved for an on-campus apartment. By next week, I'd be on my own.

Eric: *Could you pick up my phone from the Sprint store? I only asked because it is on your way. (7:15 am)*

I rolled my eyes but typed, *yes.*

Even being petty had lost its joy. He opted to have it repaired instead of replaced. Less expensive in the long run. They'd had to ship it to a repair center and then ship it back to the store. In the meantime, he was using his iPad.

I showered and packed, double-checking the checklist Khadijah had given all her maids. I was once again amazed at how much of a control freak she could be, but also impressed at how thorough she was. I added Eric's task to my checklist.

Taylor Bianca B

It was a quick stop. I was in and out in five minutes. They'd given it back dead so I couldn't check if it worked.

Rude.

The screen looked fine, so I left without pushing it. I couldn't. I wasn't willing to be late on Khadijah's big day. I plugged it up to charge and drove to the bridal suite.

When I parked, the glow of the charging screen flickered, catching my eye. The backlit screen of Eric's phone read 40%. I turned it on, opening the lock screen to make sure the buttons worked. A crescendo of notifications chimed until his phone showed 39 unread messages.

30 of them were from Khadijah.

Chapter 33: What I Already Knew

I walked into the bridal suite, Eric's cell phone in my pocket. It weighed a ton against my anxiety.

Standing amongst the cheer and the rush of the wedding party made time feel stagnant. I hadn't opened any of the messages, but the beginning of several messages were visible on his notification screen.

Khadijah Fawaz: *Please don't tell her!!!!* (11:00 pm)

Khadijah Fawaz: *It was a stupid mistake.* (11:12 pm)

I only glimpsed the notifications for a moment, but it was like I'd taken a screenshot. I searched for a context that fit the words. Only one circumstance applied.

"It's your turn, Rebecca," Mrs. Fawaz cued me to sit for hair and makeup, instead of standing in the middle of the room aimlessly.

Hair, makeup, a ceremony, photos, and champagne combined forces to usher me through the day. The messages never left my mind. I couldn't bring myself to read them. So, I spent the day trying to read Khadijah and Eric's interactions. Trying to work out how they'd slept together. My best friend and my fiancé.

Taylor Bianca B

That can't be true. I shook the thought from my mind. Or, at least, I tried to.

"Do you want to dance?" Eric asked.

His question was the first sound to pierce the echo chamber of my mind in several hours. I felt slightly confused as music and the chatter of the reception became audible, too.

"Would you like to dance?" Eric repeated.

I looked at him, completely baffled by the information I had and the parts that I didn't have. Trying to picture the action itself, the time, the place—or places.

I pulled his phone from my purse, waking it to the notification screen, where Khadijah's message still appeared.

"Did you have sex with Khadijah?" I asked, still puzzled by the what, where, why, and the how of the scandal.

He leaned towards me until our faces were a breath apart. "No, Rebecca, I did not have sex with Khadijah," he replied like I had finally asked the right question.

A web of discomfort detangled from his frame.

His answer started to pull back the edges of my anxiety. "This is a very important moment for details."

He looked up, compiling his thoughts. He inhaled deeply. "Khadijah tried to convince me to sleep with her at her dinner party. She was upset that Jamie would not ask the manager to send Juliette home. Later, she asked me to have a word with her, and I followed her to the coatroom. She started crying and then hugged me. Babbling incoherent things. *'They don't deserve us. We should hurt them.'* Then, she slipped her hands underneath my shirt, and I tried to push her away. She said she had seen you with Christian, kissing him. I asked her when. It was the morning of the fitting. Before we reconciled." He stared at me like I would figure out the riddle any moment now. "I told her that she needed to speak with you. That things were complicated. She would not listen to me. She started to get down on her knees. I pushed her off me and her nails raked against my back. I made to leave, and she dropped to the floor crying and begging me not to tell you."

There it was. I didn't need to read the messages. Every word resonated, the details pierced me like a barrage of bee stings. My skin felt hot like I had been boiled alive, but it was my blood boiling.

"While I was dancing with Dad?" I asked, staring in the distance as I worked out the sequence of events.

"Yes."

"That's why you stormed out. You were talking about her in the parking lot?"

"Yes."

My head whipped toward him, "Why didn't you tell me?"

He drew in a breath. "I have broken your heart once. I never want to do that again. She begged me not to say anything the first night, but she promised she would tell you. It was supposed to be the morning after they had stayed over, then after the Mehndi. I told her today was her deadline. I was going to tell you after the wedding."

He sat back and rubbed the back of his neck. "I waited because you just spent months protecting this wedding. I thought this was what you might do. Carry the burden, so as not to hurt everyone involved in the wedding. Jamie, their families. So, I carried it." He sighed, "I was not sure. I went back and forth on it. I almost told you a dozen times… I'm sorry."

I scanned the room.

I jumped to my feet as all the interconnected details aligned. The way Eric behaved after the dinner. Khadijah looking for us the next morning. She was trying to intervene before he could tell me.

Wordlessly, I made my way toward her, accosting her while she mingled with guests. "We need to talk."

She looked stunning in a red wedding dress with gold accessories. Her bridal henna ran beautifully from her forearm to her fingertips.

"What?" she asked, the ever-innocent victim, eyeing me with supreme naïveté. But her eyes betrayed her.

I stared at her, anger not allowing me to speak.

"What is it, Rebecca?" she asked with a ring to her voice, but it cracked a little.

"You…" I tried to make the accusation, but it hit me. The whole picture— her actions, her lie—hit me like a freight train.

"Excuse us a moment," she asked, taking my hand and leading me away. I snatched my hand free but followed her. I counted her steps, a distraction from the collision of emotion.

One, two. She tried to sleep with Eric. Three, four. But she was my best friend; she wouldn't do that. Five, six. She did. I felt it.

I felt it in the way she led me through the crowd with slow, careful steps. She was sure not to bump or engage with anyone like she was carrying a bomb set to explode.

Emotional Charades

She stopped in the eating suite—a small room used to allow the bride and groom to eat before the reception wearing garment coverings, a trick to avoid ruining their fancy attire. It was all still here, their dirty plates and stained covering.

She locked the door, and the sound made the moment real, the following conversation finite. Moments ago, I'd jumped up, determined to breathe fire. Now, suddenly, I didn't want to leave this room without a best friend, but I knew that I would.

"Khadijah." I cracked and then stopped.

I couldn't trust my intentions. Words I meant to say with fury were filled with pain instead. I covered my mouth and closed my eyes tightly. This was not the moment to cry, but of course, it was.

"You," I managed to say with some conviction.

"I…" she started, looking wide-eyed, while I waited for the story that would make me forgive her. "I didn't know you guys were on a break. I thought you were a cheater, like Jamie." She laid out her defense, ever shifting the blame, this time pointing it at me.

"What does that matter!" I yelled. It wasn't the story I needed to forgive her.

"I thought Eric would get it, what it feels like to be treated like you're worthless."

"Khadijah!" I shouted. "This conversation is not about you. You tried to seduce my fiancé."

"I know… and I feel terrible, but nothing happened." She added the last part like it was her silver lining.

"Because he said no!" I believed him, but a tiny part of me wanted confirmation.

Taylor Bianca B

Pure shame washed over her face, furrowed brows, nose pinched, the inability to look in my direction. "I'm sorry, Rebecca. I am so sorry. It's the worst thing I have ever done. I promise I will do anything to earn your forgiveness."

"It's not the worst thing you've done. You sat on my couch while the whole story unfolded. You never decided to confess. The days after, you let me think he betrayed me again. You asked him to lie. You were willing to let me endure all the pain that you say caused you to come on to Eric. You let me think that Eric didn't love me. You were going to let my relationship take the fall to protect yours. That's worse."

"Goddammit, I was just so confused…" She sobbed." You two are strong enough to make it through this. You two were already working it out, already having healthy, honest conversations."

She was missing the bigger picture. I could see my part in her delusion. I had given her the impression that she could treat my relationship like a fallout shelter.

"Khadijah, I can't do this anymore."

"What?"

"Us."

"I made a mistake."

"A mistake? You broke this friendship!" I screamed at her. My heart felt more seared than when Eric had broken it. "I have bent over backward to accommodate you the last few months. You've been so fucking fragile!" I lost my composure, yelling like there weren't 250 people in the next room. "I allowed you to be this way. I've made you worse, and so has Jamie. Now, you manipulate us. Weaponizing your pain to control me. And I'm…I'm done with you."

"What about you and Eric?" she asked, her tone switching. Suddenly, she was serious. Her type A persona returned. "No, no, no, it wasn't his fault. You know that now." She pleaded earnestly. Her eyes were big and focused, like a child begging her parents not to separate. "I begged him not to tell you. I got on my knees. I told him about my abortion. Please don't blame him."

"I heard you were already on your knees," I shot back.

Her head dropped, and she wrapped her arms around herself. I turned my back to her. Her self-pity had no purchase here.

"Were you pretending at our dinner?" she asked.

"What?" I asked, surprised by the question.

"Were you and Eric pretending to be in love at my dinner?"

There was a clearing, like the Red Sea, where all the emotions I was juggling split.

"No." And it was an absolute. What did that mean for me and Eric?

"Everything between now and that cocktail party was my fault. I've messed up so many things." She broke down into sobs again. Her tears did not pull sympathy from me. Instead, the truth of them triggered another emotion.

"I should drag you around this room by your hair," I threatened, taking a step towards her. She took an intimidated step back.

Knock, knock.

"Sweetheart, are you okay? Our guests are starting to miss you," Jamie said through the door.

Her face turned to ash.

"Please don't tell Jamie," she begged, wiping her eyes and cheeks.

I looked at her in her gorgeous dress on her wedding day with disappointment, "You don't get to ask me for favors."

I backed toward the sound of the knock, contemplating what version of the truth she would entangle with tears to control the narrative. A version where she was the victim. Where tears equaled accountability.

"Rebecca! What's wrong?" Jamie asked as soon as I opened the door.

I dragged my fingertips under my eyes, smudging the mixture of eyeliner and tears. He took in the whole room. A bride and her maid of honor locked in a room crying.

"What's the matter?" he asked.

Tears budded in the corner of my eyes. I glanced at her one last time. "It was her. She left the marks on Eric's back. She wanted to hurt us. He turned her down."

I turned back to Jamie. A half smile raised his cheek. Like I'd set up a joke but hadn't delivered the punch line. As he stared at me, the smile faded out. His eyes darted to her. He covered his mouth with his hand.

"It was me." Khadijah admitted, eyes closed, fists clenched. "I scratched him."

"What?" he asked, his tone in falsetto.

"I wanted a way to hurt you. To repay you," Khadijah answered.

He stared at her.

"Bye, Rebecca," Jamie murmured with grit in his voice as he walked past me and into his marriage, reaping what he had once sowed.

Emotional Charades

"I don't want to think like this anymore. I think I need help," she cried as I closed the door.

Where I thought I would find vindication, there was a biting back of my own tears. For years, I had wanted Jamie to pay for hurting Khadijah, but this didn't break even. It was like watching a new person take the fall for a person that no longer existed. But you couldn't pick which versions of you dealt with the repercussions of your actions.

I made my way back to the reception. The music grew louder, reminding me of the festivities still in full swing. I stopped short of the double doors leading to the reception, making one more attempt to right my appearance.

Pushing the double doors, I walked into a room of wonder. Bright colors, coins, group dancing, hair whipping around with spins and turns. Laughter and smiles and the hum of chatter beneath the music.

A cloud of positivity.

I walked in feeling like I was poisoning the energy in the room. Whatever Khadijah and Jamie decided about their future, I didn't want to be involved. Not even as the bridesmaid, whose attitude dampened the wedding. I made my way by the gift table and discreetly took back the air fryer.

Grabbing my jacket from the table, I snuck away before any guest could interrogate me. Eric spotted me. He tried to flag me down, but I needed air. I staggered away from the celebration into the frigid atmosphere. A light coat of snow dusted the pavement. My breath made white clouds against the night sky.

A new pain ached and rippled through my chest. It wouldn't just go away; I couldn't bury it with silence or move past it with willpower. I needed to get through it and let it out. I walked out of hearing distance.

"That fucking bitch. How the fuck could she think this was forgivable?!" I shouted into the night.

"My name is Eric Bennett Bridgeport," his voice rang out from behind me, startling me. I dropped the gift and turned in the direction of his voice.

Eric was standing there, out of breath, cupping his side, his face contorted with discomfort.

"My name is Eric Bennett Bridgeport. I am 23. I want a pet. I want to see my siblings more. I hate wearing cardigans and dress shoes. I will only wear hoodies and gym shoes from now on. I don't like trying to live up to the expectations of strangers, and I am comfortable being classified as weird or abnormal. I have loved you since before I knew what it meant—before I could put a title to the pulse I feel when you are around me. I will never betray you again."

He was introducing his new self. Sharing the ways he'd changed.

"My name is Rebecca Anisha Dangerfield. I'm 22. I hate straightening my hair. I don't like reading books tandemly anymore. I'm done with people-pleasing. I have a mean side. I don't want to be an *it couple* or *perfect* anymore. I just lost one of my best friends and during one of the worst fights of my life, I couldn't say I didn't love you." That Red Sea of emotion parted again, and I needed to tell him. "Eric, I have been head-over-heels, crazy in love, Elisabeth and Darcy, Dewayne and Whitley, in love with you since you kissed me on my doorstep."

He beamed, then his smile pulled back tentatively. He stepped towards me, grabbed my hand,

and squeezed. "Rebecca, I'm immensely sorry about Khadijah. I thought if she was honest with you, you two might be able to work it out. I'm sorry. I will never withhold anything from you again."

I looked at our hands. There wasn't any animosity or resentment tied to his touch. "Eric... I'm not mad at you."

Khadijah had manipulated me for months; I knew what it was like to go against your self-interest for her.

"You're not? I know you were planning on leaving me after the wedding. When you showed me the hero story, you were saying goodbye." he said, a confused panic in his voice.

"I was," I responded lightly.

"And you are not anymore?" He titled his head.

"I don't think so."

"Rebecca, I do not understand," he said, still clutching his ribs, wincing when he inhaled.

"Eric, do you need to sit?" I released his hand and moved to his side to let him put his weight on me.

He pivoted to face me. "Rebecca! Please clarify your answer."

The suspense was clearly causing him more pain than his bruised rib.

"Oh." I switched back to the topic at hand, "I *was* saying goodbye because I thought that we couldn't grow with each other. I thought you cheated again and refused to admit it as a strategy to assuage my anger, that you were treating me like a prop in your pre-arranged arguments, always trying to win the fight. That you were making the same mistake again."

I quoted my list from the library, from my decision from that night. My reasons to move on.

Taylor Bianca B

"Rebecca, that is not an answer."

"Eric, you've changed: you tried to protect Khadijah, even though it didn't serve you any purpose. You didn't cheat again, and you didn't try to control me with a strategy. You didn't try to win this fight. You went into it knowing that you couldn't. Yet you still tried to fight for us." My chest lightened. An ease coursed through with the realization that we'd grown with each other.

He smiled, breathing for the first time in minutes.

"Would you like to dance?" he asked, extending his hand.

"Eric, you don't like to dance," I said, attempting to absolve him from appeasing me.

"Would you…like to dance?" he asked again, this time implicating that it was my choice alone.

I took his hand.

He pulled me into him. My head rested against his chest. We swayed in the cold. The anger and resentment toward Khadijah temporarily abated as I listened to his heartbeat. From rapid to slow and steady.

"I had a speech prepared," he admitted. "Not to win a fight," he said quickly. "An apology with action. I wanted to ask you to dance in front of everyone, while sober." He spoke in my ear. "You enjoy dancing, and I enjoy making you happy. I think I wanted to show that we could test my boundaries. That I am not this fixed point you need to adjust to. You are my point; I will meet you anywhere."

He stopped our soft sway and tilted his head down. His eyes bore into mine; his hand cupped my neck. His lips pressed mine. It was an apology, a promise, and a step into our future. My heart raced. I ran my hands through his hair and stood on my tiptoes to push into his kiss.

I pressed my hand against his chest, "Wait, I want you to promise me a few things." I said breathlessly.

"Anything," he promised, looking at me with elation. His eyes locked on mine, his smile bright.

"Promise me you

will leave me if I try to make you hide who you are, dictate how you behave, when to speak, what to say, try to convince you to lie to your family, or isolate yourself from them." I recited the list of my mistakes from my guide.

I looked into his mixed eyes, wanting the promise to be binding.

"No, that is absurd."

"If we are together, we are equal—"

"I will never just leave you. I will communicate and grow with you," he explained, serious.

I smiled and bit my bottom lip. "Then, I promise to commit to communicating, to growing with you."

He looked into my eyes; his breaths heavy, "My side really hurts."

We both laughed. He grabbed his side. His other arm rested on me for support. We hobbled to a curb and sat.

"Laughing hurts."

"Are you okay?" I asked.

He looked at me, his eyes big and shimmering, "You love, *love* me?"

I smirked at him, "I always have."

"My promise is that I will never question it again."

Epilogue –Six months later – Results Day

"What is the matter, Rebecca?"

My pen froze mid-sentence. I glared at him.

He cracked a smile. "You are waiting on your MCAT results. I know. I just want to distract you. You look so tense."

He sat a plate and mug in front of me. An omelet with a side of avocado toast, and my coffee concoction. He grabbed his breakfast and took the chair to my left. He was dressed comfortably in a summer sweatsuit. Teal shorts with a matching short sleeve shirt. His new comfy style was filled with monochromatic sweat suits. His collection ranged in thickness to function throughout Michigan's true seasons.

"Thank you, baby." Without taking a bite, I began writing in my legal pad again. He gave me a pointed look.

"I'm not overreacting. I'm proactively picking a second test date, just in case I failed. Also, I'm creating a detailed study schedule."

He gave me a look that meant *exactly*.

I looked at the bullet-pointed, color-coded schedule and I dropped my head. He had a point. My results were due within the hour. I didn't need to make a plan until after I got them. I put the pen down, ignoring the Khadijah-like voice in my head telling me to stay ahead of my schedule.

I started to eat my breakfast. My eyes were locked on my cell phone screen. I refreshed the results site impatiently. My nails tapped distractedly on the table. All I needed was a 511 score.

Eric laid his hand on mine.

"How about we do our check-in?" he asked, applying gentle pressure to my hand. Ease radiated from his touch. My shoulders relaxed. I sat back in my chair, which eased the tension building in my lower back.

"Of course." I laced our fingers.

After the wedding, we didn't just rest on our laurels about the health of our relationship, or individual growth. After a little research, we decided to do monthly check-ins. Throughout the month, we answered questions to ourselves and shared them.

Three months ago, the process yielded its first life-changing answers. Eric answered the question: *How do you feel about your career path?*

The first month he was confident in his path, then it changed to comfortable with it. On the third check-in, he realized that he didn't have any passion for psychiatry.

He told me, "I think I selected a medical field to fit into your relationship with my dad. I am great at the academic side, but I will not enjoy a career in the field. I think I have known it for a long time, but I thought it was just life."

We talked about it. He decided to finish his undergrad degree but to withdraw his graduate applications. A couple of weeks later, he started a coding program online. He earned a few certificates. Now, he worked remotely coding for a startup.

He loved it. I loved seeing him thrive.

Before I pulled up my check-in, I refreshed the site one more time. *Click here to review your results* flashed on the screen.

I stopped breathing, clicked the link, and entered my ID.

I got 519. My whole body shook. Excitement, pride, and a little fear ran through me.

I looked up at Eric with my mouth wide open.

"You passed." He shot to his feet, pulled me out of my chair, and lifted me into a hug. He spun us. I laughed. My heart raced like I'd run a marathon.

"I did it!" Tears blurred my vision.

He sat me down. I grabbed my phone, eager to share the news. I opened my contacts and started to type *Khad…*

No matching contact. My shoulders sank a bit at the sad acknowledgment. My eyes cast down. This was bittersweet. I took a breath. Reclaiming my joy, I turned to Eric.

He was on one knee. A box open with a gorgeous princess-cut diamond ring with a gold band.

"What? What are you…" I tried to ask.

He smiled big and bright. His mixed eyes danced in the light.

"Over the last six months, I have felt more comfortable and certain of myself than I have in my whole life. I love myself now. Within that peace, I find I love you even more. I have been trying to think of a way to tell you that. The only thing I can think of is this," he said, nodding to the ring. "So, would you, Rebecca Anisha Dangerfield, marry me?"

All my love for him bubbled up. Frizzy excitement coursed through me. I felt the same way about him. This chapter in our lives wasn't perfect, but it was right and honest.

I clapped my hands over my mouth and nodded. My heart felt so full and light.

I extended my left hand. It shook like I'd downed three Redbulls.

He slid the ring on, and it fit with my other engagement ring. The diamonds looked like they rested on a double band.

I dropped to my knees and crushed myself against his chest.

"I'd marry you today."

He pulled back to stare at me. His expression posed a question. *Are you sure?*

Was I sure? I loved him, believed in us. I wanted to be his wife. It would be easier than planning a wedding while in med school. It'd be cheaper. Best of all, no pushy, nagging wedding party.

So yes, I was sure.

I returned the expression. *I'm sure.* The smile that spread on Eric's face was pure joy. I echoed it.

And wouldn't you know it, you could get a same-day marriage license in Ohio.

Taylor Bianca B

About the Author

Taylor is a debut author with a passion for complicated characters and engaging storylines.

Tweeter: @TaylorBBrown1
TikTok: @TaylorBiancab.author

Printed in Great Britain
by Amazon

27686961R00205